Sweet Tea

A perfect heartwarming romance
from Hallmark Publishing

PIPER HUGULEY

Sweet Tea
Copyright © 2021 Piper G. Huguley

This is a work of fiction. Names, characters, places and incidents are either the product of the author's imagination or are used fictitiously, and any resemblance to actual persons, living or dead, business establishments, events or locales is entirely coincidental.

ISBN: 978-1-952210-64-8

www.hallmarkpublishing.com

For my father, Neal Huguley, Jr. who cried when
he heard I was being published by
Hallmark Publishing:

Goodnight, sweet Prince. And flights of angels
sing thee to thy rest

Chapter 1

Thirty-two-year-old Allie Dailey had everything she'd ever wanted, but she could not sleep.

Her favorite things to watch during these sleepless nights were the infomercials, especially with the same brunette lady who did all of the half-hour ones, making apple pies out of Wonder Bread and pressing her sandwiches into technological gadgets that amazed.

When the sun came up, Allie could finally rest. For two hours.

Then she had to get up and go to work at the law firm of Pichon, Boar and Ellis—soon to be Pichon, Boar, Ellis and Dailey, with her name added onto the end, because she had just made partner.

Everyone in the niche world of intellectual property law was excited about a young woman, one of her age, caliber—and color, if she were honest with herself—coming to be part of a firm. She was one of a rare few in New York.

Except Allie wasn't excited.

She couldn't put a finger on quite why. The thing she had been working for all of her life was beyond her caring just now. It made no sense. This ho-hum feeling she had toward her life made no sense.

The one perk she had worked so hard for—to have a car to drive her to work—was hers now. She had a regular driver who would come for her, so she could work in the car. Every minute of her time had value and was accounted for in some way.

And today, the car wasn't there. And it was raining.

Stepping in front of the apartment building away from the doorman, her heart beat a little fast at this strange turn of events. Something must have happened, but she couldn't imagine what. Her driver was always on time.

Ahh, there was the car. Her usual driver, Frank, an elderly Italian gentleman, had been replaced by someone who had the same tone of brown skin she did.

Frank spoiled Allie something fierce, and she usually enjoyed his supercilious manner and saw to it he was richly rewarded at Christmas and his birthday, ever since she had first qualified for this perk two and a half years ago.

Today, this new person pulled the car up to the curb and sat there.

She watched.

This gentleman didn't get out of the car to open the door for her. This gentleman didn't seem to be looking for her. This gentleman just sat, as if it were up to her to teach him how to do his job.

She bent at the waist and looked into the car. The man looked at her and waved, but went right back to his phone.

She couldn't have been more offended if she had been smacked by her grandma. This ignoring of her needs somehow felt as if she had been. Smacked by reality.

But no, it was Frank's car, right down to the midnight

blue, the number on the Empire State license plate, and the heated fuchsia lumbar cushion in the back.

On rainy April days like this one, Frank would greet her with an umbrella so her shoulder-length black bob would stay smooth and relaxed and not frizz out à la Angela Davis.

Allie had no umbrella and no way of negotiating the space between the awning of her apartment building and the curb. The doorman gave the car a look and stepped up, wielding his umbrella.

"Miss Allie, it looks as if you have a substitute on this rainy day. How about I take you to the curb?"

Relief washed up on her. "Yes. Thank you. So much."

The doorman had a huge black-and-red striped umbrella, one of those inside-outside marvels, and with a flourish, he assisted her to the curb, where she uncertainly knocked on the window.

The window moved down slowly and the shining face of the driver appeared. "How do?"

It was the twang in his voice that hit her upside her perfectly coifed bob, threatening to shake it. And her.

"Here is Miss Allie," the doorman said.

"Oh my, yes." The driver reached over and opened the door for her. For the seat next to him.

The doorman scowled and led Allie to the back seat, where her fuchsia cushion awaited. Frank would have had it plugged in, ready to smooth out the kinks in her back with warmth. But when she sat upon it, the cushion, ice-cold and stiff, gave her no love.

"I hope Frank is okay," the doorman said.

A mixture of alarm and surprise began to stir in Allie like nothing had for at least a decade. "Me too."

The doorman gently let her in and went around to the front, where he gestured and shouted at the driver.

"Get along there! Come on!"

Once Allie was encased in the car, the driver started an apology tour, something she could have done just as well without.

"Sis, if I'd known you was who I was supposed to pick up, I would have been here sooner. I'm so sorry. You Miss Dailey?"

"I am," Allie said with the chill of January in her voice, even though it was April.

He began to go on the apology tour all over again.
Sigh.

"I'll be late." Allie smoothed her bob. "Let's just leave."

She held up her hand to quiet him, because there was something in the twang of his voice that unsettled her. She tried to focus on her tablet to get some work done, but the pitch of his voice, his word choice kept burrowing into her head like a screw. "My wife is going to want to hear all about this for sure."

"Hear about what?"

"You. Me driving you. Ain't this something?"

"Why would that be newsworthy? I'm no one."

The driver peered at her in the rear view mirror, which made Allie a little nervous. "Naw. You a Smithson. Aren't you? I saw on the call sheet. It say Althea S. Dailey."

With a sweaty hand, Allie closed her tablet, then wiped it on her Burberry scarf. Was there nowhere she could go on this infernal planet without being recognized? Would she never be shed of her Georgia red clay roots? She cleared her throat so that this man could hear her clearly. "There are a lot of people named Smithson in the world."

He chuckled. "Yes, but with the shape of your nose, you a Smithson all right."

Sighing, she moved plastic surgery up higher on her

mental to do list items. She hadn't wanted to take the time off for a nose job in her chase toward partnership at the law firm of Pichon, Boar and Ellis, soon to be Pichon, Boar, Ellis and Dailey, but now that she had checked off that goal, she would go out to California to those *Botched* doctors and get her nose altered. Narrowed. Fixed. Something un-Smithsonable.

Breathe.

Do your exercises.

Allie drew in deep breaths and blew them out through her mouth to slow down that familiar awful feeling that came whenever a panic attack started. One hadn't happened in a very long time, because she had learned how to control them, but this recognition came without warning. Came without expectation. She thought she was safe from being recognized here in New York.

She was wrong.

"I didn't mean to cause you any offense, ma'am," he said.

The breathing was working. She calmed down enough to fend off the panic attack. She blinked her eyes in gratitude. "Oh no. I just never expect to be recognized here in New York City. When did you graduate from Milford?"

Judging from his voice, he didn't suspect how shaken she was. Good. "Class of '95, and my wife was '97. You graduate from there?"

"No. I came north. For school. I went to Columbia."

"I see. Well, it sure is good to see home folks up here in the cold north."

Allie gave a wry grin. "What about the 'return to Milford?'"

"What do you think I'm chauffeuring rich folks for, ma'am? I'm trying to save my money for a little patch of land to retire to down there. I can't wait. I'm about four years away from my goal. My wife is a teacher. She'll have put in her thirty years and then we'll both go back home. It's sure good to see you here, though. Which branch are you?"

Allie sighed. "Miss Ada is my grandmother."

The man nearly ran up into the back of a taxicab in his excitement. She reached her hand out to brace herself for certain impact. "You don't say? God, that woman is a pillar. I enjoyed every mouthful of her home cooking she put into my belly while I was in school. As if you couldn't tell." He patted his rotund belly. Fortunately, he was quite near the subway stop where she noticed her executive assistant, Connie, making her way toward the building. Connie, who was a few years younger than Allie and of West Indian descent, appeared to be pregnant with three babies, instead of the one they all knew was in there.

"Can you pull over and pick up that woman there?" Allie pointed Connie out.

"'Course, God bless her."

Allie pressed a button to let the window down. "What have I told you?" she called.

Connie stopped her walking and straightened up. "Hey boss! I was trying to get there first."

"It doesn't matter. Get in."

Allie slid over off of the back cushion onto the cool leather seat. Connie eased herself and her bulk inside, leaning back into the heat of the pad. "Man, you live the life, boss woman."

"I'll get you one."

Connie opened her eyes. "You do enough for me. No more."

"No more of your stiff-necked pride. I'll do what I want."

The driver up front chuckled. "You just as stiff-necked, Miss Allie. That's how Smithsons are." He glided out into the traffic with a smooth gesture. People who could drive like that were rare indeed.

"Who's he?" Connie pointed to the driver. "Where's Frank?"

"He's off today, ma'am. I'll drive you in so you are nice and dry."

Connie waved. "Yes, I appreciate that, sir. Heaven knows what I would have done without you nearby."

She made comedic faces in Allie's direction that made her want to laugh—a refreshing change from the chest-tightening anxiety that had threatened to come over her just a few minutes before. Her heart gladdened at the sight of her work tower coming into view.

"You cook like your grandmother?" the driver asked.

"Oh no. I can't even boil an egg." Allie flipped her hand.

Connie gave her the side-eye. *Why is he all up in your business?* her expression plainly conveyed. Connie knew all about how the legend of Allie's grandmother overwhelmed her. Suffocated her. Frightened her.

The car fell silent. What was wrong with what she had said?

"I just pursued other things. That's all."

"How is she?"

"Oh, Granda is fine. As feisty as ever. She's getting ready for the Graduation Day feast." The picture of her active little grandmother popped into Allie's head. Had it been four years since her last visit? Maybe five? What a shame. How much time had gotten away from her?

Connie's hand, swollen with the late-stage, late-in-life, unexpected pregnancy, slid over to hers and squeezed. *You don't have to answer these questions*, Connie's eyes said.

Allie shook her head, keeping any anxiety at bay. "Indeed. I know it would have to be a little different in these strange times, but I'm glad she is still doing it." It occurred to her, then. She was in her thirties and had not seen her Granda in years. Well, now that she had achieved her goal of making partner, maybe it was time to go see her.

"She's busy, all right."

Pulling into the garage so that they could get out of the car without worrying about the rain, he parked, came around and opened the door for them. Well, at least he had some sense. "It was so good to see you, Miss Althea. So good."

Connie ambled out past him, cutting her eyes at the driver, almost making Allie laugh out loud.

His large arm reached out and squeezed her to him before she could stop him. When Allie pulled back from his embrace, she was mortified to see some of her brown foundation left behind on his black suit.

"I'm, I'm sorry." Allie didn't know what else to say.

"No worries. When I tell my wife I saw Miss Ada's own grandchild, she won't mind. You take care now."

Fairly skipping back to his driver's seat, the man drove off, leaving Allie there in the garage with her face half made-up, half unmade.

"You look like Two Face from Batman," Connie informed her.

"Of course I do, and here comes Mr. Pichon." Allie held up her hand over her face.

"Good morning, Allie. Got a new love interest?" Mr. Pichon turned to see the car driving off.

"No, Max. An acquaintance from back home." Allie turned so she could get into the bathroom to repair her sliding face.

"From home?" The older man gave her a new look, as if he had never seen her before over the ten years she had been with the intellectual property firm. "I thought you were from here in New York."

Allie linked her arm through Connie's so that she didn't slip on the slippery pavement, or slick marble flooring inside the lobby. "No." She shouldered her computer bag and turned around so he wasn't facing her bad side. "I'm not." Something pierced her soul. And she said it. "I'm from the South. Georgia. Coastal Georgia. Milford."

Mr. Pichon followed them.

Unfortunately.

"Well, isn't that interesting. I would have never taken you for a southerner."

Her heels had clicked on the hard quartz floor, but then she stopped and the echo resonated in her brain. Allie opened her mouth, but Connie spoke for her, as she so often did. "What's a southerner like?"

Allie lowered her hand and faced him full on.

The sprinkles of brown aging spots on Mr. Pichon's balding pate stood out as he turned crimson. "Well, you know. The voice, the manner, the expression of a southerner. That's not you, Allie. You're a very—well—classy woman. Graceful."

Connie scoffed. "She's not like a country hick, then?" They had arrived at the elevator bank and she pulled her arm out of the crook of Allie's, freeing her to go to the lobby bathroom.

Thanks.

"Yes," Mr. Pichon said. "I mean no. Just classy and elegant. Not…"

"Southern." Connie tapped her foot. Her ankles had disappeared a couple of weeks ago.

Smothering another laugh, Allie added that cushion for Connie to her mental list. Pichon didn't like to deal with Connie directly, so he had gotten what he deserved. Allie stepped briskly down the hall to the women's restroom. Best to do the repair job here before she went upstairs.

Pichon was trying to compliment her, she guessed, but it was hard, taking a look at herself in the mirror, not to react to all of these comments on her appearance today.

Her nose, something she had seemed reconciled to lately, appeared wider than ever. She held down her nostrils with her fingers, imagining what it would look like at that width. Yes. Call Dr. DuBrow today. Good thing she did have a nice figure. Of course, she worked on herself like mad and made sure to do all of the healthy things whenever she could.

She dug her compact out, repairing the mess the driver made, as the words about her nose resonated in her mind, and she focused on covering up the ache that comment had caused her by dusting her skin over with the cosmetic puff as she applied the acceptable shade of copper, taking the tone of her skin down two shades.

It was extra effort, but worthwhile, to make sure her neck was made up to match as well. Her fingers were a little slippery and she gripped the puff a little harder.

Had Pichon seen her natural color? What had he noticed?

So much time. She spent so much time every morning performing this exercise. And for what?

What if she took it all off?

What if she abandoned the two-tones-lighter copper foundation?

What if she let her hair grow out of her head as it was?

What if she kept her nose as it was, without contour,

shading, highlighting, hiding it in plain sight?

The questions chased themselves around and around in her mind until they caught up with one another in a tangled mess.

Allie's laugh echoed throughout the bathroom chill, as she fixed her face and hair, in that order.

The nose, as well as Connie's cushion, was something she would look into as soon as she got upstairs.

Chapter 2

ALLIE COULDN'T WAIT TO REACH the womblike haven of her office, where she could breathe for just one minute. To not have to mask for one minute.

What was with her today? Why today? Why was she so bothered?

That new driver—he was at fault. Allie had long succeeded in putting Milford, Georgia to the back of her mind, out of her heart, out of her head, and that man had made her think of it today.

Right now was the point when Milford would start to get summer hot, not achy spring cold like here in New York. The subtropical heat would have come last month, while New York would still be overcast gray with lots of shadows from the tall, overwhelming buildings.

Meanwhile, the tallest building in Milford was Porter Hall, which was also the oldest building on the Milford College campus. Three floors high.

When she entered the suite of offices, Connie had already settled her bulk at her desk outside of Allie's office. Lowering her voice, Connie twisted her lips, and said, "The Horsemen are looking for you."

Allie's private name for the other partners. Of course they were.

"I…I'm fine. I'll be in the conference room in about five minutes."

"Shall I tell them to wait?"

Allie took in a sharp, soul-deep breath. *Yes. Tell them to wait. Tell them to leave me alone. Tell them…*

"I'll be right down."

Allie entered her office, putting down her things, and took off one of her shoes, wiggling her toes. Why did she have to wear heels? Hateful things. She put the shoe back on again and picked up the cup of coffee Connie had brewed from her personal Keurig. Then the youngest and most colorful partner of Pichon, Boar, Ellis and Dailey ignored the chill of her toes, and took herself and her tablet down the hall so that the Three Horsemen of the Apocalypse would be able to receive their daily infusion of diversity from her.

Her nickname for the men wasn't especially kind, but the firm didn't boast the high percentage of IP wins for nothing. They had plucked her up when she was in her first year of law school at Columbia and brought her right in. She had known nothing else, and their guidance and support over the years was the very thing that had brought her riches like she had never dreamed of.

So why did she feel so empty once she joined the Three Horsemen?

"Good morning, gentlemen." Making her voice smooth and non-Southern, Allie slid into the chair, third down on the right, nearest to the door.

"Good day, Althea." Pichon said. *All-thee-a.*

She tried not to wince at the way he insisted on dragging out the pronunciation of her full first name. He was the White Horseman. Not because of his flesh, but because he always wore a white flower in his lapel, no matter the weather. He was one day older than God himself, but refused to retire.

She wanted to tell him that her appearance had nothing to do with her capacity to handle the meeting, but she nodded at him.

Boar and Ellis nodded eagerly as well, given that they never spoke until old Pichon gave them leave to.

"We have just the IP case for you, my dear. Here are the particulars." Pichon shoved the folder at her. He was not into technology. He'd struggled a bit in recent years, but he had intermediaries who were willing to risk their lives to keep him fully apprised on all of their cases.

"Mama Cassie's Home Cooking restaurant chain is bringing suit against Sherry Holiday of Sherry's. It's a trade secret case in Charlotte, North Carolina."

Allie had to refrain from snapping her neck back. "A chain?"

"Yes. Mama Cassie's is worth about four million a year. Holiday is barely breaking even."

Allie opened the folder and looked at the contrast. A classic David and Goliath-type case. She swiftly, professionally looked through the papers. Then she found what she was looking for. "Wait. They are fighting over…iced tea?"

Pichon clapped his hands like a small child. "I knew this would be the perfect case for our newest partner. Get it settled. Sherri needs to give up the ghost, and we're counting on you to make her disappear."

Allie sat back. A trade secrets case. "This is in North Carolina. Trade secrets aren't easy to define in North Carolina."

"Well, back in the Obama days, they passed an act protecting companies' trade secrets that helped to firm up things with certain kinds of trade secrets, like recipes. Mama Cassie's iced tea recipe is one of its main specialties."

"Sweet tea." The proper name issued forth from her. Not from her lips, but from some other deep place in her.

"Excuse me?" Boar looked at her over his glasses. Then they all did.

Allie blinked, unable to stop herself from translating. "Sweet tea. It's very important in the South."

"Isn't it iced, though?"

"It is. But everyone already knows that. The important thing is its sweetness."

He scoffed. "Well, whatever. This Holiday woman is way out of line and she must be stopped. You need to stop her. Go down there if you have to."

Allie put a finger out, then pulled it back into her fist.

"This is the first case you want me to take on as a partner in Pichon, Boar, Ellis and Dailey?"

Pichon nodded.

"Why?"

"This is a case worth a great deal of money. You can handle it with your special touch," Ellis said. He was the one who had the crush on her. She could tell.

"Trade secrets are not my specialty."

"They are for this one," Boar said. She knew he had probably been the holdout on making her full partner.

"Because I'm a woman?"

They all stopped manspreading and straightened up. "Please, Althea," Pichon said. "No one can handle this as you could."

She shut her tablet cover with a sharp snap. "Fine. I'll go to Charlotte and take care of this. But when I get back, I'll want to return to my specialty of intellectual property tax attribution."

"Now see here. We can only assign the cases that come to us," said Boar.

Now was the time to frighten them. In her best *Real Housewives of Atlanta* voice, Allie brought her index finger out and gave them her finest neck roll. "I said what I said."

They were all properly horrified, except for Pichon. "There. She'll do it, boys. All-thee-a, you're magnificent. Connie has all of your arrangements made and you have the Black AmEx card. Take it and Godspeed, All-thee-a."

Yikes. Allie stood up and returned to her office.

Getting sent back to the South on the same day that the driver from Milford had brought her in was a two for one in anxiety. She pressed her hands to her stomach. Maybe if she worked out that tight ball, her bad feelings would go away. She called out for Connie. "When am I leaving for Charlotte?"

"Tomorrow morning."

"When is your due date again?"

"Not for six weeks." Allie knew already, but she also knew the question got on Connie's nerves and she liked to joke with her. But she also wanted some reassurance.

It was safe to go.

"Due dates meant nothing for my other two, but who knows with this little surprise one who popped up in our empty nester phase."

Allie sighed. So, not safe to go.

It would be criminal for her to be two states away and not go see Granda. She remembered what the driver had said, and what had been repeated about Milford ever since she was a small child.

People who come from Milford always return. They can never stay away.

From the time she was twelve, Allie had been determined

to be the first one to prove that stupid saying wrong, so that anyone and everyone could be liberated from Milford's so-called charm. But it wasn't going to work. She could not be three hours' drive away and not see her Granda.

She sat down in her office chair, an affair worth more than a term's tuition at Milford College, picked up her iPhone, and pressed the contact for Granda.

"Good morning! Praise Jesus, who is this?"

The use of her conventional greeting made Allie smile. "It's Allie, Granda. How are you today?"

"Althea Louise." Allie couldn't stop herself from smiling as the sound of her real and true name sounded through the phone. So many people in this world called her Allie, it was easy to forget who she was. "Blessed be. I'm fine, honey. I'm so glad to hear your voice all the way up there in New York City. I've got something to say." Granda's voice notched just a bit higher. "I'm going to be in a movie."

"A movie?" Her sweet little grandmother? Who would want to film her for a movie?

"Yes indeed. There's a right handsome white man who wants to make me a star in his movie. What you think about that?"

"That's wonderful."

I'll be in Charlotte for a case. Thinking of coming by. She opened her mouth to say the words, but they wouldn't come. For some reason.

"You want to come to see me film? He said you could. Maybe you could even be in the movie with me." Something in her heart sank at the yearning tone in her grandmother's voice. But the burning feeling in her gut kept the words glued inside of her.

"Maybe sometime."

The sigh from Granda was long and loud. "I know. You're a big shot partner now."

Finally, the gravity of Allie's achievement had sunk into her grandmother's mind. She'd had to explain it so many times, but now Granda finally understood. Yay?

The realization that she did not have to explain herself anymore didn't help. Allie sighed.

"You okay, baby?" Granda asked.

"I'm fine."

"She's fine." Granda repeated, *sotto voce*.

"Who are you talking to?"

"Jack. He wanted to know you were fine too, and I just told him."

"Jack?"

"That's the name of the director who is making the film. He's going to put Milford on the map."

Milford? Poky old Milford?

That wasn't nice.

More guilt. The way she had neglected her hometown and the college named after the town shamed her. The hope in her grandmother's voice brought a warmth to her heart that she didn't know she needed. The pain of tears welling up from her ducts pricked her eye sockets. Who was she anymore? "I hope so. I really do."

Then her grandmother moved on to another topic that she dreaded.

"Are you seeing anyone, up there in New York City?"

"No ma'am."

"You thirty-two years old, little girl. Time to get moving on that husband front, if you are having one."

"I don't have time to date, Granda. I've told you that."

"Yes, but I also recall you saying that now you a partner, you might have more time."

Allie put the pen down. More of what she said stayed

with her grandmother than she thought. "I guess so."

"You want someone like you, so you're equally yoked. That could mean just about anything. My goodness, we have a lot of stories in the Smithson family about being equally yoked. Think about Virgil and Amanda…"

And there her dear little grandmother went off on a flight of fancy about Allie's great-great-grandparents and their love story. Allie had heard the story so many times that she tuned it out, thinking about a new piece of art that she might purchase now that she was partner. Maybe a Romare Bearden, or who was that artist who did Barack Obama's portrait in the National Portrait Gallery? She always liked the sensibility of his work. She Googled him as Granda went on and on. Ahh, Kehinde Wiley. She would have Connie seek him out and see when he might be able to do a portrait of her. She preferred his work over what that female artist had done with the Michelle Obama portrait, which, to her taste, left the former first lady looking too grayed-out.

"And when they made the school together, you see, they was equally yoked, just as it says in the Bible. So, if you want to be happy, you need to find that man. Even if he's white. Granda don't care."

"Granda, why are you saying that?"

"I just want you to know. And Jack is standing right here, so I don't want him thinking I'm opposed to such. We've not had that in our family before, but it's all acceptable to me."

Granda lowered her voice, whispering loudly. "You need to come here and see him. I mean, this director man is a looker, and I never thought any of ours would be inclined that way, but Jack could change many a mind."

At the mention of traveling to Milford, Allie went to end the call. No doubt her Granda could see inside of her, all the way from Georgia. "Yes, ma'am. I need to get back to work."

"Of course you do. I love you."

"Yes ma'am. Goodbye. I love you too." Allie blew a kiss to the telephone and slid a well-manicured finger across her screen to hang up the call. She did love her grandmother, but when she hung up, she felt like a failure, in spite of the enormous achievement she had just unlocked in her life. Anyway, she didn't need to hear any more pleas to get married or any more of those Milford stories again. They were so boring. Still, the thought that her grandmother was going to be in a movie was something. What kind of movie? Did she have to sign a contract? She should look into that.

One more thing to add to the note to herself. The portrait, along with the nose job, the cushion for Connie, and the details for Charlotte in the morning. Bringing her hot spot would help. She could get some work done.

Chapter 3

WHENEVER HIS DADDY TOLD HIM that Jack didn't have a care in the world, he meant it. Andrew Jack Darwent III didn't care. Not about his daddy's world. He had other concerns. That's why the two men, who carried the same name, separated only by some pretentious Roman numerals, didn't get along. Jack didn't care anything about what Drew Darwent cared about.

This attitude about their caring meant it was better for them to part ways. So after Jack had refused to settle down with one of the girls they had matched him up with out of his frat's sibling sorority at Vandy by the time he was 30, he had pretty much distanced himself from the bulk of his family's old Southern society and cut himself loose enough from the lot of them, save his sister Bethany who, because she had married a half-Japanese man, found herself relegated to the fringes of the Junior League golf-playing richies.

It was all so stupid.

In his mind.

Once his mother had died, and his nanny, Miss Luly, had been cast out of the Darwent home due to old age

21

and the arrival of a new beehived wife on Drew Darwent's arm, Jack quit everything, bought a houseboat with the ill-gotten gains from his one year as a too high-paying attorney job, and went to the rivers of the South.

He spent a few years in his late twenties and early thirties going to—*gasp*—culinary school, working in hot kitchens as prep and sous chefs while he learned. He did pretty well for himself, but working in a restaurant, no matter how high-end it all was, didn't capture what he was looking for in life. He came upon it once when he had eaten at a small, out-of-the-way combined restaurant and gas station, where they served him a humble plate of sorghum grits and frog legs. The lady with the smooth brown skin of a teenager, but who was babysitting her two small grandchildren, apologized as she served him the food on one of those paper plates that was supported with a basket-woven plate holder.

She gave him two napkins and a plastic fork. He proclaimed the simple stew the best he had ever eaten.

"How you make it?" He kept his language loose and lax. One of the things he had learned in these meanderings around the South was that being a pretentious, stiff know-it-all like his Daddy was not going to get him to the food. He spent an afternoon in her company, and after she showed him how to make it, and he filmed her making it, and he made cat's cradles many times with her grandchildren, he had the recipe. Once he was in the car, it all dawned on him.

Who was going to show people this cuisine, this pure Southern food?

This woman, and her showcase of humble food, wasn't the only one. There were maybe a hundred of these women, maybe more of these people across the South with these recipes of the *real* Southern cooking. Who was collecting these treasures?

That's when Jack got it in his mind to write a cookbook and to film a documentary of his travels. He would call it *Southern Treasures*. He pitched the idea over the phone to a friend of a friend of his law firm, had an agent in two days, and in two weeks, captured a very nice deal to write a cookbook and travelogue for publication the next year.

His advance check of $145,000, plus his trust fund money, would get him a start on his film. He would write grants to obtain additional funding and work his way across several of the Southern states looking out for these treasured women who held the secrets of true Southern cooking in their hands and heads. When he was finished, then he would settle somewhere and start his own restaurant and show the entire cooking establishment what real Southern cooking was about.

He had heard about Milford College when he hit a small town in South Carolina where he had picked up on a recipe for peach teacakes. One gentleman, the husband of the lady who had baked the tender teacakes, told him about a meal he'd had at the college, which was a once-a-month gathering in the student cafeteria at the small coastal Georgia institution.

"They don't just let anyone in the monthly meal at Milford. The meal is to raise funds for the school." He punctuated his statement with a sharp nod.

"It's a smart way to raise money."

"You better believe it, son. There's been many a time that school nearly died, and those meals were the difference between life and death for my alma mater."

"You went to school there, sir?" Jack moistened his fork to get the last few crumbs of teacake. It wouldn't be polite to lick his plate, no matter how much he wanted to.

"Sure did. It's a preachers' and teachers' college. It's not doing too well right about now, but Miss Ada is still making the monthly meal."

There. No more crumbs. Jack eyed the gentleman. "Can you get me in?"

The man looked at him. "Well now, I don't know. They just had the last meal for April. Next one will be May, and it's the last meal of the year. They do it up special. They decorate outside and have it on the square instead of inside in the cafeteria."

"They close over the summer?"

"Yes. They can't afford to keep the school running over the summer. But Miss Ada, who runs the meal, she's a pillar of the school. Must be nigh on ninety years old now. She seemed old to me when I went there thirty years ago, when Milford was a happening HBCU. You go there, let her know I told you about her. Miss Ada Dailey. I worked in the kitchen and believe me, I learned a lot at her hands. She's a legend."

"Sounds fascinating." Jack could hardly restrain himself from running out the door to get right to Milford.

The man picked up his little china plate, holding it up. "Plate so clean it can skip the dishwasher."

Jack grinned, and said goodbye to the couple. The more he'd heard about the monthly Milford meal, the more he wanted to go. He had been kind of purposeful in selecting recipes and stops. The peach teacake couple was only his fifth stop, but now, he drove the rental car back to Enterprise, ready to weigh anchor in his two-story houseboat and make straight for Milford, Georgia.

Something tugged at him when he heard the word "Milford" and the gentleman's story of how a young missionary lady had come South to teach the recently freed enslaved people at the Milford plantation how to read and write. She stayed, married the town's mayor, and established the school there. Her determination to make sure her people attained literacy made him feel he was doing the right thing by capturing the stories and recipes of the Southern past.

When Jack sailed up the inlet up the Savannah River toward Milford, he could see how rich the low land was with potential. It was marsh land, but it was also colored with rich vibrant varieties of green and brown. He could look down into the waterway and see how thick the river was with fish. The air was clean and one could breathe easy. He inhaled, remembering the gentleman's words. "Once you come to Milford, people have a hard time leaving." Now that he was here, he could see why.

There was a boathouse and dock and he sailed into a space. He made arrangements for the payment of the rent and connected with Enterprise for the delivery of a rental car. The man at the dock, called the Milford Seapond, gave him a strange look when he asked about Miss Ada. "She's not someone who takes to strangers, sir."

"I'm a filmmaker, and I want to make a film about Southern foodways. I've heard that she's someone to see. Mind if I take some notes while we talk?" Jack whipped out a small notepad he kept handy.

The man, middle-aged with a beefy red complexion and dressed in a stretched polo shirt and khakis, seemed not to mind. "Have you ever experienced the monthly meal?" Jack asked.

"Once. 'Cause it was my birthday."

Jack gave him a startled look.

"You can't expect just to get in. Those tickets are premium and are purchased a year out in advance.

Families have held spots year after year, generation after generation. The money all goes to the school. This place would have been closed up years ago if it weren't for those meals. School's having a hard enough time now as it is."

"It is?"

"Why yes. Well, anyway. The meal. It's the best Southern food you've ever had in your life. The angel biscuits are so light they float in the air like pillows. The cornbread crackles in your hand and has just the right sweetness. Miss Ada makes a special butter to go with them. And as for the peach cobbler…" The man stopped.

"Yes?"

The man's eyes narrowed. "I don't know why I'm telling you all this."

Jack wasn't concerned about that. He had his ways. "I'm taking notes from your perspective. For my film. What did you have?"

The man calmed down. "The fried chicken, of course. It had the thinnest coating that melted in your mouth and the chicken was so juicy, the juice ran down my chin."

"Why don't they make the meal bigger? Sell more tickets?"

The man laughed. "You best not ask Miss Ada that. The meal is a spiritual experience. She wants to be able to look into the face of all who eat her food. Do you believe in God?"

"I have my good days and bad days." Jack shrugged.

The man shook his head. "That won't do. It's a religious experience. You have to go with purity in your heart, mind and soul." He held up a hand. "That's all I've got to say to you now. I'm happy to watch out for your boat here, but I don't think you are going to get too much information for your movie."

Jack still shook the man's hand and went up the dock to the landing, which had small houses and buildings. A lot of it was student housing, and some of it was office buildings for Milford College. He didn't mind the Georgia red clay scuffing his white Sperry gliders as he walked the beautiful quadrangle of the campus, laid out in a long green lawn with buildings on either side bordering the lawn. When he'd looked up the school's website online, he'd learned it was finals week, so there was a scattering of college students, some of them wearing a rather anxious look of furrowed brows paired with earbuds as they rushed past him.

He wanted to reach out to them and say it wasn't all bad, that it would be okay, but he knew that his overtures of comfort would not be welcome. The owner at the dock had said that the cafeteria was in Porter Hall. Porter Hall, the largest building crowned with a white dome, was the heart of Milford College, and was the place where students ate their meals and where the cooks who prepared the lesser meals during the week now reigned supreme.

Sunday was Miss Ada's day to cook weekly, apart from the feast, and it was only Wednesday. He headed in the direction of the huge building, opened a side door and smelled. Yeah. A little spice, a little sweet cinnamon smell, and roasting caramelized onions wrapped around him like a warm hug. Who caramelized onions for students? Cooks who cared, that's who. He rubbed his hands together, and by following his nose, like Toucan Sam, he found the cafeteria.

As he paid, he noted the appearance of the student workers. They were dressed for restaurant service with open-collared shirts and pressed pants. No young men with slouchy pants, no half-dressed young women worked here. Their appearance proved that this was a top-notch operation.

Jack, a bit rumpled in a blue polo, khakis and his boat shoes, felt the red creep up his arms and neck, ashamed to be dressed so casually as a white man in such a place. It had been a long time since he was the minority in a place, but he didn't feel bad about it. It made him feel as if he was investigating a place and time apart from his usual life, and he liked it.

He selected a Salisbury steak, green pole beans and a dish of stewed okra and tomatoes. For dessert, he had a slice of egg pie.

Everything he ate gave him great pleasure. Every mouthful of food burst with freshness. No canned ingredients used here. How did they manage to cook this quality food for a student population? Why would they bother? The egg pie finished off on his tongue with a silky milk nutmeg spice quality that was so rich, it was almost as if his mama had risen up off the hillside where they had buried her and embraced him.

There was practically no need for his dishes to go back to the dishwasher. They were clean as when he had selected them. As he left, he saw a sign by the cashier that had been facing in the opposite direction when he came in.

"Hiring kitchen help."

Perfect. They must have been hiring temporary help for the graduation meal. He would get a job and work in the kitchen and get to know Miss Ada that way.

When he asked for the application, the cashier looked him over once…twice…three times. Then she made a tsking sound and dug around in a drawer for a pad of applications, the top ones crinkled and stained with coffee. "We don't have a pen."

"That's okay. I've got one." Jack held it up and went to fill out the application, which looked like the campus dog had tried to eat it. "Who should I give it to?"

"Come back tomorrow at two. After lunch. They'll be doing interviews then." Her gaze went behind him to ring someone up and to make sure their ID was correct.

Whistling, Jack waved a hand at the student cashier who had rung him in, and took the long way back to the houseboat, examining the main quadrangle of the campus, enjoying the beauty of the drooping trees and fountains with historical plaques and statues of prominent people who held a place of honor in the history of the campus. It would be wondrous to work here for the May feast meal, and a better shot to learn from the bottom up. It had been years since his sous chef days, but he didn't mind revisiting them to learn at the feet of a master.

His first day in Milford had gone better than he'd planned. Typing up his notes that night, he took a moment and looked up at the stars, feeling the magic of Milford wrap its arms around him.

Just as if he were home.

Chapter 4

AFTER SUCH A LUNCH, JACK knew he didn't need to have anything fancy for dinner, but made his specialty grilled cheese sandwich, listened to jazz and watched the moonlight shoot beams through his window while he thought about his research on Ada Dailey.

Ada. She had been a civil rights activist in the 1960s, whose reputation had grown far and wide by the end of that decade because she had been responsible for feeding the young people and civil rights leaders meals when they came to Milford College. Even both Martin Luther Kings, father and famous son, had been known to sneak down from Atlanta, looking out for her yeast rolls, caramel cake and collard greens. She had been offered membership in the James Beard Society sometime in the 1980s, and had shocked everyone when she showed up to cook her famous fried chicken bringing her own seasoned flour in a Ziploc bag.

"I know y'all want to know what is in here," she was reported to have said, "But I ain't telling none of y'all." Once she'd tasted the James Beard meal, she'd proclaimed that his food wasn't anything special and left her award behind.

Jack folded his hands over his belly, making sure that it wasn't widening too much, and fell asleep thinking about what it would be like to marry such a feisty woman.

The next day, he made sure to carefully groom his hair with product, to shave, and not splash on too much cologne. He put on his best cerulean blue Brooks Brothers oxford cloth shirt, pressed khaki pants, and Sperry loafers.

When the appointed time came, after the lunch rush, he told the cashier what he was there for. After he endured her close scrutiny, he was ushered through a large, modern, state-of-the-art kitchen and a series of smaller rooms in the back. Finally, they went through another door and back out across a hallway, where, in a large carpeted office, there was a conference table surrounded by chairs. Jack sat down in one of the side chairs and waited. And waited. And waited some more.

Ada Dailey was late. Or maybe she couldn't come. She was an old lady, after all. Finally, when he was about to stand up and see if anyone remembered he was there, the door opened, and she appeared with a young woman in tow.

He had only seen Queen Elizabeth in video footage, but this woman, with the smoothest tan skin he had ever seen, topped by a crown of white feathered curls, was every bit as regal as the English monarch. She wore a crisp white chef's jacket and black pants, with a pair of small black chucks on her tiny feet.

Ada fixed Jack with a sharp look, then turned to the other woman. "Go on ahead now. Let me talk to him."

The younger woman with long braids seemed to hesitate, but Ada Dailey shooed her off. "Nothing going to happen to me. Will it?"

Jack stood. "No ma'am. Let me help you in."

"Why do folks think that when you old you can't walk? I can walk."

Now he had to endure the scrutiny of a woman old enough to be his grandmother, but she certainly wasn't looking at him as if she were related to him.

"You're a big one." Her posture was a bit bent over as she moved toward him and examined him on all sides, like he was a side of beef. "Nice eyes. Good thick hair. You dressed well. Hmph." She came behind him, and he was tempted to turn around.

"Aht, aht."

She didn't stay looking at his backside long, but she did look at it. She must have. Her gait was slow but she brought herself back around to the front of him and smiled. "Yes. You'll do."

"Ma'am?"

"I said you'll do. You want the job or not?" She folded her hands over her middle.

"Why yes, but I just thought you wanted to ask me some questions."

Her look pierced him through like a cleaver. "What do you think I should ask? About what cooking school you been to? I've never been to cooking school. I cook by feel, sight, taste, smell and touch. I see them nice large hands you got and know you've been gripping large pots with them. You're a nice shape, not too skinny, but you look like you have a hearty appetite. I don't trust no skinny cook."

"Yes ma'am."

"Your face is nice. I see you've got some burn scars here and there, on your arms. Those are the marks of arms what have reached in and out of ovens. Now. You want questions or you want to show me what you can do?"

"I'll show you what I can do."

"Fine. Let's go back to the kitchen."

Jack stood, willing his knees to be still. Why should he be nervous in front of this queen? He knew. Something, the cock of her head, the way she spoke, her halting movement, something reminded him of Miss Luly. The only mother he had ever really known. He did the thing Miss Luly would have expected, by stepping to her and offering his arm. "May I escort you?"

He thought she would like that.

She did.

"Oh. My. You have manners, too." She put her slight, shaking hand into the crook of his arm and he covered it with his. "A firm arm as well. Thank you, Jack."

He did not correct her. He'd had enough of being called Mr. Darwent. He preferred to keep the Darwent legacy far away from him. She led the way from the conference room. It was a nice enough space, but he wanted a closer look at the kitchens.

Since it was just after lunch, the shining silver of the kitchen sparkled and shone. Miss Ada pointed to a stool. Jack guided her to it and watched as she eased herself onto it.

"Now. Your audition, Mr. Jack."

"Whatever you wish, Miss Ada."

She fixed him with a laser-sharp glare and pointed. "In an hour, I want to see a pan of biscuits on the counter. Right in front of me."

He rubbed his hands together. This he could do. "That's it?"

"Yes. But be warned, Mr. Jack. I have a very high expectation for any biscuit that comes out of this kitchen."

"Oh, I understand that. So, by 3:55 p.m., you want some biscuits. Can I get a jump on understanding where the pantry might be located?"

Miss Ada beckoned someone with her little finger. A young man with thin dreadlocks stood to attention. "This is Roy. He'll help you get what you need."

"Fine. Roy, please show me the pantry."

Roy took him to a room off to the left that was cool and dark. Jack flipped on a switch and saw what he wanted in front of him. A row of flour bins, six different kinds, were lined up in front of him. Fortunately, they were all clearly labeled. He asked Roy to take the one labeled "Camellia Flower Flour" to the front.

Jack also retrieved a fresh tin of baking powder, some powdered milk and a package of lard, and looked for salt. There were several kinds: Kosher, iodized, pink Himalayan. He took up the Morton's and went out front to where Roy waited with a bowl and several cooking tools lined up. Jack scoffed. He wouldn't need a lot of that.

"Any grease from the bacon left over from breakfast?"

Roy blinked, but he retrieved a small glass dish with the liquid gold.

"No butter?" Miss Ada leaned forward from the stool where she sat, watching him.

"No ma'am."

"How would you get your biscuits that buttery flavor folks love?"

"I put it on at the end."

Washing his hands at the commercial sink with liquid soap and hot water, Jack dried his hands with the provided toweling and examined the layout in the kitchen. He stepped forward and scooped out two cups of the Camellia Flour into a bowl.

"Interesting choice for your biscuits."

"The best choice, ma'am."

She tsked and then sat back watching him. He made a well in the middle of the flour and took out two good pinches of the baking powder, a lesser one of salt and a big pinch of the powdered milk. Using his fingers, he worked the ingredients together and made another well, this time to work in some lard and bacon fat.

"Lard? Isn't that dangerous?"

"You asked me for the best biscuits, ma'am. That's what I'm going to do."

He took a cupful of cold water and poured it into the well, starting to work the ingredients together into a soft dough. A soft touch, not a rough one. Biscuit dough had to be handled like a lady. Pull it until it just came together, but not too much or it would be tough.

He saw Roy had laid out a metal 9x9 dish. He went to the refrigerator and surveyed what was inside. There it was. A stick of butter. Jack took it up, working the butter inside the wrapper to soften it. "Well, there's a technique I've never seen," Ada commented.

"It needs to get soft, ma'am."

Her eyebrows went up. "Indeed. That butter has no choice but to obey, I'm sure."

Roy laughed a bit, as did Jack, who opened the wrapper and spread the now softened butter all over the pan at the bottom and sides for that buttery taste. Then, he pinched off blobs of the soft dough, gently shaping it with his hands until they were laid out in the pan, four by three. A dozen biscuits.

"Don't they need to touch? So they rise high?"

"They will, ma'am."

The oven had been preheated to 350, but Jack preferred the heat higher, at 425. He adjusted it and put the biscuits in. Closing the oven, he went back to the refrigerator and plucked out a cold baked sweet potato and some apple cider.

"What you doing now? I only asked you to make some

biscuits." A slight frown appeared on Ada's tan features.

"Oh, just something a bit extra. Where is your cinnamon?"

Roy pointed out the spices and Jack selected the ones that he wanted, along with the sugar jar. Picking up a small skillet on the stove, he mixed together a sweet potato butter.

Ten minutes left.

With cheddar cheese, chopped red pepper and some Duke's mayonnaise and spices, he whipped up a small vat of pimiento cheese.

He retrieved the biscuits and put them in front of Miss Ada, whose eyes went wide at the pan full of golden goodness. "Not too bad. You were right about the biscuits rising. Roy, get us some plates and knives. What is this other stuff you made?"

"Sweet potato butter and a pimiento cheese spread."

Once he had finished, some of the other workers wandered in, gathering at the smell of the baking biscuits and the spicy cinnamon smell, no doubt. Everyone reached for a biscuit.

Ms. Ada pulled a hot biscuit from the pan and examined it. Looking at the layers, peeling them back one by one, tasting them as she went. "Not bad. Not bad at all. Now let me try this butter and pimiento cheese spread."

Miss Ada helped herself to the butter. Jack's heart lurched as he watched the older woman eat and enjoy his food. The appreciation moved and spread among the other kitchen workers who had gathered. Yes. This was the very thing that kept him going, even when there were times he wanted to give up—kept him living for the moans of appreciation, nods, and exclamations of joy that broke out from the people who enjoyed his food.

Much better than being a lawyer.

But Miss Ada had said nothing.

All of a sudden, the older woman held up her hands and her staff silenced at her command. "These were wonderful. You're hired."

The entire kitchen erupted into applause and congratulations to Jack.

Thank God. He had passed the test. He was on his way.

Chapter 5

F ORTUNATELY, THE FLIGHT TO CHARLOTTE was uneventful and when Althea landed on the plane tarmac, she was able to find the gentleman holding up a sign with her name on it. She always hired drivers. Professional ones.

The middle-aged gentleman sporting a yellow polo shirt and baggy shorts to accommodate his large stomach gave her a friendly smile and made sure that she had a smooth-as-silk ride to the headquarters of Mama Cassie's Home Cooking. Mama Cassie's was a place where Southern food was chain-made for a wide dispersal of the Southern food experience. Doing a little market research in the car, Allie spoke pleasantly to the driver, who was an older Black gentleman.

"Would you recommend Mama Cassie's as a place to eat Southern food here in Charlotte?"

The good gentleman laughed. "If you like that tourist notion of what Southern food is, it's fair enough. You from the North?"

"Originally, I'm from Georgia."

She didn't know what caused her to admit to that.

Usually she didn't say that, but it felt important to be extra candid today.

"Well, Mama Cassie's has all kinds of tasty food." The man looked around as he was driving. "But honestly, people go there for the sweet tea."

Allie rearranged the things on her lap and paid attention. "Well, it's funny that you should mention that. I'm here because of their tea."

"Lord, yes. That tea cures everything. It's wonderful. I buy a jug of it a week."

"Why is it so good?"

"It's, I don't know. Healing. It reminds me of my mama. I can't say."

"Well, let's hope they can continue to make it."

The man pushed his foot down on the brake hard, and Allie went sliding up in her seat just a bit. "Say what?"

"Nothing." Allie waved her hand. What was in this mystery tea? "I'm sure it will be fine." The man pulled up to the gates of the headquarters of Mama Cassie's. "Please, return here in an hour. I have another stop to make."

"To be honest, I feel like hanging out here with a sign begging for a sample."

"I'll convey your thoughts to the CEO."

He gave her a prolonged look, up one side of her jeans and high-heeled boots and down the other to her crisp white shirt and peach ragged-edge cardigan. "Well then. I'll wait."

Allie smiled.

Entering into a space as a woman in charge of things was an exercise she should have been well used to by now, but being back in the South made her stomach knot up a bit. Was Charlotte like New York, where people stared at her in a boardroom as if she did not belong? Or as if she should do something to herself to fit in?

Before she could really wonder about that, she was whisked in to the well-appointed beige-decorated office of Cassandra Shrum, the president and CEO of Mama Cassie's. Along with her was her daughter, Sandy Lou, her mother's executive assistant in running the business.

"Thank you so much for coming to handle this matter personally, Ms. Dailey. It's very disturbing." Allie shook her slight, small hand. Cassandra, a thin blonde, did not appear as if she had any part in eating the Southern cooking she sold, and that made an alarm bell go off in Allie's mind. For some reason.

She shook her head to clear it so that she could attend to her present business.

"I can imagine. Matters with the law aren't ever easy, but I'm glad to help." Allie shook Sandy Lou's hand too, and sat in the chair she indicated.

"Good," Sandy Lou chimed in. "We've been through enough."

"So, let me ask a few questions." Allie set up the Evernote app on her phone and her recorder as she took notes. "How old is your company?"

"Twenty years. I started it while Sandy Lou and my son were in high school. I was a single mother trying to make a way in the world, and I began to cook some Southern dishes and to sell boxed lunches to ladies in beauty parlors. Getting your hair done can take all day. You understand."

Allie did not understand.

"What beauty salons?"

"Oh, the ones that were helping ladies with braiding, weaves and the like. Those styles can take hours and people can get very hungry."

Who were these clients? Allie wanted to talk to them

for the case. She leaned forward to listen to Sandy Lou, who interrupted her mother. "We did all right, but it was when we brought in the tea four years into it that we were able to buy our first location. Now we have fifty stores across North Carolina, Virginia and South Carolina."

This, Allie knew. Interesting that their chain didn't take off until the tea arrived on the scene. "Okay. So. I don't know how to say this any more plainly, but we've got to get to what is in that tea."

Mother and daughter looked at one another. "Oh, does the lawsuit require that?" Cassandra asked.

"I'm afraid it does."

"We make all of the tea here and ship it out. Maybe Sandy Lou should take you to the production line and you can watch it being made."

Allie nodded. That sounded reasonable. Still, she wasn't surprised that they clammed up. Trade secrets were secret for a reason.

Waving a brief good bye to Cassandra, Sandy Lou took Allie to a changing room where she put on protective equipment, complete with face mask and helmet, before she and Sandy Lou entered the vast production room, filled with similarly attired workers, tall shiny silver silos and large vats with strange colored liquids with steam rising into the air. "When we first started, Mama used Lipton tea bags. Now that we are a bigger operation, we do our own contracting directly with the best tea plantations in Ceylon. We buy the best black tea and brew it with the purest filtered water and sugar." They moved along the production line. "It moves down through here, where it cools and is put through our aging process."

Sandy Lou pointed to the finished product of steaming tea ready to be cooled. Allie felt her pores open up like she was on the receiving end of a much-needed facial.

She noticed Sandy Lou's face flushing in the heat.

"Once it has been aged over three days, then it's put through these chutes and packaged in recyclable gallon jugs to go to our shops."

"Is that where you can buy it?"

"Yes. Only in the restaurants. We've been approached about selling it in grocery stores."

"That's where the suit came in." Allie encouraged. "Sherry wanted to sell it too."

Allie didn't think the young woman's face could get any redder, but it did. "Her part of the suit, as I'm sure you can see, is complete foolishness."

"Do you know Sherry?"

More face flushing. "Of course not. What would make you think I did?'

Her defensive response told Allie volumes. Yes they did. Of course they did. But how?

Allie untwisted her lips. "Yes. Well, thank you." They returned to the changing room. Once Sandy Lou showed her where to divest herself of her protective gear, Allie said her goodbyes, and went back out the gate to where the driver was waiting for her.

She gave him the next address. "Well, I saw how they make it. Pretty straightforward. It's just tea."

"Didn't they offer you any?"

No. They had not, which was strange. Very strange.

The car drove through a different part of town, a part that brought back memories to Allie of when she was Althea. The houses were older ranch styles, made of brick, with well-kept fronts populated with gardens. The gardens bloomed with flowers like geraniums and impatiens, but she could see the beginnings of vegetables being grown there as well. Her mind pulled up many memories of picking tomatoes and collard greens in

Granda's garden. Happy memories. Sunny ones before the dark days came.

The car pulled up to a gravel-covered lot. The squat white building had a white plastic sign reading "Sherry's," with a pink-that-was-once-red Coca-Cola symbol.

"You sure this is it?" The driver looked uncertain.

"I'm sure."

"I never heard of this place before."

Allie realigned her purse, and decided that she would like another opinion. "How about lunch?"

"I thought you would never ask." The driver, who told her his name was Derek, made all kinds of show leading her into the diner.

Once inside, it was clear to see that Sherry's had been hanging on for a while. The red and green and black and white pleather booths were cracked, the black-and-white linoleum tile, while clean, had seen better days, and the menus were covered in plastic. Allie picked one up and it felt tacky to the touch. When she pulled back her hand, for some reason, her perfect French manicure seemed outrageously out of place.

Most of the booths were irregularly placed and featured some cracked and duct-taped seats. Derek gestured to the one booth that was not yet cleared off, but had a table full of dirty dishes. Probably because it had the least cracked, taped seat in the restaurant.

A pleasant-faced woman with wide lips wearing khakis and a short-sleeved green shirt and apron, came up and cleared the dirty dishes away, balancing the dishes in her free hand while adroitly grasping the cloth in the other.

Allie's mind went back to the days when she waited tables, and she appreciated the woman's skill. "Thank you all for coming," the woman said. "I'm Sherry. I'll return to take your order." Her voice, low and unmistakably Southern, put Allie right at ease. Maybe it was because she was here and could be acclimated to the accent, instead of feeling jarred by it like she had in New York.

Derek eased his way into the booth, took up the menu, and marveled. "Whew. She got some dishes that take me back a way. Butter beans? Who does that anymore?"

"I wonder if she's the Sherry who is the owner."

"Wouldn't do any harm in asking."

Allie could tell she was, though. It was in the way she kept that Handi Wipe moving across the counters. Yes, the place was worn down, small, and dark, but it was clean. Sherry returned, a notepad poised before her.

"What would you all like?"

"Are you the owner of this here fine establishment?" Derek batted his eyelashes at Sherry in an exaggerated way.

"I sure am, big man."

Derek frowned. "How come I've never heard of you? Been living in Charlotte almost ten years now."

"Well, I get along on word of mouth a lot. But it's just enough for me."

"Ain't that something?" Allie watched as Derek's gaze wandered all up and down Sherry in a way that she had not been on the receiving end of in quite a few years.

His frank appraisal of Sherry's rather generous proportions tugged low and deep in Allie. Bathing in the glow of obvious attraction when you weren't part of it tended to do that. When had she been on a date last?

Now here she was at thirty-two with no one. That world seemed to have slipped past her. Oh well. She didn't begrudge it to anyone else. Clearly, it wasn't for her.

"Well, I'm still deciding, but I'll take a glass of your tea while I wait," she said.

"Is it that good?" Derek looked at Allie.

Now Sherry's face, arranged in a flirtatious way to match his, shifted as if rain were coming into a sunny day. "I'll pour you one for free. Let you decide for yourself."

Sherry went away and immediately brought two tall frosty glasses of iced tea with long straws in them. Allie leaned over and took a sip. The smooth, cool sweetness of the tea quenched all of the hot parched patches in her throat. The hint of mint sweetness made her feel as if her breath were refreshed and new. It took everything in her not to sag and say "Ahhh" after her first sip.

"My Lord," Derek said. "This tea tastes just like…"

"Heaven." Allie interjected. "Pure heaven."

"Thank you." Sherry's face was now pleased. "It's my grandmother's recipe from a long time back." Yes. Allie knew that. The offhand revelation caused her to make a small fist in her lap. She took their lunch order: smothered pork chop, butter beans and collards for Derek, and a veggie plate for Allie.

"You a vegetarian?" Derek asked after Sherry hustled away.

"No. I just didn't feel like meat right now. I like side dishes."

"Got it. I was about to say that the tea tastes just like Mama Cassie's."

Allie nodded. A familiar feeling tugged at her soul.

But why? What was the story behind this recipe? She would bet good money that there was a connection, probably a work or family connection between Cassie and Sherry with that grandmother. For the first time in her stellar career, she felt that she would rather not know.

Now she realized why Pichon, Boar and Ellis had sent her down here.

Jerks.

She wanted to throttle the Three Horsemen even more as the soft, slightly vinegar tang of the greens hit the back of her throat. They echoed with the taste that made her think of Granda's greens. These had the same degree of tenderness but less of a meaty taste. They were probably cooked with turkey or some different meat. The sweet potatoes had a caramel butter taste that made them slightly sweet, but not so much like dessert. She had opted for a corn soufflé that was pillow-light on her tongue with chunks of real fresh corn, not canned corn, and a bit of a kick from jalapenos. She regretted not ordering the macaroni and cheese, but she had to think about her thighs. She enjoyed the buttery richness of her angel biscuit, chosen instead of the cornbread.

Sherry's was a special place.

Which probably operated on thin margins.

And would be destroyed by a lawsuit from a big money corporation like Mama Cassie's.

The lawsuit that she was bringing.

"Dessert?" Derek offered after she had eaten every single bit of her lunch.

"No."

"You know you want it."

"That doesn't mean I should have it."

"I hear you. I'll go ahead then and have her bring two forks." Derek gestured and right away, Sherry brought them a thick hunk of red velvet cake with comfortingly crooked swirls of frosting and pecans pressed into the top layer. Homemade. And two forks. They asked for new beverages: a tall glass of milk for Derek and a cup of coffee for Allie.

The crowd had thinned out; they were the only ones left in the place and Sherry stood over them, arms folded. "I been trying to figure you all out."

"Have you now?" Derek's cheeky manner made Allie want to laugh as he lifted a big chunk of the red sweetness halfway to his lips. Allie regarded him as he ate the bite, eyes rolling into the back of his head.

"You're going to have to drive my car after this, Miss Allie."

Sherry's finger wavered between them. "So she ain't your sister?"

"No ma'am." Derek smiled.

"And I can tell you ain't dating her." Sherry winked at him. He returned the wink.

Allie felt left out.

"He's my Uber driver."

"And you having lunch with him?"

Allie shrugged her shoulders. "I didn't want to eat alone and it was lunchtime."

"Well, that's mighty nice of you. I might have thought that you were a stuck-up Northern chick by the way you had them shoes on, but you've clearly had some raising."

Here was an opening. "I had a grandmother raised me properly. Did whatever she had to do to keep us all fed and clothed. Worked as a lunch lady for years. " Allie said, forking up a small piece of the red goodness for herself, with just a swipe of frosting on it, glad to take in a bit of sweetness with the sour tang of the loss of her parents. She ate it. Oh yes. Sheer heaven.

"Mine too! Where?"

"Milford, Georgia," Allie admitted more easily than she usually did. Something about the air in Charlotte made her speak more readily.

"Lord, that's where Ada Dailey is." Sherry touched her generous bust.

"Who's that?" Derek looked perplexed as he kept whacking on his cake with his fork.

"Who's that? The best Southern cooking in all the world comes out of Miss Ada's kitchen. Next to my own grandmother of course."

Allie nodded. "Ada Dailey is my grandmother."

Sherry bounced up and down as if she got the Holy Ghost. "If I had known! Was my food…? I mean…?"

Allie waved her hands. "Everything was delicious, Sherry. Look at my clean plate. You have nothing to be ashamed of."

Sherry sat down at one of the counter stools across from them. "I would have made something better if I had known."

"It was wonderful. And I'm not in the family business, so you have no worries from me on that." But Sherry did have worries in another way, about something else. And that knowledge made Allie, for the first time in her life, ashamed of what she did, instead of who she was.

Chapter 6

S O SHE SHOULD HAVE GONE to Milford.
But she didn't.

The fact that Allie neglected to visit her grandmother when she was only three hours away manifested itself in that burny feeling in her middle whenever something came up about Milford. She wished she had her Tums handy. Or Sherry's red velvet cake.

She could call and get Tums delivered, but given that things were winding down at the firm in advance of the summer slowdown, maybe she should make a prolonged visit to make up for her recklessness.

She picked up the phone to call Granda, knowing full well that on a Saturday morning, she would not be that busy. It was the one day when the students slept in until noon and the cafeteria opened up a brunch later in the day for them. That didn't mean that Granda was asleep, though.

The phone rang a long time, and at first, she was a bit afraid something had happened to her grandmother. What would she do? Would she have to move there? She was the only one in the family who would do anything to take care of Granda.

"Hello?" Her grandmother answered the phone, clearly in the middle of a laughing spell.

"Granda. It's me."

"Oh, Althea. How you doing?"

"I'm fine, Granda. Sounds as if you are in the middle of something. Something fun?"

"Oh my, yes. Jack is over here and we're baking, and…"

A deep booming voice came over the phone. The kind of voice that made women melty and warm inside. Allie hadn't felt that way in a very long time, so when it hit her, she was a bit confused. "Who is Jack?"

"I told you before, honey. Jack Darwent. The moviemaker man."

"Movie?"

"He calling it *Southern Treasures*. He say I'm one."

A niggling remembrance from their last conversation crossed her brain. Oh yes. Granda had told her that she was going to be in a movie.

"So is he filming now?" Allie leaned forward as if that would help her to hear that male voice again.

Granda giggled. "Naw. We making beaten biscuits and Jack took the rolling pin to the dough too hard, and…"

"And…?"

"Well, that dough and the rolling pin got beaten up for sure." Her grandmother's voice came more faintly. "I told you your arms was too big to beat on that dough that hard."

The person named Jack said, "I didn't know, Miss Ada. I swear."

"Child, we are going to have to throw this dough in the trash, 'cause the pin done broke. What you want, sweetie?"

Her grandmother never called her sweetie. She always called her by her given name, dragging the syllables out in her Southern way with no "th" in the middle. Al-TEE-a.

"Granda, have you been drinking?"

"Of course not, child! Why would ask me that? Your grandmother?"

Oh dear.

"I didn't mean to judge you, ma'am."

"That's better. Your words have me thinking you done forgot your Southern upbringing altogether, now you a big shot in New York. Look. I've got to go. We got to start up another dough, although I don't know what we'll roll it out with."

"I can go carve something!" Jack declared. He didn't sound drunk. He just sounded like a man. A real man.

Allie had always been a bit of a sucker for a deep voice.

"Bye now, sweetie."

And before Allie could get a word out of her mouth, the call beeped out with that maddening red circle popping up on her smart phone.

She stared at it for ten minutes.

What should I do?

Her grandmother was laughing and talking with a strange man. She surely didn't seem to need her right now. She could ask her friend Monique what was going on. Her old school chum was Allie's appointed and paid spy in Milford. She worked at the college library, went to the same church as Allie's grandmother and saw her nearly every day of the week. If there was anything unusual happening, she would have called. And she hadn't.

Due diligence time for the Mama Cassie's case loomed. Connie's baby loomed. But given technology, Allie could work from Milford if need be.

She turned to her MacBook Air and googled this Jack Darwent person.

Andrew Jackson Darwent III. An impeccable Southern heritage. The Darwents were a big deal family in Tennessee. A fistful of Darwents had existed, including his father, Drew Darwent the second, who had spent time in the Tennessee legislature. One of them had gone all the way to the lieutenant governor position in Tennessee, but a scandal had derailed a run to the governor's mansion.

Figures.

Drew Darwent had been a big-time civil rights lawyer and had spent his life working towards uplifting the rights of Black men and women, and had worked on voter suppression cases throughout the South. Well, Jack's graying father was certainly someone to see. His law firm's online presence sported the picture of a blue-eyed, handsome, gray-haired silver fox all dressed in a suit.

There were no pictures of his son, though, which was strange. All she could see on him was that he was some sort of gadabout who had graduated from Vanderbilt and engaged in all kind of frat boy opportunities.

He probably lived off his daddy's money. Looking for something to do. Or someone to exploit. Like her helpless grandmother. Allie kept clicking on links and typing. Her laptop grew warm with all of the searching she was doing.

Clicking on the *Southern Treasures* website, she could see he had a GoFundMe attached to his project. It wasn't nearly at what it could be, only a few thousand K for a $50K budget. Why didn't he just ask Daddy for it? She clicked through a few more pages, and then…

There he was.

On the contact page.

A blue-eyed, blond man with perfect teeth, dressed very casually in a fisherman's knit sweater with a pair of the most snug blue jeans she had ever seen on a man, smiled back at her. The GoFundMe link repeated just under his picture.

Of course.

The Devil went down to Georgia.

Jack Darwent's visage brought back a line from an old song her mother used to play called "Somebody's Knockin'."

Somebody's knockin', should I let him in? Lord, it's the Devil, would you look at him? I've heard about him, but I never dreamed, he'd have blue eyes and blue jeans.

Jack Darwent. The very Devil.

Which meant Allie needed the Lord's help to fight him. Someone she had not bothered to call on in a long time.

She stood. She could work from her grandmother's. It was time to get some answers. "Connie," she marched out to talk to her executive assistant. "I have to go away for a few weeks. Are you sure that you won't be due for six weeks?"

Connie rubbed her belly. "Five. But my other two came just on time."

"I need to go see my grandmother."

"Is she okay?"

"Yes. She is. But she seems to be…happy."

"Well, that's a problem." Connie never missed a beat.

Allie shook her head and explained the situation to her assistant. "Make sure to arrange the driver for me."

"All the way from Atlanta to Milford?"

Allie gulped. Such a lot of driving. "I guess I can do it."

Connie's face softened. She knew. "You can do it, Allie."

"I suppose I can. If I have to. I've got to get to my grandmother."

"I'll make the arrangements."

Allie turned from her and went back into her office. How had this Jack person gotten that kind of exclusive access to her Granda? Why hadn't Monique called her? She had better go see for herself.

That old burny, swirly feeling came alive and stirred in her stomach, making tracks up her throat centimeter by centimeter.

It should have been you.

Okay. I know that.

You didn't care enough about Granda to go back home and see to her.

I was busy.

Were you?

The burning swirl went away and a bright flush of intense red replaced it. How dare this Jack take her grandmother's time, love, and attention from her? Who did he think he was? All it would take was one French manicured tip of her fingernail to the right button on the phone and it would all be well—just one, and Jack Darwent, whoever he really was, would wish he had never set foot in Milford, Georgia.

Within the day, Allie was on a flight to Atlanta, ready to land on the ground so she could drive the few hours to Milford in her rental car. The weather was perfect for May, with a blue sky. The air at the world's busiest airport, tinged with gas, invaded her nostrils, but the fresh country was just a half hour away.

She loved that Connie knew her so well to arrange the right kind of car, outfitted in the latest technology, with enough distractions to occupy her as she drove. That way she didn't have to worry about a car accident. Equipped with an audiobook, Sirius XM, Bluetooth, she had everything she needed to focus on her driving, but enough so that she didn't get a panic attack on the way. It all worked. Before she knew it, she was pulling off on the Milford exit.

Nothing about the college town was obvious from the road. That was on purpose with the design, she knew. A school like Milford College was best hidden near the waterway, because someone might want to do the school or its students harm. That was one thing that had always hung over her head as an anxious child.

Her father, a former soldier and head of security at the school, always promised her he would protect her, but when danger came, it took him and her mother. Together. Nowhere to be found.

That's when she left Milford for an Eastern boarding school. To avoid the danger.

And now she was here again, fulfilling the saying that she hated the most.

Milford. The town no one ever really leaves.

Sigh.

The town square was bordered on one side with small shops of all sorts of things that students needed. The McDonald's was also cleverly designed to be a part of the small-town décor. At the end of the street was the sandstone brick building of Milford AME, her family's home church. The beginning of the campus was on the other side of the square, the side that faced the water.

The biggest building on campus, as well as the oldest, Porter Hall beckoned. That was where her grandmother had worked for most of her life in the main student cafeteria. On a Friday afternoon, just about four p.m., she would be leaving Porter, walking across the square toward her home on the back side of the strip away from where the students lived, toward where staff and faculty lived. Allie could sit on her grandmother's porch and wait for her, but everyone in the neighborhood knew who she was. It was better to be quiet and just wait on a bench.

She answered some calls and worked on her computer a bit. Then, walking along, laughing and talking, came her dear sweet grandmother on the arm of this drifter person. He resembled Apollo more than the devil, now that she could get a close-up look at him. His hair was not as short as it was in the picture on the website, and it curled around his head. His hair, like some kind of god from Greek mythology, made him appear to be otherworldly. She had never seen a man like Jack Darwent, and the fact that her grandmother was giggling and laughing like a teenager didn't give her any comfort.

Slipping a Tums between her lips, Allie chewed on the chalky fruitiness to help calm her, to keep the acids in her stomach from eating her up from the inside. She stood and faced the two of them, her grandmother in her little chef's coat, bent over but walking on the protective arm of this man, who wore a tightly fitting polo shirt with the expensive logo on it and more snug jeans with navy blue deck shoes.

Oh yes. A devil for sure.

Standing there, Allie pushed back her chicly cut bob over her ear. "Granda," she called.

Her grandmother froze in her steps. "Oh my Lord. It's Tea. She come home to me, like I've been praying."

The tremor in her grandmother's voice stirred Allie in an unexpected way so that she didn't realize Granda had called her by her old childhood name. A lump rose up in her throat as her grandmother uncertainly tried to cross to her on the uneven pavement. Allie went to her instead, taking big quick strides down the sidewalk in her Jimmy Choos, but when she reached her, Granda stumbled a bit. In order for them both not to fall crashing to the pavement, Jack Darwent reached his big arms out, steadying both of them.

At once.

"Whoa there, ladies," his voice boomed.

"Jack, you are making a specialty out of saving the Smithson women," Allie's grandmother purred.

Allie shook his hold from her, because all of a sudden, she felt dizzy, and she didn't like any fizzy feeling fuzzing up her head.

"Always happy to help, Miss Ada."

"Tea, meet Jack Darwent. Jack, this is my grandbaby that I raised up, Althea, but when she is in Milford, I call her Tea."

"Nice to meet you, Tea."

"What are you doing here with my grandmother?" Allie spoke entirely too sternly, because if she didn't, her legs would turn to egg noodles at the way his voice sounded when he spoke her old childhood nickname.

"Excuse me?" His eyebrows raised up.

She gulped at the surprise on his face.

"Tea, that is no way to be. Excuse her, Jack. She been living up in the North with rude Yankee people and forgot her upbringing I gave her."

"Granda, I didn't mean to be disrespectful. I just want to know who this…this…man is. He's been here for a long time."

"It's so he can make the best movie of me that he can."
Her little grandmother straightened up and Allie's heart
danced. She didn't want Granda to be mad at her, so
she softened her tone.

"He's making a movie of several subjects, Granda,
not just you."

"I film at my leisure, Miss Tea. Your grandmother is
particularly fascinating." An amused smile formed on
one side of Jack's lips.

Once again, Granda giggled.

Tea, Allie, whoever she was, had had enough. "Let
me get you home in the car."

"No indeed. I like walking and Jack is making sure I
get home safely. I don't know what you are doing here,
but you probably have your things in the car. You're
welcome to drive to the house, but I look forward to
my daily constitutional walk with Jack."

Her grandmother put her hand in the crook of the
man's arm and with that, walked away from Allie.

She ate another Tums—a wildberry one, the kind
she liked least of all.

Chapter 7

A LLIE STOOD THERE, SHOCKED AT the bait and switch
that had just taken place in front of her. This man,
this Jack man was far more cunning than she had believed. Well, she'd just better follow them and…

Wait.

No. That would add more to Granda's sassy attitude.

She sat down on the bench, looking up at the statue
in the square, of Pauline, yet another Milford ancestor of
hers, cast in bright copper that still shone under certain
light, dressed in the attire of a slave woman. Everything
about her—the kerchief on her head, simple shirt, long
skirt—all sought to highlight the determination in those
eyes. Pauline's one hand was clutched in a determined fist
and her other hand was stretched out, with a pointing
finger, showing her determination to be free.

Milford students kept the statues bright and coppery so
they didn't weather into green like the Statue of Liberty.
The upkeep of the statues had been one of the reasons she
wanted to go away to college. Why should she have to clean
up statues—even if they were legendary pioneers—when
she must study?

Besides, Pauline's story depressed her. She was the one who was shot by stray fire, right here on the square, on Election Day when she tried to vote for the first time. A sad story, but what could Allie do about it? The woman had been dead for a long time. It had nothing to do with her, right?

Her gaze shifted to the retreating figures of Granda and Jack. She clenched her hands. She ought to throw the book at him, but clearly, that would upset Granda and she didn't want that. No. The thing to do was to stay close to him, close as his underwear, which were probably some tight boxer briefs.

Allie sighed. Maybe putting off dating for so long was doing things to her. This man might be some kind of con artist out to get her grandmother's recipes and use them for himself. What could she do to stop him?

Her hand smacked her forehead, wiping a sheen of perspiration away. She would put together a contract, or carefully look over anything her grandmother had already signed, and fight it, if necessary. But first, she needed something to refresh her in this Georgia heat. She went across the street to the convenience store, where she bought a slushed Coca-Cola from a young student who wore a tee shirt that said, "I am my Ancestor's Wildest Dream."

When she paid, Allie noticed the girl had the nose.

Was this young lady a cousin?

Probably, but she had no time to find that out. Allie sipped at the drink, reveling in the cool slush going down her throat, and went to the car. Yes, she would stay close, close as two fingers together. And the benefit of it would be that she would get to spend the time that she had been meaning to spend with Granda.

Driving off with the slushy Coca-Cola frosting

between her legs so she could get some relief from the heat, she wondered something she had never thought of before, never cared about before.

Would Pauline approve of me?

I don't know.

Even driving very slowly, she arrived at her grandmother's bungalow before they did. Now she could glare at the two of them moseying up the street, arm in arm like old chums: little Ada, small hand tucked safely into the crook of the huge arm of Jack Darwent, whoever *he* was, laughing and talking. Her grandmother finally, finally, looked up and saw her. Her grandmother smiled at her, so broadly, Allie's heart caught for just a brief second in the sun of someone's pure love.

Allie waved back.

They arrived while she was lifting one of her huge, protective hard shell suitcases out of the car. She had four of them.

Immediately, probably too immediately, Jack came over and lifted out the other three, wheeling them to Granda's front door. And opened it. With a key. All at once.

Allie took in a sharp breath. This man had a key? She didn't even have a key.

"Are you looking to move in, Althea? My Lord, girl." Granda shook her head.

"Granda. He has a key to your house."

"Yes. Sometimes Jack wants to experiment in my kitchen while I'm at work. He'll see to it that your luggage gets in the house. I don't know where you going to sleep, though, since Jack uses your room for work when he's here."

The sharp breath went to Allie's heart and began slicing off pieces of it for dissection purposes. "Granda. Who is this man? We don't know him."

"Honey. You don't know him. He's my friend."

"Well, I've done some looking around, and…"

Granda folded her arms and got a stern look on her face that brought back painful memories for Allie. "I don't want to hear nothing about any of your looking around. Is that why you are here? To babysit?"

"I'm here to look out for your interests. As any good lawyer would."

"But not as my granddaughter. Hmph. I see you ain't changed none. Still in that uppity frame of mind."

"Of course, as your granddaughter. What does that even mean? As your granddaughter, I see you might need legal protection. So I'm here to look out for you for a few weeks."

"Well, I guess there's nothing I can do about it to get you to go on about your business."

"Ummm. No."

"Okay." Granda unfolded her arms and leaned in. For a kiss. The proverbial Southern sugar. She wanted some.

Allie leaned in and kissed her fragrant, soft, sunken cheek.

Granda pulled away first. "Well, we going to mess round in the kitchen and make dinner. You going to join us?"

Jack came out of the house to where they stood. Could she not even get a word in with her own grandmother?

She lowered her voice. "Granda. While I am here and probably after, I'm keeping my eye out on you. I don't care what he thinks."

Granda's voice went up in reaction to hers. "Well, good. Cause while you were up North being the big money-making lawyer, I've just been here doing what I do. I would have thought that you had enough money, rather than be concerned about my little coins, but I suppose not."

Everyone fell quiet enough to hear the chirping of the marsh birds in the moss-draped trees that populated Milford and Oberlin Court, the subdivision where Granda's old-fashioned house was.

Blood rushed to Allie's head at the thought of this stranger hearing all of this and knowing her family's business, but she knew nothing, absolutely nothing, about him.

She swallowed down a ball of hurt, again, and opened her mouth. Jack stepped forward. "May I escort you ladies into the cool air-conditioned house? I have some nice glasses of sweet tea waiting."

Granda turned to him, all charm and light, no more of the darkness and sorrow that Allie had brought. "Oh Jack, thank you so much. I'm parched."

The two of them marched into the house, leaving Allie in the driveway to tussle with her computer bag and Fendi purse. She carried them in by herself, crossing the threshold, back into the world where she was small and silent. Fourteen years slipped away from her as she went inside.

The promised tea waited in two tall Tupperware glasses from the 1970s. Granda and Jack were in the kitchen, laughing and at the same time, clearly engaged in a hand-washing party. Ugh.

Allie took her things into her room and marveled at the masculine character overlaying the room that was once hers. Gone was the pink of the room; now it was toned down with a lot of navy blue that reminded her of a ship. His computer, his papers, his bulletin board, his stuff, was all laid out on the bed.

Jack came up behind her, hands held up like a surgeon.

"I'm sorry. I'll clear all of this out for you after dinner."

Allie said nothing, but stepped into her old room and started to retrieve her things.

"She's really glad that you're here, you know."

His statement stopped her cold in her tracks. "How do you know that?"

"Well, I've been here for a few weeks. She hasn't stopped talking about you yet. I feel as if I know you already, big shot New York lawyer."

Something swirled up in her, but she swallowed again to force it down. "Well, I don't know you. That's what I'm here for."

"To get to know me?"

Allie strode over to him. With her heels on, she faced him, eye to eye. A wash of pleasure rushed over her at the fact that she had not taken them off. "To make sure that you aren't here trying to take advantage of my grandmother."

The blue eyes became big round pools of shock for just a second. Then narrowed. "I was hoping we could be friends, Althea. It doesn't seem as if that's something you want."

"I want to protect my grandmother."

"Well, that's good, since I can count on one hand the number of times you saw fit to care about her while I've been here. Let's just say it's something she thinks about. A lot."

She had been ready with a smooth retort, but she hadn't expected his words. She thought of the heart of the conflict between she and Granda. Ever since the accident.

She breathed out one of her cleansing breaths. "Let's just say that you mind your own business, Jack Darwent. Just know that I have my eye on you."

He was careful, so careful not to lower his freshly

washed hands, but she could tell that it was a struggle, and he had to think about it first. "I'm not here to do any harm."

"Oh, you aren't?"

"No. We're friends."

"I know who my grandmother is. And I know that you might want to take something that doesn't belong to you."

He lowered his hands, folding them across his broad, broad chest. "Well, all I know is that she is an 82-year-old woman who was too hungry for company. I'm not that deep into my Southern Treasures tour, but I've seen enough older women whose families don't seem to care about them."

Allie folded her own arms to match him. Or was it to ward any shame from coming into her heart at these harsh words? "We care."

"Maybe I should have phrased my words more carefully. *You* don't care. She gets calls from some of your cousins who seem to care."

Well, that…her breath didn't feel as cleansing now. "Some of us in the family are not that close," she balled her fists under her armpits. "And I have hired people who are from here and know our family to look in on her and report to me. She wants for nothing."

He shook his head. "Yeah, she's right. You have clearly lost your way."

Her head snapped back. "Excuse me?"

"Miss Ada says that you are the proverbial prodigal. Like in the Bible. That you have lost your way."

She stepped to him, poking a finger to his chest— damaging her nail tip. *Good Lord.* His chest was as hard as New York concrete.

She cleared her throat. "Let me get this straight. I've

lost my way."

"Yes. And it worries her. She keeps your name on the prayer list, and every Sunday in church they call out and pray over you, and all you can do is come down here to fight with her."

No. Not the prayer list. Now people would be wondering what was wrong with her, wherever she went in Milford. Maybe it was better to hide away and not leave this house.

"My being down here is none of your concern, nor is my relationship with my grandmother. Mind. Your. Own. Business."

"Miss Ada is my friend. She is my business. And I'll protect her from any harm. I don't care who it is."

Those blue pools narrowed, shooting ice jets at her.

Allie didn't have blue eyes, but she sure could glare right back at him. "Well, you'd better care. Because blood is thicker than water."

"Is it? Who is the Johnny-come-lately here?"

Standing close to him, all in his personal space, he smelled like oranges and summertime. Yikes. "Look here, colonizer…"

"Oh, cute. You're woke."

Now she was seeing red, because something in her blood vessels must have burst. "What does that mean?"

"Jack! Get yourself in here and let's get to cooking."

"Yes ma'am," he called back in his deep bass. Allie guessed his broad chest allowed his voice to resonate in a particular way, and that probably contributed to how deep his voice was. A deep hard chest made for a deep hard voice.

What is wrong with me?

She yanked herself back, as if she had stuck her finger into a hot, burning fire.

"I'm questioning why you are here," Jack said.

"Well, that's one thing we have in common, Mr. Darwent."

"It's just Jack. Even to you." And he turned on his heel and left her standing there with her finger up in the air, looking for all the world like Pauline down in the town square.

Allie shook her hands loose. Shook her head to shake thoughts loose so she could stick to her game plan.

I don't care who he is. He has got to go.

Reaching down into her Fendi bag, she pulled what she needed from it and followed him back into the kitchen, trying not to look at the way he walked: slow, unhurried, unbothered, unshaken by her.

Unlike how she was with him.

Chapter 8

T HAT NIGHT, ALLIE GOT THE first night of sound sleep that she had gotten in years. The slow, drowsy, humid heat of Milford lulled her to sleep, after a call she made to Connie to talk about the Mama Cassie's case. Once she had taken care of that, she drifted off into a peaceful slumber, which shocked her.

Once she woke up, she decided to go for a run before the sun got too high in the sky and too brutally hot. Her workout clothes were in her navy hard shell case, and once she dressed in her Fabris one-piece romper and athletic running shoes and swept her permed hair into a bobbing ponytail, she got going.

Her old hometown looked much the same. She knew if she jogged around the square, around the campus and back to her grandmother's house, that was a half mile loop. She had gone around on the loop three times in peace, making sure that she exerted herself to the point that she had a nice comfortable sweat, when she saw another person coming in the opposite direction.

No.

Jack Darwent.

Yes, it was him, wearing some teeny tiny shorts with his bare chest gleaming in the morning sun—looking most Apollo-like. That chest she'd broken a nail tip on last night.

Biting the tip of her tongue, she folded the uneven nail down, knowing she would have to go to a nail salon to fix it. She ought to send him the bill for the repair.

Allie knew men who jogged in Central Park without their shirts all the time, especially in the summer, but she had always resented it. Why should men take some privilege that women could not? Jogging around half-dressed was not cool.

Unfortunately for her, Jack Darwent was one of the not-cool ones.

Oh. Dear. Lord.

He waved like a fool, and once he reached her, changed direction and started jogging alongside her.

"Beautiful morning, isn't it?"

"It is. I wasn't looking for company, though." Her quads were beginning to tire, but he would never know.

"Of course you were. Who wants to jog alone? If I had known that you run, I would have made an appointment with you."

"Well, this is Milford, not New York, so I don't need company."

"Well, Allie, I can jog as I wish and I prefer to jog with you."

"Try to stay out of my personal space, please."

That would get him some distance from her. He dropped back just a bit and jogged behind her.

She kept on her loop and would only jog two miles today. From now on, she would jog in the evenings when the sun went down. She did not want to jog anywhere near this man. Who looked like that anyhow, in real life, like her teenage dreams of Apollo the blond sun god come to life? She increased her stride.

He caught up with her.

She ran faster, feeling the sweat pour down her armpits.

He matched her again.

His sunny blond curls pasted themselves to his forehead. It was harder to concentrate and think with him running next to her like that.

You haven't dated in years.

"Do you mind?" The words burst forth before she could stop them.

"Am I running too fast for you?"

"No."

"Good."

The turn to her grandmother's street came up, but she stopped at the corner to stretch. He didn't realize she had stopped, so he ran on, but then he turned around and stutter-stepped, watching her stretch.

Still stutter-stepping, he said, "This reminds me of something."

Allie continued to stretch, paying him as little attention as possible. How annoying.

"I was really into Greek myths when I was a kid," he continued.

Her head inclined to him. "Me too." She hated that her voice squeaked, but who else knew about Greek mythology these days?

"You were?" He sounded as if he was that kid. The stutter-steps ceased and he stretched next to her on the park bench.

"I mean, who wasn't?" She tried to play it off that he hadn't reached into her mind somehow and pulled out how she was thinking about him.

"Anyway, you remember that one about the chick who outran the guys who were all competing for her hand? Wasn't her name Al something? Like you?"

She stopped stretching and stood. "Her name was Atalanta."

"Ahh, yes. I knew she had an A name like you."

Allie remembered the tale well. A beautiful young princess who had vowed to remain a virgin huntress told her father that she would marry the man who could outrun her, knowing full well no man ever could. "What about it?"

"Well, your grandmother has told me you have no one special in your life."

He *had* reached inside her mind. An extra layer of sweat that she knew didn't come from the workout came to the surface of her skin. "I don't have time."

"Well, you're thirty-two. Make time."

"What about you? You're thirty-four. Granda always said any man who isn't married by the time he's thirty-five doesn't want to be married. For reasons."

He stood, keeping his body parallel to hers, and now, without her four-inch Jimmy Choos, she could see how much shorter she was than him. "I've been engaged. You?"

"Why didn't you marry her?"

"I didn't want to be engaged to some empty-headed woman from an appropriate Tennessee family who would not make good pillow talk." He grinned.

Pillow talk? "And you've been single ever since?" Allie tried to look elsewhere as she brought her leg up behind her to stretch her quads.

"I haven't found that woman who could engage me in enough intelligent conversation to intrigue me."

"Maybe your standards are too high."

"Could be. So who have you not let catch you, Ata-lanta…I mean Althea?"

"There have been some." She dropped her leg and picked up the other one.

"I see. So no golden apples in your future."

She stood up. Straight. "No man has been smart enough to toss any in my path. I don't expect any at this point."

"You never know what could happen, Miss Tea. Race you back to the house."

He took off without warning and she had to drop her leg so that she could right herself to run in that direction herself.

Only because it was time for breakfast.

"I'm not racing you!" she shouted after him. She wasn't *that* hungry.

He beat her back to the house and greeted her, smiling, as her grandmother waved to them from her porch. "Jack! You're the winner!"

"We weren't racing, Granda." Allie's curt words came forth before she could stop them. She was not here to engage in any silliness with them.

The two of them found her response funny for some reason, and collapsed in laughter as they went into the house. She followed them as her grandmother held the screen door open for her.

"I hope you didn't cook, Miss Ada." Jack said. "I thought this would be a great time for me to show your granddaughter a few things."

"Well, of course I did. That'll have to be some other day, Jack. Of course, now that I think about it, it has been a while since a handsome man cooked me breakfast."

Oh, did they laugh at that one.

Allie retrieved the ingredients for her protein shake

that she had packed in her tan hard shell case. She never ate much in the way of breakfast. Well, at least her grandmother's efforts meant that she had dodged Jack Darwent's attempts to capture her stumbling cooking efforts for two more days. With tomorrow being Sunday, breakfast was served at Milford AME church, and that—having to attend church—took on a whole new meaning.

By the time she'd had fixed her drink and was sipping on it through a recyclable straw, Jack had shrugged himself into a polo shirt and come back out. Granda fixed her with a wide-open stare.

"What is that?"

"It's a protein shake. I have them for breakfast every morning."

Jack made a green-looking poison face and crossed his eyes, which made Granda laugh all over again. What was this man, some kind of court jester for her queen grandmother?

"What's wrong with a protein shake? They are quite good." The internal talk she had given herself over and over again worked. It did taste good.

If there was nothing else to eat.

"This breakfast your grandmother fixed. It's fit for a king." He gestured at his plate of scrambled eggs, sliced red tomatoes and cantaloupe, with some kind of greasy link sausage at the edge of the plate.

"If I ate that, it would upset my stomach."

"I told you she don't like my food." Her grandmother pulled together some food on a saucer and ate from it. Allie knew it was her regular practice to eat very lightly because she nibbled on food throughout the day.

Jack gave a half laugh, shook his head and went back to using a piece of Texas toast as a trencher, scooping up bites of egg, sausage and tomatoes together.

Allie sauntered back to the bathroom, glad to be the first to take a shower and to ready herself for the day. Thinking through the paperwork she had to organize on behalf of Mama Cassie's, she showered, put on some yoga pants and a large tee shirt that she knotted on the left side, and swept up her hair, and it was hers, into a fresh ponytail.

She called in to Connie: "Any word on the baby front?"

"No, Allie. Still fat and waiting for my little oopsie to arrive."

A ping of a memory echoed in her mind. "You and Eric, you'll love the baby, right? I mean, I know you joke when you call it an oopsie."

"You okay, Allie?"

She took another one of her breaths. "Being here in Milford makes me…well, it makes me not myself. I'm sorry." She didn't say anything else, and hung up.

When she went back into the living room, she could see out of the corner of her eye that Jack and her grandmother were talking out the day. She couldn't help it; she had to eavesdrop. Besides, Jack's voice was too deep to be kept contained in the confines of her Granda's small kitchen.

"I would like to get some desserts captured. Something with fruit, a pound cake, teacakes."

"Whoa. Now you are going for it, Jack. Yes. I think my cold oven pound cake will do the trick."

"Cold oven?"

"Yes. You start it in a cold oven instead of a preheated one. You'll see how it works. Teacakes are easy, but are you sure about that? Everyone's teacakes is different."

"They are a central dessert of Black culture. I want to see your version." The insistence came hard in his voice, Allie could tell. A pound cake was the measure of any

Southern cooking, she knew. She hadn't had one in years.

"Makes sense. And you right. I should have known that you thought about that. So thoughtful."

Allie's eyes narrowed at the thought of Jack's thoughtfulness.

"What else you say?" Granda asked.

"Something fruity."

"Oh yes. Well. Maybe you need to learn the grape pie recipe."

Say what?

Allie dropped her tablet, making a cracking sound on her Granda's coffee table.

They both turned toward her and hot blood roared into her ears, blocking her hearing. She could not have heard what she thought she did.

"What are you doing in there, Tea?" her grandmother asked.

"Granda, the grape pie recipe. Are you going to tell him about that?"

Jack put down his own tablet and a strange look crossed his face.

"Baby, Jack is making me a Southern Treasure. I have to tell him what's in those things."

Allie got up and crossed to stand between her grandmother and Jack. "The grape pie. That's, well, that's special. That's Smithson. You cannot put that one in."

Jack spread his arms, looking very cavalier, as if nothing mattered to him. "I need dessert recipes for the cookbook too."

Allie stood, fists clenched. Enough was enough.

"I did not know you were going to write a cookbook. I thought this was all about his documentary."

"We need to raise funds for the making of the documentary. The cookbook with the recipes in it will help get those funds together, Tea."

Allie whipped around to face her grandmother, blocking Jack's view of her. Even though she was in her bare feet instead of Jimmy Choos, Althea Dailey, JD was in the house. "Did he have you sign a release?"

Now it was her grandmother's turn to look confused. "Tea, I don't see what you are mad about."

"Did he have you sign any papers? At all?" Her words, clipped and hurried, were weapons of destruction.

"No, but…"

She exhaled. *Thank God.*

Then she shook her head. "But what?"

"There was a contract to publish the cookbook."

Allie's hand reached out, making the flattest of surfaces. "I want to see it. Now, Granda. Where is it?"

"I think it's up in my bedroom, honey."

Allie turned to Jack, who had the chair back on two legs, looking entirely too relaxed. Her finger came out, Pauline-style. "No more giving papers to my grandmother, or for that matter, to any other grandmothers. I don't know what you are about, but I'm going to put a stop to it. Right now."

"He don't mean any harm, Tea." The dear old face wrinkled up in confusion.

"Granda. No more words about the grape pie. Nothing. Do you hear me?" Allie stomped to the other side of the house where her grandmother's bedroom was, searching on her nightstand for a contract, praying that it wasn't too late.

Chapter 9

Okay, maybe he was laying it on a bit thick. If his sister Bethany were here, she would probably have smacked him in the head at how thick. Jack knew he could be charming, but it had been a long, long, long time since he had run into a woman who was not impressed by him.

So he did lay it on with Ada, who he knew appreciated it, but he knew it was getting to Althea Dailey.

Something should get to her. Ice princess.

He had put up with having to hear how wonderful Althea was for weeks from Miss Ada, and now that she was here, she matched everything that her grandmother had reported on her and more. Only one detail was missing.

First, why the attitude? What was going on with that?

Second, and more importantly, she was the most beautiful woman he had ever seen.

Okay. Two things. That clashed.

All the pictures around the house were of Althea as an awkward teenager. Everyone had an awkward phase. So he hadn't seen the way she had blossomed—and wow, had she blossomed.

He went to Miss Ada's kitchen sink and scrubbed his hands down, as if he were going to do surgery on the fish, but maybe he was scrubbing away the bad taste of Allie's attitude. How dare this woman get to him?

"Althea say something to you, Jack?" Ada's kindly face peered around at him.

"No ma'am."

"I see you. She said something. Althea can have a sassy mouth, so if she's rude to you, you need to let me know."

He smiled to himself as he reached for two select-a-size paper towels. One was never enough for his hands.

"I just wondered why she has to be so rude to me." Jack looked up at Althea stomping into the kitchen to the cheap dining set.

Miss Ada glared at her granddaughter. "She's always had a free mouth. Her mama was like that."

Allie stopped. Her countenance changed. Was she trembling? The lovely curve of her arm made a slightly wavy line. Yes. She trembled. "I don't think you should talk about my mother." Her voice shook.

Her grandmother kept preparing the fish and the quiet, the heavy quiet, came down in the room like Plymouth Rock.

"Let's get this fish going. Lucky we got enough for Tee Tee. We was going to save it for breakfast, but we can have some streak o' lean instead."

"Ma'am, excuse me, what did you say?" Jack asked.

"I was talking about the fish and how we didn't have enough for breakfast."

"No, your name for Althea. Tee Tee?"

They laughed together as if it was the funniest thing in the world. The New York lawyer lady sat at the table fuming, probably doing social media, punching at a tablet with a stylus that looked like one of her dragon lady fingernails or something. Why did women insist on putting stuff on them that was noticeably fake? Her hands were a nice enough shape without all of those nails. Those nails probably got in the way of everything.

"Yes, I used to call her that when she was *little* little. Excuse me. My mind went back a ways."

Jack patted her shoulder, reaching over her to pull the fish closer. "It's okay. I like any and all childhood nicknames."

"People call me Allie now, if you must know."

Miss Ada leaned forward. "People in the North call you Allie. Here at home, we call her Tea."

"OK. I'll do the same, although I'll try to resist doubling up on it, since she clearly doesn't like it."

Allie gave him a swift look of something other than contempt and it shocked him. Her face was like a sun, and all her features were in perfect proportion to each other. Her nose tipped up so pleasantly, and her eyes were wide and brown. Her lips, full and pink, were so gorgeous she could be a lipstick model, and her skin glowed with a luminosity that made it appear as if she had swallowed the moon. More like Diana the huntress, the goddess whom Atalanta had vowed to serve.

That face was a perfect oval, and he could see the traces of Ada in the shape of her eyebrows, the point of her chin and the way she held her head up, like she was afraid of nothing.

So this is how he would play it. He would charm her expensive shoes off her pretty feet.

He winked.

She scowled.

Well, that was over.

Nice while it lasted. He and Ada got down to preparing the fish, which Miss Ada advocated rolling in

Piper Huguley

pure cornmeal, and he seasoned it with his special spice mixture and turned the oven up to 400 so that it would fry quickly. He oiled a pan and laid the fish on it, sprayed it with cooking spray and slid the tray into the oven.

He rubbed his hands together, washing them once more, fiercely, as if he could scrub her pretty face out of his mind. He would show her a thing or two.

"Okay. Side dishes now. What are you thinking about, Jack?" Miss Ada rinsed her hands free of cornmeal crumbs.

"Why ma'am, I thought it was your choice."

Allie put in. "I'm really not up for a lot of fattening food, to be honest. I was glad to see that you oven fried the fish instead of the other. I'm not a fan of grease." She held up some expensive looking phone, punching numbers into it, and started talking to someone.

"I guess she's watching her figure," Jack commented.

"Tea ain't got nothing to worry about. She just don't like my cooking."

"Umm, ma'am. What did you say?" Jack leaned down to the old lady so he could hear her over Tea's talking on the phone in loud, broad tones. She stood on those impossible shoes and walked back in the direction of her room.

"Tea. She don't like my cooking, so when she's here I keep it plain and simple for her. Nothing fancy."

"Well, we'll make it nice. Give me that okra and some of those fresh tomatoes, and we'll stew them." Ada gave him the ingredients and she stood back, watching, letting him do all the work. In a few minutes, he had made a ragout that was ready to pour over the fish, and some small sourdough biscuits with a sliced peach conserve he had whipped up.

The time went fast enough that he hadn't noticed

Allie walk back into the room with a disgusted look on her face.

"You okay, Tea?"

"I'm fine, Granda. Just work pressures."

Jack noticed one of her beringed hands go to her middle, pressing inward. What was that all about? Was she ill? That could explain a lot about her attitude if she were ill.

No, not with that gorgeous skin.

He shook the thought from his mind.

Time to focus.

Jack came around and pulled the cheesy plastic chairs out one at a time. "Have a seat, ladies, and I will serve you your plates." Miss Ada sat down, giggling a little. Allie plopped down in her seat and he practically dashed into the kitchen, eager to get out of her personal space before he fully took in the intriguing scent of her perfume, floral and fragrant.

He brought in the plates, already prepared, and served them all. He poured fresh glasses of the iced tea he had made with a strawberry infusion.

Sitting next to Miss Ada, he prepared to lower his head, but Allie picked up her fork, hardly noticing her grandmother's glare, but dropped it with a clatter to her plate when she noticed Jack's slightly lowered head.

Miss Ada clasped their hands in hers and prayed. "Lord, we thank you for this wonderful day, when you have brought my granddaughter home. Thank you for the gift of her presence here. Thank you for the friendship of Jack Darwent, and give me the strength I need, Lord, to get ready for this end of term dinner that's coming up in a few weeks. In the name of Jesus who helps us with all things. Amen."

"Amen." Jack sounded out.

"Amen," Allie muttered. She picked up her fork and started scraping off the ragout.

Jack leaned forward, shaking the glasses on the little table. "Excuse me, what are you doing?"

Allie looked up in shock. "I don't like okra. It's slimy."

He cleared his throat. "It's slimy if prepared the wrong way. I roasted this okra, so there's no mucilage. It's safe to eat. The flavors are designed to go together: acid versus sweet, crunch versus soft. Enjoy."

He really didn't care what she did, but he was not going to stand for her treating his hard work that way. She watched as the two of them, Jack and Ada, plated perfect forkfuls of fish, okra and heirloom tomato and consumed them.

"It's so well balanced, Jack, praise God. Perfect."

"Thank you, ma'am."

He pulled another bite together with his knife and fork as Allie struggled a bit to get it all on her fork and put it into her mouth.

Well?

But he didn't dare speak it aloud, because he didn't care.

Except he did, because he *had* spoken the word aloud.

"It's okay. I see your point about balance."

Ada beamed. "Yes. Jack been to a fancy cooking school, so he knows about all of that kind of stuff."

Jack gestured, not on purpose, with his butter knife. "Try the biscuit with butter and a bit of the conserve."

Tea didn't say anything, but actually did it. "Oh. It's like a little dessert. A peach shortcake."

"Something like that."

She said nothing else, but ate everything on her plate, leaving the fish bones white and a few red scrapings on her plate.

"Humph," Ada said as Jack picked up the plates. "You haven't forgotten your upbringing, so you remember how to eat fish with bones, I see."

"No, Granda. I haven't forgotten that."

"Well, praise Jesus for small favors." Ada's slightly bitter words, uncharacteristic ones from her, he thought, changed when she turned to him, plate uplifted in a slightly trembling hand. He caught it. "Baby, your biscuits are too small today. Let me have another half of one."

"Coming right up, ma'am. And some conserve?"

"Of course." Ada dimpled and he served her plate again.

Allie held herself away and apart from her grandmother, almost on the other side of the table, and now he got it.

She was in pain.

What was the source of this woman's pain?

She's coming down here to derail your movie and cookbook project and you are thinking about her pain?

Yes. Her pain was Ada's pain, and that interfered with his work.

He turned to her. "Do you cook, Althea?"

Allie stood up, holding up a hand, shaking her head. "The meal was lovely. I appreciate it. I'll be happy to do the dishes." She stepped out from behind the table in one swift move and crossed to the kitchen, finding where the gloves were, and donned them quickly.

"She don't cook, Jack. Somehow she always thought it was beneath her."

"That's not true, Granda. I'm just not talented in that area."

"Oh, come on. Everyone can do something basic. Scrambled eggs. Baked chicken," Jack urged.

Allie bowed her head to her task and ignored them both.

"Leave it be." Ada had finished tucking into her second helping. "She don't want to eat what I do and she doesn't want to cook."

"What if I filmed a lesson for her?"

"What you mean, Jack?"

"A cooking lesson. You passing on your knowledge to her. What if I wrote a little scene where your granddaughter learned how to cook something from you. A Smithson recipe from your family, maybe."

Ada's fork went to her plate after she had licked all of the peachy goodness from the tines. Her eyes went excessively shiny, all of a sudden.

Allie scrubbed a dish with extra vigor. "I don't know who you are, Jack Darwent, but you don't need to be so concerned about my cooking abilities. I've managed to keep myself alive over these years."

He regarded her well-shaped but thin frame. *Barely.*

"Don't you want to be in *Southern Treasures*? You'll get a per diem and your name in the movie, any way you want."

"No."

"Who doesn't want to be in a movie?"

She shook out the soap stick after she had scrubbed off all the plates and stacked them to dry. "I don't. Now." She peeled off the yellow gloves. "If you will both excuse me, I have some work to do before I retire to bed. Good night."

Jack and Ada sat there in the silence.

He broke it. "Was it something I said?"

"No. She's just a puzzle. Always has been. We can do some work before *Family Feud* comes on."

"Good. Let's talk pound cake."

Jack went to the living room to get his setups and Allie breezed past him, phone to her ear again. When he stared at her figure going past him, she held up a hand, opened the door and went outside on the porch, keeping up her rapid-fire dialogue, all at once engaged in her professional world.

She was a puzzle, all right.

Clearly one worth the mental challenge.

A puzzle worth solving.

Chapter 10

O NCE BREAKFAST WAS OVER ON Saturday, Allie sat down on the couch to work on her computer, but a flurry of activity from both her grandmother and Jack, whom she was doing her best to ignore, took place. Looking up from the screen, Allie blinked when her grandmother emerged in a denim dress and matching flat blue espadrilles.

"Where are you going?"

"We go to the farmers' market in the city square every Saturday. We've got to get there early for the freshest produce."

"And…" Jack came in with a tote bag over his shoulder, looking for all the world like a casual vacationer. "We have to get some of the farmers in line for this month's feast."

Ahh, yes. The feast. This one was the special May one, because it took place after graduation, to celebrate the class of 2021. Many rich donors who helped Milford graduates line up jobs were invited. It wasn't as publicly available as some of the other meals, but it was still very important.

Allie logged off of her computer and shut it down. "I'll come with you both."

Granda tsked at her outfit of pajama tights and over-large tee shirt, and Allie got the message. "I'll change."

"You can catch up with us. We've got to get moving," Granda shouted out behind her. "Just close the door, Althea Louise."

She would not, no, *no*, let Jack Darwent get the upper hand over her. She put on a fresh yellow sundress decorated with sunflowers and a pair of wedge-heeled espadrilles with beige ties that crisscrossed up her leg to the knee. It was the kind of retro look from the 1970s that she always liked to wear on such a Saturday. She enjoyed the farmer's markets in NYC, but Jack Darwent should not think that she was not going to protect her Granda and see what they were up to.

She dashed out of the house, walking as quickly as she could on the heeled espadrilles, swishing her skirt around her legs. Granda and Jack had set a good pace and were halfway to the square, but she caught up.

Granda stopped in her tracks to get a good look at her. "I'm glad you put on a dress. You don't have any makeup on, though, but I suppose you'll do."

The old burny feeling swirled around in Allie's insides again. *Was that about her skin tone? Had she tanned this short time in the Southern sun?*

She took a breath. No. Her grandmother couldn't have meant that.

Jack's look said something different, however, and she wasn't sure she liked what he thought. His gaze appraised her, from tip to toe and back. "She doesn't need any makeup, Miss Ada. None at all."

"Bah." Her grandmother waved a hand. "I guess not. Let's get going."

They continued on as a little trio, Granda and Jack up front, looking like the long and the short of it, and Allie, lagging behind them. As they approached the people who were setting up on the square, a chorus of hellos went up, greeting Granda and Jack.

Allie giggled to herself at her grandmother's tenacity when she approached stand after stand of heirloom tomatoes for sale, as she haggled and selected what she wanted to take home with her.

"This your granddaughter?" an old man said. His afro was a beautiful stark white.

"The very one."

"My, my, my." The man appraised Allie. "She's a beautiful one. Smart too?"

"Yeah. And rich." Granda sounded bored.

"The perfect trifecta in a wife, praise God." The man rubbed his hands together and smiled at Allie.

"Too bad you been married for forty years," Granda snapped.

"Yeah, that's true. I'm talking about your friend there what's been accompanying you here to help you cook. He looks like he could make you some beautiful great-grandbabies."

"Oh," Allie and Jack said at the exact same time. He had just come up behind her to hear this unwelcome pronouncement.

"I mean, no!" Allie shouted above the growing din of the farmers' market. "I'm not looking to marry."

"Oh, honey. Everyone is looking to marry." The man shook his head. "What is wrong with these young people today?" he appealed to Granda.

Granda's white curls shook. "I've got no idea."

"Why are folks afraid to procreate? I mean, that's what we here for and people are forgetting." He said *afraid*

in that old man Southern way: AFF-raid, Allie noticed.
Wow.

"Oh my God. Is that you, Althea?" The sound of a
familiar squeal took her away from this uncomfortable
conversation.

Thank you, Sweet Baby Jesus.

Allie turned and looked off to the left, where a small
card table had been erected. It was covered in books. The
young woman who had squealed wore tiny bantu knots
all over her head and had on a white sleeveless top with
a long denim skirt and espadrilles almost like Allie's.

"Is that you, Monique?"

Old habit made her squeal too at the sight of her old
middle-school chum. She ran to her table and their arms
flapped as they talked fast to each other.

"Are you a hugger?" Monique flapped. "Wait, I don't
care!"

"Yes!"

Monique's arms went around her and the warmth of
her friend's hug almost brought tears into Allie's eyes.
Monique pulled back and looked at her, openly crying.

"You look so beautiful, all grown up and citified.
Come here." Monique hooked an arm through hers.
"Come sit with me. You know they're going to shop for
a long time." She waved her hands toward Jack and her
grandmother, where clearly, at an artisanal breadmaker's
stall, they were in a world of their own.

"How are you?"

"The question is, how are you? And why haven't you
been keeping me posted about this Jack Darwent?"
Allie gestured to Jack. "I've been paying you to keep
tabs on my Granda."

"I have been. She's fine."

"Is she?"

"Look at them. She's happy." Monique's tan face sported a wide grin. "Girl, if Ada Mary was a few decades younger she would be all over that. And who could blame her?" The grin turned lascivious.

"He's a jerk. A bona fide jerk." Allie insisted, forcing her voice into confidence. "We don't know him."

"Jack is not a jerk. He's kind, and patient, and fits in, and…" Monique stopped, peering at Allie. "He's been a good friend for her. And maybe you, too."

Allie shook her head, drawing in her lower lip between her teeth. "I don't like the way he has taken over my grandmother. I'm here to look out for her interests, not make friends. That's all."

Monique gave her a light punch on the arm. "Every woman in town older than 18 and younger than Miss Ada has been after him. He's like the elusive Pimpernel."

Allie laughed at the reference from one of their favorite movies to the smoldering Scarlet Pimpernel. Monique, an avid bookworm as a child and now the college librarian, had made her watch some interesting stuff growing up. "Well, we don't get along."

"Why not?"

"I told you. He got an attitude with me when I came here."

Monique shook her head. "Not Jack."

"Why don't you believe me? I'm your friend." In spite of Allie's best intentions, the pitch of her voice went up.

Monique regarded them. "Yes. I am. I'm on your side in the matter. That is, until he turns around, and then…"

Allie gave her a light smack in the arm. "Really, Monique Denise."

Her friend rubbed on her arm, play-acting hurt. "Well, I'm glad to see you here. I'm organizing the library's discards and making a small amount of money for the school doing it. I'm here every Saturday. What else can I do? And I mean that I'm coming up there to see *Hamilton* one day."

"You've been saying that for years. You really should." Allie tried not to pout, but she knew how rarely Milford people traveled. For the reason of the town slogan: Milford—the town you can't stay away from."

"I know. I have ties here. Family. Friends. It's all I need."

Allie shook her head. "I admire you in your satisfaction with it all."

Her friend hugged up against her. "And you in going after what you wanted. And look at you. You're partner now."

Her smile came as fast as she forced it to. "I am."

Monique pulled back and looked at her with a suspicious side-eye. "Aren't you happy?"

Allie sighed. She couldn't hide her feelings as she might like here in Milford. The Georgia humidity had a way of peeling her armor away. "I'm just wondering what else there is. That's all. It just seemed so easy to reach a lifetime accomplishment, and now I'm thirty-two and there's no fun anymore."

When Monique's elbow poked her side, Allie rubbed it in response. "So, try to start a little fun with old Jack then," Monique suggested

She gave her old friend some side-eye of her own. "First that old guy trying to pair us off, and now you? What? You all better watch *General Hospital* and leave me be."

"Well, you could date. Think of that." There had been many a phone call with Monique, talking about her dating issues in New York.

"Men don't like me."

"No. They do. But you scare them with your dragon lady lawyer side, Althea. As soft and pretty as you are today, who could resist you?"

Now Allie elbowed her back. "Well what about you, Monique? Where is your Prince Charming?"

Her friend gestured out to the community. "He'll be here on his white horse in a matter of hours."

They laughed like the old friends they were, collapsing in each other's arms. Allie stayed at her stall, helping Monique sell her antique books.

More people came by the table to welcome her home than to buy books, but it was enough of them for Allie to feel welcomed.

She hadn't felt that way in a long, long time.

In all too brief a time, Jack wandered up to them with two heavy bags full of produce and a loaf of bread sticking out. "You want to help?"

"You can't carry it on your own?" Allie's eyes wandered to his arms, bulging out with the weight of the bags.

Wow.

"I could, but I thought you just wanted to help your grandmother. We're about to leave." Jack inclined his head toward the elderly woman.

Allie replanted herself in the folding chair next to Monique, heart beating a little faster. More Georgia humidity, she supposed. "I'm catching up with my girlfriend. You can go on ahead, since you seem to be everything to Granda. I'll be along soon."

The look on his face shifted and Jack edged himself away, back to the table where Granda stood, waving her arms, clearly in deep negotiations with someone.

"I saw that." Monique scolded. "Gurl, why were you rude to him?"

"I don't need anyone else regulating my time. I get

enough of that from the Three Horsemen in New York." Allie folded her arms and kicked at the grass.

Monique stared down at her.

"What is it?" Allie craned her neck up.

Monique was nearly six feet tall, and Allie, at a rather tall five foot nine, always had to look up at her, even today in her three-inch-heeled espadrilles.

"Look. We've known each other since we were kids, right? I know it's been a while since we have seen one another, but I'm going to tell you straight. You got something for this guy."

She shook her head as if someone had put her brains in a blender.

"Look. It's okay. He's not an average guy. He's exceptionally charming. Ever since he arrived in Milford the attendance at church has, well, gone up. Lots of ladies getting the Holy Ghost every week, you know?"

Allie had not stopped shaking her head. She did not care if her ponytail came loose.

"Okay. Okay." Monique held up her hands. "Peace, my sister. Peace."

Why had Monique gone all New Agey on her? She gripped her sides, pleased that her old friend had stopped saying what was on her mind.

But then Monique put hands on Allie's shoulders and made her face her, chin up, "I just want to say one more thing, but first, I'm going to deal with this customer who has been waiting." She gestured to a man with a little girl who browsed over her children's collection and stepped away. Her friend tended to the dramatic, but something warmed Allie's heart, watching her friend help the little girl select a new book to take with her. The joy on the father's face reminded her of her own daddy and the times they'd spent together here on the square whenever he brought her down to campus with him. The father's smile at his child's happiness was a rare pleasure to behold, and even better, the little girl practically skipped away, clutching her new book to her heart.

I hope she enjoys this memory.

Monique returned to her previous posture of confrontation.

"What?" Allie rasped, coming out of a dreamlike stupor at watching the cute little girl.

"You're thirty-two. There is nothing wrong with you wanting a man in your life. Nothing. Stewart and Nona would have wanted that for you."

Real-life concerns rushed back to Allie, furrowing her brow. "I know that." The burny feeling swirled.

"Do you?"

"Yes. Look, I've got to go. I've got to keep an eye on him." Allie looked over Monique's shoulder instead of into her eyes.

"On him?"

"Yes. He might swindle my grandmother. Why is no one concerned about that?"

Monique folded her own arms. "He might." Her face was a mask of everything serious, but then she broke out into a radiant smile. "But what a way to go!"

Allie held up her own hands. "Okay. That's it. I'll see you in church tomorrow."

She walked off into the green grass, leaving her friend behind her in a fury of laughter. How dare she suggest that to her? And say her parents' names like that? Walking so fast, she didn't notice the thick tree root in front of her. Tripping over it, she wrenched her ankle.

"Argggghhh!" Allie growled, throwing her fists at the tree root, as if she wanted to fight it. The little girl who had been so happy with her book stared at her instead, as if she had gone plumb loco.

Maybe she had.

She yanked her espadrilles off her feet, trusting as she always had to step into the cool, sweet, safe grass of Milford, Georgia. Tying the long shoe strings together, she slung them over her shoulder and walked the road to her grandmother's house, determined not to let Jack Darwent slip from her clutches again.

Chapter 11

I T WAS TIME TO MAKE lunch, and as he helped Miss Ada unload the bounty from the farmers' market, Jack spoke. "I can whip up a quick lunch for you ladies if you like, and then maybe we can talk about the grape pie."

"Yes. Tea was very rude when I tried to tell you, but now that the Lord's cursing has worked on her, she'll have no choice but to be still."

Miss Ada whispered, even though Althea was laid out on the couch in the living room, watching a movie with her computer propped up on her lap and her wrenched ankle elevated.

Miss Ada went into the living room to watch the movie too and to talk with her granddaughter, while Jack set about making tomato sandwiches out of the summer vegetables. The heirloom tomatoes from the farmers' market were glorious, and he chose a mix of purple and gold ones to slice into thick steaks for the sandwiches. They had selected a rustic bread with a crunchy golden crust. He sliced the bread and put it to the side. The rest would make a wonderful French toast. He spread Duke's mayo on both sides of the bread and sprinkled a mix of fresh ground pepper, kosher salt and finely cut herbes de Provence on the bread, laying the tomatoes on it. He made four sandwiches, just in case.

He set up two lunch plates with sandwiches cut into diagonals and peach slices, and carried them to the living room, where Ada had changed the gentle, romantic movie her granddaughter had been watching to a Dirty Harry Clint Eastwood movie, but Allie was buried into her computer. "Lunch is served," Jack joked in his best Jeeves voice.

"This looks just beautiful." Ada marveled.

Allie looked at the plate. "Where's the bacon?"

"No bacon. These are tomato sandwiches."

She stopped working on her computer and swung her long legs around to the front of the couch. She had changed from her sunflower dress into a pair of denim cutoffs and a bright orange shirt that set off her features perfectly, and she glowed like Diana, the virgin huntress.

"We don't have to have sandwiches with no meat on them. I have money, if that's a problem."

He laughed a little and Ada joined in.

Miss Ada turned to her granddaughter. "Girl, you've never had a tomato sandwich?"

"No. And you never gave me one when I was growing up. There was always meat on our sandwiches."

Jack put his thumbs through his belt loops, trying to keep the moment light, but really wanting her to like the food. "It's a Southern delicacy, darlin'. One of my Tennessee treasures."

Miss Ada bowed her head and the two of them followed suit. "Lord, we ask for your blessings on all of us, especially my granddaughter. Keep her covered in the blood. In the name of Jesus. Amen."

The three of them had bowed and lifted their heads

so quickly that they looked like a set of bobbleheads.

"I'm hungry," Ada announced, and tucked into her sandwich. Jack knew Miss Ada liked it because she'd had them before.

"Why did I get a special prayer? I'm fine."

Miss Ada swallowed her first bite. "Because you up here questioning a meal someone done prepared for you. Eat it."

Althea said nothing, but her lips moved a step down from being pursed. She picked up the triangle and bit into a corner of it, chewing and ripping the bread off, but as she tasted, her face softened and the sight of her was a light to Jack's heart.

He loved to see a pretty woman enjoy his food.

"Like it?"

She swallowed. "Let me see." She took another dainty bite, and Ada laughed.

"You know it's good, Tea. Jack is a great chef. I'm so honored to have him help me for the May feast."

This time, Allie took a bigger bite. He smiled, but then noticed she had stopped mid-chew.

"He's helping for the May feast."

"Yes." Miss Ada ate and they watched in silence. "I ain't getting any younger, and the people I've been training have not been up to my standard. Jack does wonderful work."

Althea rolled her eyes but kept on eating, a sign that she liked it. But wasn't going to say so. "I could have hired you anyone you wanted," she said in a break from eating.

"Let me get you some tea, ladies."

"Didn't you make some for yourself, Jack? Come in here and eat with us. I know you like Clint Eastwood."

He did. He did as Miss Ada bid him to, but when he came back into the room, Miss Ada was still fussing with her granddaughter. "I don't want no strangers coming in fancying up my food. My food is for plain hard-working folks. They would put a bit of this on a plate and a spoon and swirl some stuff on. I don't want none of that."

As Jack ate one of the two sandwiches on his plate, he contemplated how the May feast, held next week, would be laid out for the right camera positions. He would be busy, and might send for a cameraperson to help him. He probably should. But if he did that, it would distance him from the story, and he didn't want that. Not at all.

"Okay, Granda."

"Maybe you ought to help me too. You so worried about Jack stealing from me. I keep telling you he's no thief."

Allie finished her sandwich and picked up a peach quarter, nibbling on it. The juice of the peach ran down her skin, and she had to take up a napkin to catch it all.

What a dazzling sight.

"Granda. Theft is different when it's IP. Jack may not mean to steal your recipes." Allie fixed him with a bold and direct look. "But that doesn't mean some of what you say won't seep into his cooking process. It happens. We just want to make sure that the particulars of your process are captured so that it would receive proper credit, no matter where it went."

"Ain't none of that necessary. I trust him."

"Well, I don't. I mean, I can't."

That's an interesting change of wording.

Jack spoke up. "She's right not to, Miss Ada. She doesn't know me from a hole in the wall."

"Well, maybe she should. I'm not one of your cases, Tea. Go on and do your work." Miss Ada pushed her plate away from her. "That was right tasty, Jack. Thank you. I was gone tell you about the grape pie, but they didn't have no grapes at the market. I was kind of surprised." She sat up. "I know. Maybe you can check the thickets. See where the muscadines are and check how they are coming."

"Muscadines?"

"It's the kind of grape you need for the pie," Althea said, smirking a little. Her smirk made the peach slippery and she had to slurp it up. Served her right. He liked the sight of her slurping in an inelegant manner.

"Where are they?" He was always ready for an adventure.

"Tea can show you where they are."

Jack looked over to the couch where Allie rested with her leg up and the bag of frozen peas on her ankle shifted. "She's injured."

Allie stood up, took in the last bite of peach, and put a hand on her hip. "I'm fine."

Yes, she was.

"Okay, but put on your running shoes. They'll provide some extra support," Jack suggested.

She gave him a hard look before she went to her bedroom.

He knew she liked his advice.

Miss Ada watched her go. She leaned over to Jack and whispered "I'm worried about her. She doesn't look too good and she keeps on pressing her stomach. Will you keep an eye on her?"

He grabbed the soft hand of his friend and patted it. "I will. I think we started off on the wrong foot. This outing will give me some time to get on the right footing with her and it'll all be fine. You'll see."

Allie came out sooner than he'd expected, and he dropped Miss Ada's hand like something hot and stood up right away.

Now Allie had dug into her vast wardrobe and had put on a snug tee shirt and some incredible-looking short shorts that made her legs look as if they went on forever.

Have mercy.

Miss Ada tsked.

"What now, Granda?"

"You need bug spray. Them chiggers is gone eat you alive if you go into the vines that way. How much of your upbringing did you forget, girl?"

Althea folded her arms. "We can stop and get bug spray, Granda."

"Well, praise the Lord for that. Y'all go ahead. Bring me back what I need, and I'll take a nap while I watch old Clint Eastwood here."

The two of them left the house and Jack jingled his keys. "We can go to the Piggly Wiggly first for the bug spray, and then to the vines. Sound okay?"

Allie nodded. He opened the door for her and she tsked, the exact sound that Miss Ada had made moments before. "I can open the door myself."

"I was raised on Southern manners. Forgive me." Jack bowed at the waist and watched as Althea slid herself into the passenger side of his rented car.

He got in the driver's side to fold himself into the car. It wasn't a big car, but he hadn't needed one. Miss Ada wasn't that big, but Althea was a whole lot of woman, and they seemed mighty close in there. Not that he minded.

But she did. He could tell by the way she fidgeted in her seat to get close to the door.

"The Piggly Wiggly isn't far," he said.

"I know that. I grew up here."

"Yes. That's why I would be interested in your take on things around here."

She turned to look out the window. "It was small and suffocating. Everything was predetermined for me, and I had to leave that behind to establish what I wanted to do."

"Did you?"

He pulled out of the driveway and looked at her.

"Did I what?"

"Establish what you wanted to do?"

"Of course I did. I'm very successful."

Jack had one hand on the wheel and held one up as she responded. "Okay. Well, maybe the better question would be, what did they want you to do here?"

Her pretty face was impassive. "It's a family tradition. Every one of us who are descendants of Virgil and Amanda Smithson have to give our lives over to the college. And the college hasn't been doing very well in recent years. So I was expected to stay, graduate from Milford and then stay home to help."

"And you didn't."

"No." Her voice stayed on an even keel.

So. She was a runaway too. Just like him. Jack gestured with his free hand. "Why not? The school is a fine legacy."

Her eyebrows, perfectly shaped ones, came together. "I just felt as if I could be of better benefit elsewhere. I make regular donations to the school coffers, but that doesn't seem to be enough for everyone around here, so they just look at me strangely."

He shook his head. "Money is one thing, but commitment of the heart to something you truly love to do, well, that's something else."

"Exactly." She peered at him. "What do you know about it?"

Jack gripped the wheel with both hands. "Oh, my father wanted me to follow in his footsteps."

"Ahh, yes. The civil rights attorney and activist, Drew Darwent."

10 o'clock and 2 o'clock. He didn't want to steer them off the road in his surprise. "You've looked me up."

"Of course. I had to know who you were."

"Well then. You know we have something in common. We're both runaways." He put a hand on his pants leg to dry it off a little.

Now she was facing him, with her arms folded. "Well, your path makes no sense to me. He built a legacy for you that you could be proud of. A law practice. You could work for him, make a nice living and help people. Sounds like the perfect combination to me."

When Jack arrived at the turnoff to the Piggly Wiggly, he stopped the car, waiting to make the left turn into the busy parking lot. "Because he built that. I had nothing to do with it. Isn't that some of what you feel with Milford College? It's not yours. It's someone in the past's burden. That's what I felt."

"Mine is *past* past. Yours is recent." She flipped her hand over and over to indicate a lot of pasts.

He made a sure, smooth turn into the parking lot and parked closer than she probably would have liked, but he had remembered her ankle. "Well, I don't like to perform my beliefs about civil rights for the cameras," Jack said. "I want to walk the walk with my law degree."

"So you did get the law degree." She gaped. A little. She had gorgeous teeth.

He shut off the car and stared at her. "Is that so hard to believe, Althea?"

She lowered her head away from his gaze and turned to open the car door.

"I'll be right back in two shakes of a lamb's tail." He walked off, away from the car. Laughter bubbled up

inside of him, but he kept a lid on it.
It would not do to gloat in front of Althea.

Chapter 12

A LLIE KNEW SHE WAS IN trouble when he came out
to the car with a reusable shopping bag containing
not one, but two cans of spray, and a bottle of Red Rock.

"I remember. Your grandmother said you liked it."

He tossed the bag to her and started the car. Something in her, a taut, taut wire, wanted to snap in two.
What was her life anymore? She had done everything
that she wanted to do in her life and she was happy in
New York. Who was this man who had beckoned her
away from her home, comfort, and safety?

She remembered her manners. "Thank you."

It was all she could do to get those two words out.

"Where do we go?"

"The Rise."

"What's that?"

"The high part of town where Virgil and Amanda
lived." The words of her lineage came out by rote because
her throat was surely parched by surprise. It was a dry
thing that even the peppery, gingery, slap-you-in-the-
face spiciness of Red Rock couldn't cure.

"Really? Okay."

The weight on her chest pressed harder at his eager tone. She palmed the drink. "Look. I'm sure you are a nice guy and all."

"Yeah, you checked that out already, Sherlock Holmes."

She took a deep breath. "I just want to know what you want. I'm pretty well off. So if it's money you're looking for…"

A deep frown appeared on his golden brow. "If you were anyone else in the world, other than Miss Ada's blood, I would call you out for that. Money isn't everything. I walked away from my father's very lucrative practice as proof of that."

She shivered at his words. "I have every right to ask you questions. Who do you think you are, coming down here trying to steal recipes from my grandmother?"

"I'm a documentarian. I'm making a movie of something that will disappear if it's not documented. You see I have equipment. I'm helping her."

"Who else are you documenting? Just her? Because it seems to me these weeks are a long time to stay with one subject."

She could see his knuckles grow whiter as he grasped the wheel. Pointing, she said, "Turn right here."

He did as she bid, but then something else loomed in front of her that had not been there before. A large swath of red earth opened before her like a scar in the land. Small lots were measured off in right angles. Clearly a subdivision was emerging here. A sign off to the right of the fenced area told her its name: "Blacksmithy Pond."

He stopped the car.

She hopped out. "No." Such a small word to capture what was happening before her. "Not this place."

"Yes, this place." Jack's deep voice boomed out behind

her. The heat of him radiated into her personal space and she knew he was one, maybe two feet from her. Interfering.

She spread her hands in front of her at all of it. "I can't believe it. I mean, this is where they lived."

Jack stepped closer to her. "I read about it in the paper a few weeks ago. There'll be a plaque. Properly named streets. Milford College needed the money and they sold off this parcel about six months ago. More people want to live in this area of coastal Georgia. So here it is. A new subdivision of McMansions."

Pressing at her stomach, she walked up to the gate. "This was the best place to find the muscadines. I mean, I don't know where they would be anymore."

The words made her legs a little rubbery.

She turned to face him, and she couldn't read the look on his face. The way his handsome features were all scrunched up, expressing something like pity for her.

She stepped out in front of him to avoid seeing his displeasure. "It's still wooded here toward the water. Let's try there."

The bright sun made her stumble to the car, and he retrieved the two cans of spray. They both sprayed their legs and arms. "You've missed some spots," Jack told her, and before she could say anything, he'd sprayed a cold stream down the back of her legs, "Spray a little puddle in your hands and rub it on your face."

She did as he bid her, and with the both of them fairly radiating the stench of Deet, began a foray into the woods. She kept examining the leaves near the base of the trees, glad to see this stretch was still wooded and that there were some muscadines. These seemed smaller than they should be. "Yes, there are some here, but the best place was closer to where they lived. I can't believe it's gone."

"That's what happens when you stay away from a place. I learned that the hard way myself." Jack came behind her with the bag as they harvested the globes of fruit.

"So you don't approve of my going away?" The way she said it made her wonder if she approved of it herself.

He shrugged. "We all do what we have to do."

"That's what I did." She kept her voice firm, certain.

"So you are prepared to accept the consequences, then? Of finding historic places gone when someone of your intelligence, drive and smarts could have found a way to save this? And I know Miss Ada must have told you about it. You knew. And you chose to stay in New York."

Swallowing down a hard lump, Allie's eyes closed in on a bigger cluster of the elusive muscadines. She knelt and snipped them off the vines with Miss Ada's sewing scissors. They had to gather the clusters in the reusable Piggly Wiggly bag since they had no other container for the large seeded grapes.

Allie took in a deep breath and exhaled. Slowly. "It was right about the time the partner decision came up. I wasn't focused on anything else. Just on making partner."

"Congratulations." Jack reached for the scissors, brushing up against her hands, causing a frisson of feeling to travel down her spine that had nothing to do with her stomach.

Time to change the topic. "So when are you going to move on? From my grandmother? I'm sure there are many other Southern Treasures elsewhere."

"I'm sure there are too. But I like it here. A lot." He stood and faced her.

"Why?"

He spread his arms. "This is a special place, and you don't even know it. How sad."

"I don't need your pity, Jack Darwent."

"No, but maybe someone needs to make you realize what you have here. Your grandmother is a lonely lady and I didn't want to leave her by herself."

"So that's your racket?"

"Excuse me, racket?"

"Yes. Scam, scheme, racket. Whatever you want to call it. You get close to old ladies, get their intellectual property and who knows what else, and their trust. Maybe change their wills in favor of you. Maybe you've married a few." Seeing another cluster, she knelt, and when he got too close to her, she lifted her scissors as protection.

He laughed. "You watch too much *Dateline*."

Well, sure she did, but who didn't? She snipped and put three nice clusters in the bag.

"You missed some." He leaned in and pushed some leaves to the side, showing some more. "Forget how to do this?"

She yanked her scissors out and retrieved five more clusters. "We don't want to take all of them. There may be more in a few weeks if we leave some behind. It's not about take, take, take, Jack."

"That's the first time you've said my name."

"So?" *So?*

She stood up straight and went down the path another way. Daytime was closed out by the thick foliage and it was darker and cooler. "I'm looking for something. I hope they've left it alone."

"More Milford past?" He came closer to her.

"Yes." She turned a corner on the path and a small pond emerged. "There's your pond."

"Ahh." They stood and admired the clean, clear area untouched by development. *Once those steam shovels and backhoes got going, you could probably hear it back here.* The thought caused her to ball her fists. "It's lovely," Jack murmured.

"This is where my great-great," Allie stopped to think. "-great aunt would come and write her music. March."

"The one who was not Amanda's daughter."

Allie turned to him. Turned on him. "She was her daughter in every sense of the word. It was Amanda's fierce love for March that kept her here."

"Really?" Jack breathed just over her head. "That's not what I've heard."

"What have you heard?"

"It was her fierce love for the blacksmith that kept her here." His voice came softer and she shivered in the cool of the wood.

"That too. They were practically strangers when they were forced to marry." Maybe if she spoke louder, she could keep control of her emotions.

"It came out all right in the end. Sometimes, you just know." The deep timbre of his voice echoed in the woods and touched an open place in her heart.

It made her think of her parents' love story and the reason why she was here. How they had met in the registration line at Milford College and married, against the wishes of his family, just six weeks later. Two first-year college students, alone in the world. Why had they done something so crazy?

Well, okay, Allie had her parents' marriage and a series of others to thank for her existence, but that was a fairy tale. A love story. Things like that didn't happen in real life.

Not in her life.

She blinked her eyes very fast, and fortunately she saw some more grape clusters to harvest. She pointed them out and stood, stretching. "That's enough for a pie and then some. We can go."

He harvested them and then stood up straight, holding out the bag. "Well, thank you for showing me where they are."

She took the bag. "Yes. Aunt March will probably come and get me for showing you where they are. You'll probably come and take the rest of them."

"I'm not sure I understand why you would say that, Althea." She turned to leave the pond area of the woods and he followed her closely on the small worn path.

"You're traveling the country taking recipes and such from old ladies. Why not muscadines?"

"Ha ha."

She walked so fast trying to get away from him, she took a wrong turn in the foliage and stopped, her heart beating. This area did not look familiar.

"What's wrong?" Jack stopped too.

"This is different." Her voice shook. Just a little. More than she intended.

"What's different?"

"The path, it's worn here and I followed it and we aren't where we should be." She took her phone out of her pocket. Of course there was no signal.

"Are we lost, Althea?"

"No," she told him sharply.

"And here we were getting along so well." His mouth tugged upward into something that looked like a smile.

She almost couldn't hear his sarcasm in her panic, hands sweating, heart pounding. How could she be lost? That wire in her belly threatened to come up her throat in tears and she turned away from him.

Cleansing breath, cleansing breath.

"Hey, are you okay?"

Her voice shook, in spite of her best intent. "I'm fine. I just. Things have changed. Nothing remains the same. That's what I don't like."

"Come on. It's okay. Look, let's go this way."

"No. I don't want to." Her rebelled-against tears slid down her face and she wiped them away.

"This is the way out, Tea." He started walking in the opposite direction. "See?"

Well. The path had forked off in a new direction.

"Come this way." His voice was gentle and low. He reached out his hand. She took it and he led her to the opening to the road within about two minutes. When she saw where they were, she let go, no longer afraid.

"How…how did you know what way to come?"

"I've been in these woods before. I just didn't know this was where the muscadines were." Soon, they emerged in the bright sunlight, back on the road with Jack's car in sight.

What had just happened?

Maybe she did need this time off.

"I'm sorry I snapped at you back there."

"That's okay." Jack jingled his keys, preparing to unlock the door. "I'm getting used to it."

Something in his tone made her bite her lip. She didn't want to be mean to him. They got in the car.

"I'm sorry, I said." She made her voice a little more firm.

"I heard you."

"I don't usually say it twice."

"Well, one way to make me know you are truly sorry is to treat me better."

The car filled with silence. Althea didn't say anything on the ride back.

"I'm not here to hurt you. Or Miss Ada. That old

lady." She turned to him, seeing him—she couldn't believe it—quiver. "She reminds me of someone I once knew. Someone who saved my life. If she hadn't existed, I don't know if I would be here."

"Who?"

"Her name was Miss Luly."

"Was she your mammy?" The words came to her mouth with a hot quickness that she didn't expect.

"I prefer the term, my substitute mother. After mine committed…took her own life, Miss Luly mothered me and my sister. Then she stepped into my life again and saved it when I was older and much more foolish. I'm making *Southern Treasures* for her."

His words came fast, and she breathed out. So they did have something in common.

He knew the same pain she did.

"I'm sorry about your mother. I lost my parents young too."

He nodded. "I know."

Of course he did. Granda had told him everything. Everything Allie would have preferred to forget. The silence between them allowed her to relive that same series of sad memories: waking up in the hospital, learning about her parents, seeing their two bodies—not her parents, but two bodies with the light in them gone, in two caskets In the church, her not being able to take the sight of them that way any longer, and the pain, pain, pain of it all. She reached for her purse, but she had no Tums.

Jack pulled up to the house and they both seemed reluctant to get out.

She pushed her purse from her and instead took a swig of the warm, peppery ginger ale he had bought for her. "Is Miss Luly dead?"

"Yes."

"I—I'm sorry," Allie stammered.

"I want her to be proud of me for one thing in my life." Jack reached into the back, retrieving the grapes. He stopped. "I'm leaving after the feast. I'm sure that will give you a lot of relief."

He went into the house and she could hear his joyous tone from the car where she still sat, stunned at his revelation.

And how it had increased her hurt from the long-ago past.

She sat there in the car, holding herself, folding herself at the pain in her middle until it went away.

Chapter 13

T HE FIRST ORDER OF BUSINESS once Allie went in the house was to rid herself of the Deet stench she had needed in the woods.

The bathroom where she had been a teenager had long been a refuge for her. Now, it looked small and cramped, but it was familiar and that's what she needed now. She had brought some of her bathing supplies, so she loaded the small tub with nice warm water and put in a virtual army of bath bombs.

Slipping in, she soaked with bent knees, but still felt a certain amount of peace, even as the warm water soaked in all of her hurt spots.

Confusion over the Mama Cassie's deal.

Embarrassment at the farmers' market.

Sadness at the excavated piece of land.

Anger at herself that she had not been there to do anything about it.

Confusion over the Mama Cassie deal.

Why did Jack Darwent, with his voice booming throughout her grandmother's house, make her so reflective about these matters?

I have everything I could possibly want. It's natural for me to think of the next step in my life.

So what was it?

She had always thought of acquiring a little cabin here as a getaway spot for herself. She had earned a large bonus when she made partner, and with some more of her cases closing, there might be another couple of hundred thousand more.

Money was just money.

Sitting in the warm water for the twenty minutes recommended by her doctor for her stomach made her sleepy, and when her phone timer went off, she dragged herself out of the tub and went straight to bed.

When she woke up, she could tell that it was later in the day, but the house smelled heavenly.

Of pie. Grape pie.

She sat straight up and shrugged into her fluffiest robe, tying the belt to create a super snatched waist. She went into the kitchen. "What happened here?"

Granda and Jack sat at the little kitchen table, eating pie and drinking cups of coffee. They both looked up at her, confused.

"We wondered where you disappeared to. I made pie. Jack filmed."

"We're good. Very good." Jack reached for the pie tin which had about a third of the pie missing. The flaky golden-brown goodness was marked with Granda's trademark edge: a coil of pie crust, brushed with heavy cream.

The jammy purple grape richness oozed from the cut parts of the pie, stinging her nose with its sugary sweetness.

Allie snatched the pie up. "I thought we had talked about this."

"Talked about what?" Granda shook her head.

She gestured with the pie. "This is a family secret. He is not family."

"Girl, if you don't put that hot pie down…"

Now Allie noticed that the glass pie dish was still hot, so she did set it down, but well out of the reach of Jack Darwent.

Granda shook her head. "Jack says you all had a good time getting the muscadines. He thought that everything was settled between you two."

"Ha! And he has a law degree?" Allie rounded on Jack. "Who gave you a degree to come to that conclusion?"

"Duke." He blinked, and his impossibly long eyelashes waved back and forth over his impossibly blue eyes.

"Duke?" She'd thought he was going to say some fly-by-night law school.

But he said Duke.

Oh.

Covering up her sweaty humiliation, she spoke with a loud voice to her grandmother. "Well, it isn't. I still need to make sure you and the work of your hands are protected. And until then…" Allie reached for the pie with the tie end on her robe, grabbing the hot dish with the fluffy edge.

"What are you doing, girl?"

"Protecting you. And us." She walked backward into her room. Now that she had kidnapped the pie, where should she put it? On the nightstand. On top of her headscarf. There.

She sat down on the bed, feeling a little ridiculous at having just kidnapped a pie. But at the same time, she felt better. Victorious.

There was a knock on the door.

She marched to it. "Granda, I…"

When she yanked open her door, instead of her

wizened grandmother, Jack Darwent stood there, tall and handsome. He held up a fork. A long dinner fork. Perfect for eating pie.

He smiled, showing all of the blinding whiteness of his teeth.

And winked at her.

Because he knew what she needed.

Because he knew her pain.

She took the fork from him and it seemed that it slid from his fingers. "Thank you."

"You're welcome, Althea." His voice drew out the syllables of her name in an altogether new way. In a pretty way.

Like she never heard her own name before.

Turning on her bare heel, she shut the door quietly, needing to be alone with her thoughts.

And the pie.

She sat down on the edge of her bed and opened up her computer, looking up everything she needed to generate protection for her grandmother, her recipes, and her stories. She sent it off to Connie for processing. Soon, her phone rang.

"So, is he as good-looking in person as he is on the internet?" It sounded like there was a full-fledged party going on. Given her popularity with the other admins, there might have been, since Allie was not in the office.

"Don't you have a baby to have?" Allie tried to steady her voice. Connie could read her like she read the *New York Times*.

"He is, isn't he? I wanna see. Get pics on your phone. Give me a reason to give birth."

"You aren't due for a few more weeks yet." *Sound bored*.

But it didn't work.

"Is he nice?"

"He's nice to Granda, but I want you to work on this contract." Now she sounded stern.

"Yes, boss lady. And then you can get to working on him!" Connie's cackle into the phone reached up to the highest register.

Allie held the phone out from her ear and pressed the red "End" sign, then she grabbed up the fork Jack had brought her and ate every crumb of that pie out of the dish. She put the dish on her dresser, covered herself with her bed sheets and fell asleep to the sound of Jack Darwent asking Granda if they couldn't make another one.

Jerking awake the next day, multiple realizations hit her all at once.

It was Sunday in Milford.

It was six a.m.

She had slept for twelve hours.

After eating a whole grape pie.

That she had kidnapped.

And she had neglected to brush her teeth.

Who was she, even?

Allie leaped up, ran to the bathroom and reached for her electric toothbrush.

No more tooth damage, please God.

How many years of pain and bother had it taken her to get her teeth into the right kind of shape? She did her whole regimen twice to atone for her sin.

Still garbed in the robe, she went out into the darkened living room where her Granda slept in her overstuffed chair with the news playing.

She touched the old woman on the shoulder and Granda jumped awake, as Allie just had.

"I'm sorry, Granda."

"You feeling okay? You need me to fix you a bicarb? Eating all of that pie yourself. You should be ashamed." A sly smile pulled across her grandmother's weathered face.

"I probably won't eat anything until Tuesday, Granda. No breakfast for me."

"Serves you right." And for once, Allie reeled. Because her grandmother smiled at her—something that didn't happen that often. A light entered her soul and suddenly, setting foot into the church didn't seem like such a chore any more.

"I need to get myself going. I have a deacon meeting before church."

The spry old woman stretched her frame and hobbled into her side of the house, where her bedroom and bathroom were located.

Allie went to get ready for church as well, donning something slightly less formal than her corporate wear of dark gray, blue, or black. She put on a summer suit of pink linen with a short-sleeved pussy bow tie white blouse. She swept her hair up in a slick French roll and secured a diamond decoration pin at the side of it. It was real, so of course she would not want anything to happen to it. It had been a present to herself for making partner. Sighing, she knew she would probably be skewered for wearing something so vain into Milford AME, but it was her reward to herself and she was going to wear it. Anyone who didn't like it could step off.

Summer church still required hose, which she put on with her pearlescent pink Jimmy Choo pumps.

She stepped out into the middle hallway and waited for her grandmother, who came out in her own pink ensemble with pink jeweled collar and cuffs. She also wore a white straw hat decorated with large pink roses.

"Oh my. Tea, you look so fine when you want to." Granda's hands clasped at the sight of her.

Allie smiled. "Thank you, Granda. As do you."

"But you still missing something."

Allie jangled her keys. "I don't want to keep you waiting. I know you have a meeting."

"It won't take a minute."

Granda ducked back into her bedroom and brought out a hat box.

Oh Lord.

Allie had been hoping that the diamond piece in her hair would be enough, but it clearly wasn't.

This, the expectation of a hat, was one of the things that had made her duck out of church attendance when she was a pre-teenager. It was all so pretentious.

But the sigh that she thought would work its way up from her middle didn't come. When her grandmother took the lid off of the large round box, inside there was a large pink straw hat, with a pink-and-white striped band around it. The brim was large and dipped to one side. She could still wear her diamond pin, and as a matter of fact, it would showcase the pin in her black hair.

"Sit down. I'ma put it on you."

"Granda. I can put on a hat."

The older woman seemed a little surprised at Allie's agreement to wear the hat in the first place. "You never wore one before. I'll pin it on this first time, so it gets done right."

Allie sat down on one of the dining room chairs and her little grandmother perched the hat on her head. Something familiar, her grandmother's soft hands working in her hair, the smell of her Chantilly perfume, the weight of the hat on her head, took her back into another kind of feeling. A feeling like, well, maybe she was pretty. Maybe she was someone. Someone who mattered.

A horn beeped.

"Oh, that's Jack. Let me see."

Granda stepped around the front and looked at her. "Perfect. It's good you had the right outfit on. I can't wear that hat as well anymore, so it's better you wear it."

"Why not?"

"It's too heavy for my neck. It's a hat for a younger woman. Come on."

"He's taking us?"

"Yes, he comes to get me every Sunday."

Allie didn't feel put out about that, but relieved instead. Tension that she hadn't known was there slipped from her shoulders. A frisson of fear from who knew where started to signal to her stomach juices to swirl about.

But then it stopped. For the first time since she had been to Milford.

Jack Darwent had come into Granda's house. He fairly danced in and embraced her grandmother, laughing, and looked over her shoulder.

At her.

And froze.

So did she. Was he connected with the burny feeling stopping?

He wore a navy blue blazer with a starched white shirt and a blue-and-white striped tie. His pants were white, as were his shoes. The blazer sleeves were snug on his arms and his eyes went wide as he saw Allie sitting there.

"Well. Miss Ada, who is this?"

"It's Tea. Don't she look grand?"

Jack stepped back, straightening his jacket. "That's

not the word for it. Wow."

Granda smiled all up and down herself. "Let's get going. Can't be late, you know."

Allie stood up, not twelve years old, coltish in her high heels, but Jack Darwent held a hand out anyway. "No. No. I'll be right back to help you."

"I can help, I mean I can do what I need to do myself."

"Girl, let him help you."

"Well, I did forget something."

Jack nodded, fairly looking as if he wanted to dance around. "I'll take Miss Ada to the car and then I'll be back for you."

They went up the walkway while Allie stole away back to her bathroom on the other side of the house to get a good look at herself.

Staring at herself in the mirror, a faint echo of the ache stirred, but a healing balm of good feelings accompanied it. Yes. She looked wonderful. Beautiful even. Old Pichon would probably lose it to see her with this hat on, which did so much to frame her features—but more than that, she recognized, she looked like her mother.

And it was okay to look like a ghost. It was reassuring. Proof that her dear mother would carry on was right there in her face. The years of blame, heartache and loneliness slipped away from her as well.

She took in a deep breath at the realization and blinked. The screen door sounded, and she knew that Jack Darwent was back in the house. She went out of the bathroom to him and he stood there, with his arm out. "Ready?"

She took his arm, shutting the door to her grandmother's house, and stepped down the little pathway with him, feeling comfortable within her skin for the very first time in her life.

Chapter 14

SOMETHING ZINGED JACK IN HIS spine when he lifted his eyes from Miss Ada's shoulder and looked at Althea all dressed up, sitting there in that chair.

My God.

He knew she was beautiful, and he had been very successful going back to his houseboat over these last few nights and noting that to himself, and then going to sleep.

Now, having seen her looking like this…vision, he would not be able to think of the times she had spoken to him in her short, curt way, as if he were something gummy she had picked up on her shoe.

Seeing her lit something deep within his innards, a feeling that his life had changed somehow, the feeling that someone gets whenever they throw open a window or open a door into a stuffy room.

Althea, this woman, was supposed to be his wife.

Say what? Where did that thought come from?

Get it together, Jack.

He was vaguely aware of saying something to her, but it was as if he were in another reality. He offered to take

Miss Ada to the car first.

At his age, he had been doing just fine.

There was no need to be paired up.

Sure, he wanted to be a dad someday. Who didn't? He was great with kids and he knew he could nurture tiny beings into a good place in this world.

But with frosty Althea? Cold Tea? Iced Tea? He tried to joke with himself, so that the sudden thought might go elsewhere. Away from him.

Walking the short older woman to the car, he cleared his throat a few times, ready to make some pedestrian remark about the weather.

But Miss Ada, in the short time they had become friends, had come to know his heart. Just like Miss Luly had. "Isn't she beautiful?"

"She is, Miss Ada." *Shake it off.* "Because she's your granddaughter, no doubt."

There, old Jack was back. *Gotta keep it together.* At least for the drive to the church. Then he could go somewhere and fall apart.

She smacked his hand lightly. "Tea always did clean up so well. She never liked to do it when she was young. I never understood why it was so hard for her."

Me neither.

Maybe he should ask her.

Miss Ada opened the back door. "You all get yourself some breakfast while I'm at my meeting. Then we'll all sit together in church."

"You should sit in the front seat." *Please.*

"No. Let Tea sit in front. Her big hat will block your rear view." Miss Ada adjusted her skirt and smiled at him.

He refrained from running a hand through his curls as he went back toward the house to escort Althea to the car, but she was already there. "Ready?"

"I'm just fine, Jack. Thank you anyway."

She walked past him as if he were a fly on the wall. A nothing. He caught a whiff of her floral perfume in the May day.

He opened the front passenger door for her. A look of surprise registered on her face, but as he slid into the driver's seat he nodded. "Miss Ada pointed out that your hat might have blocked the rearview. I think she's right."

The opportunity for levity made him firm up his resolve.

Ada waved her hand from the back seat. "It's a lovely hat, but it's a big one. One of the reasons I stopped wearing it. It was too heavy on my neck, but it's perfect for my granddaughter to carry it off."

"It's amazing, Miss Ada. And you look amazing in it, Tea."

"Thank you." Two nice words made it past her deliciously full lips, directed at him.

Calm down.

Now he was the one breathing out.

The distance to Milford AME was short, and before he knew it, he was pulling up in one of the handicapped spots off to the side, so that Miss Ada could get out and walk to the side door.

"I've got my meeting. Now you two have some breakfast, and I'll see you inside in about an hour."

Allie did not object. The look on her face was of sheer terror, and he wondered why.

They watched Miss Ada go inside and disappear behind the door.

"Well, do you want to go to the diner or something?"

"I don't want that much breakfast. I just ate a whole pie yesterday. It's fine to go to the coffee house." She smiled and he matched her. Gladly.

She got out, indicating the coffee house across the square. "Oh, let me." Jack smoothed down his tie. "I'll go there and bring back something in a jiffy. Coffee? Muffin?"

He bowed.

She flipped her hand over "Okay. Okay. I'll have a cinnamon scone if they have it. And my coffee order. Will you be able to memorize it?"

She lowered her head and looked up at him, causing a Thor's hammer to be taken to his heart. This was one occasion when his love of mythology paid off. "Of course."

"I'll have a short, half-pump mint whip, half-pump chocolate whip, double espresso with hot water and a pinch of milk chocolate shavings. If it's dark chocolate or semi-sweet, don't bother."

He jumped out of the car, after recording her order on his phone, and fairly skipped across the square to where Calvin, the owner of the coffee shop, was helping two or three people ahead of him.

The older man waved at Jack, and started his regular order of a mocha latte after his other customers left. They did have a cinnamon scone that they warmed for Althea, and when Calvin wanted to know if that was it, Jack held up a phone and played Althea's voice for Calvin to hear. He laughed. "Yep. Sounds like the princess to me."

"The princess?" Jack repeated.

"Yeah, man. That's what we used to call her. My younger brother and she were in school at the same time, so he would come home and talk about her. He had a thing for her, so we heard lots about her at the table at night. My parents were big on that eating dinner together thing."

Calvin fixed Jack's drink and put it in front of him,

and retrieved the warmed scone. Jack put the bag in his pocket.

"Of course, with the tragedy of the accident, things kind of changed."

A memory niggled at Jack. "Her parents?"

"Yes. It was pretty tragic. Thank God she wasn't with them in the car, or she would have been a goner too. The funeral was so sad. I was in the Milford College choir and we sang at the funeral. Two caskets, and there she was with her grandmother."

Jack had lifted the cup to his lips to begin sipping his latte but stopped, putting it down. He recalled her sad face yesterday when they talked about their parents, and his heart jolted, wishing he could bring her comfort.

Calvin went on. "I don't remember what Reverend Floyd said, but it was something. You know she ran out of the church that day and she's never been back since. Been like twenty years."

Now Jack took a sip of the hot liquid. For courage.

"That long, huh?"

"Yeah. The princess been away for so long, some of us wonder what she's back here for."

Calvin leaned a friendly arm on the counter as Jack processed his card for payment.

"I don't know, man."

"You in that house with her."

Jack sipped again. "You know full well I'm on my houseboat."

"Yeah, but the rest of the time, you are with her." Calvin waggled his eyebrows.

"She's visiting her grandmother."

"She hasn't cared to visit her grandmother too much, and now here she comes."

And here she came.

The bell to the coffee shop jingled, the door opened, and there was Althea in the doorway.

Calvin's jaw dropped and Jack stepped toward her. "I was going to bring everything back."

"Well, I got to thinking about it and I wanted to see this space. The pizza shop used to be in here." She stepped inside. "It looks nice."

"Thank you, ma'am."

Allie turned to Calvin, fixing him with a look. "You look familiar."

"I should. I'm Ephram Shouts's older brother Calvin. I was two years ahead of you at Milford Middle."

"Ahh, yes. I remember." No she didn't. The vacant look on Althea's pretty face told Jack that she was putting on the princess act just for the benevolent coffee shop owner.

"It's good to see you again. Got your order ready. Y'all sit down."

Jack gestured to a table near the window and pulled out a chair for her. Althea sat down and he sat down opposite her with his latte in his hand. "Where's mine?" she asked.

"It's right here." Calvin came forward with the drink in a delicate white cup and saucer with the right amount of shavings on top. "Since you're here, you don't have to drink out of the paper cup."

"I'm sure it was fine, Mr. Shouts."

"Calvin, please." He went away and came back with a scone on a plate, clearly forgetting that he had given Jack one.

How did Althea induce this kind of feeling in people? She sipped at the drink, clearly enjoying it, breaking off a corner of the scone and dunking it in the coffee.

Calvin lingered nearby, intrigued, but not wanting to act as if he was eavesdropping. But he was.

"Calvin here wanted to know why you came back to Milford."

Jack smiled as the warmth of his chocolate coffee spread in his mouth.

"I came back to protect my grandmother from intellectual property theft." She looked over her cup at him, sipping her special drink, blinking her lovely lashes. At him. Without hostility. The warmth of the scone in his pocket spread all over him.

"Theft?" Calvin came over and pulled up a chair to sit with them. "No one would harm Miss Ada in these parts. We wouldn't have it."

"Yes, I know. But it seemed to me that when someone came into town and wanted her recipes, well, that was when I knew I had to use my training to help my grandmother."

"Oh, you talking about Jack's movie? It'll be nice for those recipes to be kept somewhere. Those things can disappear without the proper care."

Allie set her cup down. "Yes. But they are the property of my grandmother and should remain as such."

Jack drained his cup. "They should. And they will. Calvin, I'm feeling like a cinnamon roll. And a refill of regular coffee. With a shot of warmed milk."

Calvin stood. "Coming right up."

Jack didn't take his eyes off Allie and she didn't take her eyes off him. "I promise you."

"Do you? Such promises should be signed into reality."

"Anytime you say, juris doctor. Anytime."

"Good."

"One of the reasons that I'm doing this project is because, well, when an older person dies, especially a renowned cook like Miss Ada, it's like the library of Alexandria burns down."

With her love of ancient history, he knew she would get that reference.

"So, all I'm doing is trying to save all of those scrolls. Because, as we both know, death leaves a huge hole in the lives of the loved ones left behind."

Her eyes went down to the scone on the table and he was almost sorry he'd said that. When she lifted her face, her eyebrows were drawn together.

His hand shot across the table to her arm. "Althea. It's okay. You have people to support you."

"That doesn't make it any easier." She set her coffee down, looking out at the town square.

Calvin set down a huge cinnamon roll, thick with icing that dripped onto the table, and another paper cup of steaming hot coffee. Jack could tell this was no mass-manufactured roll, but the real homemade kind. It fairly oozed butter and it was warmed up, just a bit, so that cinnamon tingled his nostrils, mixing with her perfume, and it was all home to him.

"Would you like some?"

Smiling at him, she shook her head slowly. "It's obnoxious."

"It's delicious." He smiled. "Look at all the turns in that dough."

"Turns?"

He drew his eyebrows together. "How much do you know about cooking, Althea?"

"Enough."

Nothing, he would wager. Cutting the buttery roll with a knife and fork, he offered up a small bite to her, dripping cinnamon and vanilla.

To his surprise, she took it and ate it, licking her lips. Then a dazzling smile.

He cut off a bigger piece and ate it, and then another

of equal size and let her take it in. And she did.

She sipped at her coffee, laughing. "Enough. I'm buzzed on sugar already."

"I was hoping for that." He took another bite and put the knife and fork down, defeated already. He inhaled. "Althea. I lost my mom at twelve, too. I know what it's like. I'll go in there with you. You won't be alone."

Calvin stood. "I'll go with you. Close down the shop if I have to."

"That's very gracious of you, Mr. Shouts. But you need to keep the shop open for others."

Allie stood. Then she asked Jack a question he would never have thought she would ask when she first arrived, when she would glare at him with bare hatred.

"Are you ready, Jack?"

He had to actually think about keeping his jaw shut. He nodded.

"Good. Let's get it over with, then."

He took her hand in his arm and left everything, even the delicious cinnamon roll, behind, so that he could walk with Althea out of the coffee shop toward the hulking stone edifice that was Milford AME church.

Together.

Chapter 15

T HAT BUILDING HAD GHOSTS IN it, Allie knew. And now, the moment had arrived when she had to confront those ghosts.

Jack spoke up. "Why don't you show me the inside? Miss Ada told me how historical it is, but she's never had time to show me."

The May morning had slowly warmed since they had left the house, but once she stepped into the narthex of the church, cool air surrounded her, enveloped her and pulled her in. This place, this church, carried more than one hundred and fifty years of her blood, and she felt it. The escape that she'd made when she was twelve was her attempt to break loose from obligation, to break free from tradition, break free from sorrow, but like the old saying, she was back.

Strange. Instead of feeling defeated, there was something comforting about being here now. "There," she pointed upwards to a line of large portraits. "The line of pastors of the church goes all the way back to my great-great-grandfather, Virgil Smithson."

The painting of a carte de visite portrait featured a

Black man with a Van Dyke beard and a suit and tie in the old-fashioned style. "When I was a child, I thought he saw me whenever I misbehaved."

"You? Never." Jack shook his head. "Well, he sure was quite the pillar. He's everywhere."

Allie stepped away. "He built this church when there were slave people here in Milford." The burning feeling in her stomach stirred. Something in her always, always, felt the suffering of her people here. She took a deep breath and felt it shake in her very veins. "As well as the college."

"A remarkable man."

"He was. He bought his own freedom from the Milfords but, because of the laws at the time, he had to leave. He wanted to buy his wife and child, but he had to earn money to buy them." She turned away from him, holding onto the bannister of the stairs that led to the worship space. "I can't even talk about it. The words—it's too hard."

His hand was on her arm and instead of making her want to pull away, his touch soothed her. For some reason. "Let's go upstairs."

All of the old hens of the church awaited her there. All the judgment, the tsking, the questions about the way she hadn't come home, had run away from all of this. Suddenly, she felt the large hat on her head surround her and weigh her down.

But then she turned and saw, like a shining light, the other portrait, the one that faced Virgil Smithson: a woman with a kindly brown face and a high-necked dress. The warm eyes of the carte de visite of Amanda never failed to soothe her. Amanda's face wore the care of a mother, and that's what she was—a Madonna of Milford.

"Who is that?"

"Amanda Aurelia Stewart Smithson. She was one of the first educated Black women in the country to get a college degree before the Civil War."

"Stellar."

"Yes. And she used it to help her people. She came here and was the guiding muse of the school."

"There's more. Don't forget," Granda came up to them. "Nothing here, nothing at the college would have been accomplished without Mama 'Manda." The older woman's short arms reached out. "She believed in our people enough to give up all she had to come here to start a school. And Papa Virgil didn't always make it easy on her. But she didn't give up." She put her hand on Allie's arm. "We got her strength. We've got her resilience and love. All we need is to know our purpose, Tea."

Then, Granda did something she had never done before. She laced her fingers with Allie's. "Come on, Tea."

With Granda on one side of her and Jack following closely behind, Allie went up the stairs and entered the worship space of Milford AME.

The hard wooden pews of her childhood were gone, replaced with softer individual chairs that were arranged in a semicircle. The same vibrant red carpet remained, but something about the look of the place seemed warmer, more welcoming, and not foreboding and sad.

"When did they do all of this, Granda?"

"A few years ago. I probably told you, but maybe you didn't remember."

Or she hadn't listened. Allie picked up her feet and started in to the space, touching the soft hand of her grandmother, who guided her in. "What happened to the dedication plates?"

"They are in a display in the library. We didn't think

they did the job to welcome folk enough to the church, so when we got rid of the pews, we took them off too. We have to reach out and welcome people in so they don't feel as if they are taking up someone else's spot."

"Still, this is just about where the Smithsons always sat."

"Yes, approximately. But you can see I made room for Jack. And for you."

The service music, instead of being played on the heavy organ of her childhood, was instead performed on a piano and guitar. The music provided a lighter sound, one that appealed to her heart, one that made her steps lighter and the burning feeling in her stomach go away. "Thank you, Granda."

There were eyes on her as they eased down the pathway to their seats in the left front. That show-off, Jack Darwent, waved and smiled and shook hands. Somehow, though, it didn't irritate Allie. Instead, it brought to mind the fact that this church, one that was peopled with many of her skin tone, was able to welcome someone like Jack with open arms, and without question.

To her, that was God. That was a wonderful, splendid thing.

The long line of pastors at Milford AME had led to a man of about her age, Reverend Michaels, who was handsome enough, and seemed friendly.

"He seems nice, Granda."

Her grandmother nodded. "He's a bit young, but time will fix that problem."

Allie could see the college president and his wife, Jim and Sarah Jasper, near the front. Jim Jasper had been the president of Milford College ever since she was a small child. He was a much older man now and his lovely wife, the first lady of the college, had silver streaks in her well-coiffed bob.

"Is Reverend Michaels married?"

Granda shook her head. "That's a sore topic around here. There is nothing so hungry for a man as a woman in a church." She turned to her granddaughter, looking at Allie with new eyes. "Maybe you should meet him."

"Granda, you know I would not make a good first lady of any church. I don't like anybody."

"She didn't suggest that you get married. She just said to meet him," Jack whispered.

Monique came down the aisle and sat behind them with her parents, Mr. and Mrs. Mason. "So, you see our new hottie minister?" she whispered.

Allie nodded her head. "I do."

"He's sure eyeing you."

"That's because I have this huge hat on."

"Oh, yeah. It's also because you are a hot thang."

"Monique," Mrs. Mason breathed.

Her friend shrank back into her seat, and when the minister called the church to order, Allie did notice that he was looking at her, but it was with a regard for who she was, she was sure.

"Now. Will all visitors identify themselves so we may welcome them?" The minister looked right at her.

In her peripheral vision, Allie could see everyone was looking At her,

There were probably holes in her hat from people who were looking at her from behind.

Oh dear.

Then, all of sudden, Granda stood up next to her, casting a little shadow on her legs. "I want to say something to all of you while we are here in the Lord's House."

"Speak, Sister Ada. Please." The look on the minister's face was reverent and respectful. A little bit of the weight

Allie carried lifted from her. Older people were so fragile, so vulnerable. She didn't want strangers coming in to her grandmother's life and hurting her. Even if they didn't get along.

"Welcome to God's house." Everyone, to a person, answered her Granda with a welcome. Their respect for her was deep and unswerving. What would it be like to be such a person that everyone listened to? That people didn't look over as if she were an ornament.

Because that's what Allie was in the world. A well-oiled, well-spoken, pretty—by some standards—ornament.

"You all know me. I've been a member of this church for my entire life. I was baptized here when the church was brand new. Got married here. My husband's casket, right here. And, God help me." Her grandmother swallowed. Hard. Just like she did when things were rough. "The casket of my only son and daughter-in-law here. Now for a long time, my granddaughter, Althea, didn't feel as if she was welcome here. That why," Granda turned to her. "I want to say she's welcome here. I, I…"

Allie's grandmother, the pillar of strength in the family, covered her mouth. "I don't know what I did or said that made her take twenty years to come back here to the church. But, on my soul, right here before the Lord, I won't ever do it again. Never."

She turned her slight person toward Allie, who was completely shocked to see tears rolling down her grandmother's face. "I needed to say this before I lost the courage. 'Cause being here, in this place, gives me courage. I see the places where my grandfather and uncles shaped metal frameworks for the stained glass. The pictures on the wall of my great grandparents. Knowing that Mama 'Manda came to my christening and blessed me before she died at nearly 100 years old. Having organized marches here in this very sanctuary and finally, needing the blessing and love of all of you before I plan this feast. I just wanted my Tea to know I love her. Right here, before God and everyone."

Something in Allie jerked her to her feet. Something tugged at the iron in her soul, and melted it down into a hot lava that sought to cover and soothe that spot in her belly that would burn like fire sometimes when life felt hard. Granda turned to her and wrapped her arms around her. "Forgive me, girl. Please Jesus. Heal us. Heal us now."

For Allie, public shows of affection needed to be real. Rare.

Well, not unless she was in the courtroom, savaging someone over the peculiarities of trade secrets. So, even as she felt soothed, it was hard for her to wrap her arms around the pillow-soft old woman and hug her as she needed to be hugged.

The moment was awkward and clearly disquieting. Jack, sitting next to her, clapped and his applause resonated throughout the sanctuary.

Granda pulled back from Allie, taking out one of the handkerchiefs that she insisted on carrying because she felt Kleenex killed too many trees, and wiped at her face. "It's okay, Granda. It wasn't you. It was never you." Allie managed to get out.

"I just had to let you know how I felt and I couldn't do it anywhere else," Granda whispered as she sat down, pulling Allie down with her. "Jack said I should say it in a place that gave me my strength. That was right here."

And, to her mind, it was. Tea squeezed the soft hand. For comfort. For joy.

The minister smiled at them. "May I take up my text

now, ma'am?"

Granda waved her arm. "Go 'head, boy."

Everyone laughed, but now, Tea turned to Jack, fixing him with a questioning look. What had Granda said to him about their relationship? How could it be that this blue-eyed stranger knew so much about her, but she knew so very little about him?

And how could she make it right?

Chapter 16

AFTER THE SERVICE, JACK AND Tea had to stand to the side while many of the older people in the church came forward to greet Granda like the queen she was. When people wanted to talk to her, their discussions grew into twenty-minute diatribes.

When they finished, they would come to where Tea and Jack were standing and say nice words. Some of the older ladies liked to get a kiss from Jack, the only white person in the entire church.

"Why are you kissing on them?" Tea said after one woman went on her merry way up the aisle toward Mason's for lunch. Everyone in Milford had lunch at Mason's after church on Sunday. It was a ritual that made her wish that Mr. and Mrs. Mason would just bring their ribs and sides to the church basement. But no. They all went there. The paint on the sidewalk between the corner where the church was and Mason's was practically worn down by all the low-heeled pumps and loafers that would make their way to the rib shack.

"They love it and so do I."

"Y'all look good together standing here." Mrs. Michaels,

the reverend's mother, said.

"Oh no. He's just. Well, he's Jack," Tea stammered.

"Tea. There is nothing wrong with standing next to a good-looking man," the woman purred. "That's all I meant." She held her cheek up to Jack and he obediently bent down to kiss it. When Mrs. Michaels drew away, it was crystal-clear to her that the woman's intentions were not honorable.

Hot fury bubbled up in her.

"Don't you see? That was manipulative. She's not that old to think that kissing on her wasn't something else."

"Well, for some of these women, Mrs. Michaels excepted, that kiss is all they will get from a man. It may be all the touch they get from anyone all week."

The warm lava of emotion cooled. "I just don't think it's a good idea."

Granda came over to them, the church sanctuary empty, and held out her arm to Jack. "I know everyone goes for barbeque, but we saw everyone. I need to get to the school."

"Whatever you wish, Miss Ada."

"I can go home," Tea suggested.

"No, Tea. I'm counting on you to help me for the feast."

Well, that was a request that came out of left field. "I'm not a very good cook."

"I know. We gone fix that this week. Finally."

I don't want it to be fixed.

"Come on," Jack implored. "I've got some planning to do and it will be fun. We can grab lunch there. I'll fix it."

"Shouldn't I change?"

"Absolutely not," Granda said. "I have aprons and you'll be fine. Come on."

They made quite a little parade as they crossed the

square cattycorner to Porter Hall.

"Did I tell you that going back to Virgil and 'Mama Manda, it was a thing in our family for couples to fall in love at first sight?" Granda offered up to Tea as Jack opened the door for them both.

Tea shook her head. "I didn't think they fell in love at first sight."

"Yes they did, and if they were still alive, they would tell you so."

"But Granda, he didn't like her when he first saw her." Tea looked over her shoulder to see if Jack was listening.

He was.

"He was in love," Granda insisted as they marched on to her workplace. "The old blacksmith was too stubborn to know what he wanted."

The cafeteria was nearly empty of students at the end of the brunch hour. The line had a remnant of hard scrambled eggs, no more bacon, dry sausage links and hard rounds of English muffins. Granda set up a table for them in the dining room and went back to her office, retrieving three large aprons. Tea took off her hat and secured her hat pin in it, smoothing down her French roll.

"What would you ladies like to have?" Jack tied his apron on.

Granda looked at her. "Go on and order, Tea."

"There's no menu."

"It don't matter. Jack will make it."

"A mimosa?"

"Now you know we don't have no alcohol here on the campus." Granda rolled her eyes.

"Okay. My special coffee order from earlier and huevos rancheros."

"Okay. And for you Miss Ada?"

"Eggs Benedict over easy."

"Sounds delightful." Jack scurried away and grandmother and granddaughter were alone, for the first time in a long time.

"He's the best. Such a help. I have so much to do for this feast coming up and it will be such a help to have him with me."

"Is he filming it?"

"Well, of course. It's all a part of the movie."

Tea swallowed. "What are you serving?"

"Ham, turkey, a side of beef. Ten side dishes. Three kinds of pie, three kinds of cake. Angel rolls. And, well."

"Well?"

"Our tea purveyor has not been as reliable as we might like. We throw the feast on a shoestring budget, but I just can't imagine serving them some ordinary Lipton. We have the soda fountains, of course, but these people are looking for the real Southern meal. Serving them tea out of the fountain would be a crime."

Her grandmother bowed her head over a notepad, scribbling down notes.

Tea's heart knocked about inside of her. "I may know of a way to help, Granda. I met a fan of yours in Charlotte. Her name is Sherry. She's known for her sweet tea there. She's lovely, wonderful. Maybe if she can bring sweet tea or make it here. Being associated with you would help her a lot."

And it would. The introduction of Sherry's tea at the meal might be enough to boost her fight against Mama Cassie's, even though she knew that was not the way to actually help Cassie.

Somehow she was fine with that.

"And well, the tea recipe is her grandmother's." Tea smiled and Granda smiled back at her.

Tension she didn't know she had carried left her shoulders. It felt good to help someone.

Granda kept writing. "Well, you welcome to invite this Sherry down here if you think she has the goods."

"Oh, she does. And she cooks too. She said she puzzled out your broccoli and rice casserole."

"Oh she did? Well, I would like to see that. Tell her to bring some of that too."

"Thank you, Granda." *Cleansing breath. Whooosh.*

Jack came towards them, balancing three plates. He had made huevos rancheros for the two of them and eggs Benedict for her grandmother. He put the plates down, went back and fetched a steaming hot coffee beverage for Allie and water all around, balancing everything in his wide palms.

Another swallow.

"Jack, this is wonderful." Granda dug into her eggs Benedict, which featured a warm square of cornbread on the side.

Tea took a bite of her own cornbread and found it not too sweet, but not savory, either. The crumb of the cornbread was soft in her mouth, and a sigh escaped her.

Jack's voice startled her. "Let us pray first."

There went his dazzling grin again. She shook her head as they all joined hands and prayed. "You must have been hungry, Althea."

"She was, in spite of that pie last night." Granda smiled in a conspiratorial fashion. She uttered a thoughtful prayer and they lifted their heads when she was through.

"I knew you didn't eat enough this morning. Dig in to these huevos while they are hot," Jack urged.

"That don't look like anything Southern." Granda said with a frown.

"It's not."

Jack winked at Tea. "No. It's fancy appropriated Nueva York food for brunches. Makes the people feel as if they are eating fancy when it's really rancher/cowboy food."

"Jack, you know so much." Granda giggled.

Usually Tea might have felt irritated at his comments, but the scent of the spices tickled her nose, beckoning her away from a bad feeling to a good one.

"Yes, Jack, you know too much." Tea dug in, relishing the way the runny yellow egg yolk thickened the slightly spicy salsa and the toasty earthiness of the corn tortilla underneath it all.

"Well?"

She chewed thoughtfully. "It's pretty good." She heaved a sigh, knowing that the acidity of the salsa was probably the worst thing for her stomach. But her request had been the first thing out of her mouth, meant to test Jack Darwent to see if he could truly whip up anything out of the college kitchen.

He could.

"This cornbread sure hits the spot," Tea said.

"I put in a little sour cream." Jack looked over at her, who did her level best to ignore him as he spoke to her grandmother. "It really softens the crumb, as you suggested."

"But no fresh corn this time?"

"No. I didn't think Ms. Tea could take it in."

"Well, we putting it back in for the feast." Granda ate every last crumb.

"What will everyone say?" Tea joked, between mouthfuls of her huevos.

"It will be fine. I'm allowed to change."

"So we are deciding the sides?" Jack was the kind who used his knife and fork to create the perfect bite, Tea noticed all of a sudden.

"Yes. What do you want?"

"Hold on." Tea put down her knife after she had made a perfect forkful. "Why does he get to decide?"

Granda sat up a little. "Because he's going to be my wingman. We can't do the same thing every year."

Her eyebrows came together. "You have the same meat every year."

"The Coca-Cola ham is traditional. The fresh sage turkey is what we do. And then the rosemary beef."

Jack speared his bite, chewed and swallowed. "We need to go to the butcher's this week."

"We will, we will." Granda turned to her. "I've been doing a thing over the past few feasts where the change-up is in the sides."

Tea felt a little guilty about not being available and knowing of this innovation. Granda reached over. "Of course, we will have dressing, and I'll make a whole cranberry relish."

Now, Tea composed her perfect forkful and ate it, content. It had been years since she'd had any of Granda's dressing. Even though she was eating, her stomach rumbled at the memory.

Jack and Granda managed to clean their plates as they squabbled over the side dishes. "When you have sides that are prepared without side meat, then you are making room for folks who eat vegan."

Okay. But she still had to ask. "But are they good?"

"Yeah, of course they're good," her grandmother echoed. "And Tea is making her own contribution. She's having a special person come in and make tea from Charlotte."

Jack pushed his clean plate from him. "Mama Cassie's up in the Queen City? Man, that is some great sweet tea. I had a glass there, and…"

"No." Tea kept her voice chilly, even if her mouth was full of warm huevos. "There is a local woman who makes the tea."

"Excuse me? You can get a load of Mama Cassie's tea at one of the restaurants and ship it down."

She put her utensils down. Because she was done. "Well, I think it's better to have the woman I know come down and make it."

He sat back. "That makes no sense."

"To you, maybe."

She was glad she had no huevos in her mouth, because if she had, her mouth would have hung open and food would have dropped on her plate, which was not a good look. Picking up her water glass, she took a few sips, cooling her hot mouth full of spice.

Chapter 17

U P UNTIL HE CAME TO Milford, Jack thought that life as a cavalier bachelor/filmmaker/intellectual foodie was quite appealing. Living on a houseboat, à la Cary Grant or something, made things that much more fun.

Until he ran into Althea Dailey. And somehow, his life wasn't all that much fun anymore.

She showed him something else—the flip side of his life.

He was unrooted.

He was lonely.

He had nothing to look forward to.

So when she gave as good as she got with the quips, he was able to respond just as cuttingly, because even though he was trying to be nice, he didn't appreciate how this woman made him think too much. He shook his head and focused on his work the next morning, sitting there in the office with Miss Ada. Maybe he was a bit out of it because he hadn't had his run this morning.

Yes, that was it.

He held up a notepad. "So, here's what I have. Corn casserole, fried green tomatoes, collards, dressing, sweet potato soufflé, broccoli and rice casserole, cabbage, mashed potatoes, pinto beans, squash casserole."

Their morning plates were pushed off to the side where a student helper would come and take them to the conveyor belt to go back to the dishwasher.

"Pinto beans? Why?" Tea scrunched up her nose. It was a well-shaped nose. A pretty nose. An expressive nose, all rolled into one.

"You need some kind of beans on the buffet for those who don't like too much meat." Miss Ada nodded to Jack.

"What about a three-bean salad? Not pintos. That doesn't make any sense."

"I'm open to that." Jack spoke up. "Sounds like a great idea to me."

"Okay. So we need an additional side then."

"Pole beans," Allie chimed in.

"Yes, that will do. There's another kind of bean for folk if they are interested, and gives us three green sides."

"Brilliant." Jack noted it down. Not that he needed to. He had a great memory and knew what he was about. But it was more important to him in this moment to show her that her words had impacted him in some way.

"Won't fried green tomatoes be hard to get? It's not peak season yet," Allie put in.

"No, it isn't, but they can be red too."

Now, her beautiful face contorted, nose straight now, but lips twisted up, and her index finger tap, tap, tapped on her temple. The fingernail on that index finger shone with a natural pearly kind of color. It was simple, not showy at all. Perfectly chosen for the courtroom. He recalled well that women lawyers had to take care with that kind of thing, because red nails might make them appear harsh. "Who is going to do all of that frying?"

"I have helpers I hire for the feast," Miss Ada said,

her tone gentle and corrective.

Jack offered, "I'll do it."

"I thought you would be at the carving station. Will you be some kind of Jack-in-the-box, popping in and out of places?" Allie's smile broadened, and she looked at him askance.

"Ahh, that's a good one. You've been looking for a place to use that all along, but it just now fit. Bad news is that it kind of fit, but it's still hanging off sideways a bit."

"I'll get there yet."

Miss Ada waved her hands. "You two."

The student helper, a young man Jack knew named Trent, came to get their trays. He cleared the table and Jack noticed that Allie thanked him quietly.

"You're welcome, Miss." Trent beamed.

So, she knew how to talk to people. Jack's mind went back to the encounter she'd had at the coffee shop this morning, when she had briefly flirted with Calvin. It was *him* she had the problem with.

Well, she's been saying that. I just didn't believe.

"That was nice." Jack nodded. "Trent's a fine young man. An economics major."

"Nice? What?"

"You speaking to him."

"I speak to everyone. That's how I was brought up." Allie folded her hands, in a neat, delicate way.

Miss Ada nodded. "That's right. If she didn't do right, I would take her out behind the woodshed."

"Well, what about when I made the huevos rancheros? Why didn't I get a special thanks?"

"You tried too hard." She raised up her eyebrows, grinning.

Jack folded his arms at this riposte. "You thought you would trip me up when your grandmother said 'anything,' and you tried to name something you thought was out of my wheelhouse. Admit it."

She turned to him, full on, just like he wanted. Oh, how he wanted to bask in the sun of her regard, warming in it like a fat-bellied cat in the sun, stretching and yawning lazily, but satisfied. "I admit to nothing. I pay my taxes. That's what I admit to."

"Good for you. I'm still trying to evade them." He flashed her one of his best Jack smiles, but she turned from him back to her grandmother. The sun had gone away. "I'm just kidding."

"Of course you are, Jack." Miss Ada laughed at him. "You're a devil."

"Yes. Trust fund babies can well afford their tax burdens, especially after their families have provided ways for their means to be protected." Allie turned to her grandmother. "I'm worried about all of that oil and everything out in the sun. Can't we do something better?"

Jack didn't mind her critique, because she was correct. Still, the barb about his trust fund stung.

He told her, "We can make things in advance and reheat them in a series of air fryers."

"Hey yeah, that's good. Before Jack come here, I had never seen one of those. Now he got me hooked on them."

Allie's hands, her long, slender, tapered hands, curved around a special-looking pen and made a notation in a Moleskine notebook. "Fine. I just don't think anyone should be inside frying tomatoes."

"We've got it. Don't worry."

"Okay. Now what about the dishes with the dairy?" She stopped writing.

"Hey." Jack stopped watching what her hands looked like holding the pen. It was best not to think about it because then he might be thinking of what those hands would look like on him. "You're making some good suggestions. But I'm here to capture the full-fat, full-sugar, full-lard and grease experience of this feast."

"Fine." Allie held up her hands.

"No, I mean it."

"I heard what you said."

Did she just back down that easily? And here he was, all ready to spar with her—and she backed down. *Wow*.

She had moved on. "What stops do we have to make, Granda?"

Miss Ada nodded. "Most of the things are coming to us. The art department is going to create the settings and tablecloths, make everything look nice since we are eating outside. There will be ten tables of five each. We'll have a meeting with the staff on Friday. That's when I'll hand out the jackets to everyone. I do want to make sure that I get pecans."

Jack pointed to Allie, moving his hands back and forth. "We can take care of that for you, ma'am."

"What is this 'we'?" Allie drew back.

Jack's palms went up. "I'm more than happy to go. I just thought you would help as well."

"It will be good for you, Allie. Get you some fresh country air."

Allie fixed him with a side glance, something that would have made the perfect internet meme. Took a breath deep enough to flare her lovely little nostrils out and said, "Fine. Okay. And you can call me Tea."

He drew back at this new bit of information. "I don't want you to hurt yourself or anything."

Miss Ada held up a hand. "I think we are done here. I'm going home for my afternoon nap. Y'all are giving me a headache right now."

"I'm sorry, Granda." Tea patted her grandmother's hand and it gladdened Jack's heart to see a tender gesture from her. Finally, the ice was beginning to thaw.

His mentor did look tired, all of a sudden. He went to help her up from her seat and escort her to the door. Tea followed with her giant hat. They walked back to the church parking lot as a silent little group, but they passed Mason's, where a merry crowd had spilled out on the street and into the square waiting to get inside. Tea paused.

"You all go on ahead. I want to chat with Monique."

Before they could stop her, there she went, long legs striding with purpose across the lawn to the restaurant.

Jack couldn't help but watch the way she strode, being able to tell just by her walk, the high way she held her head and the slight movement of her hips: this was a woman who won many a case.

He and Ada stopped at the crosswalk. He was trying to make sure that they took care crossing the street, but that happened to coincide with Althea crossing the square to go into Mason's.

"You like her, don't you?" Miss Ada shifted a little in her walk.

Jack's head swiveled so fast to face his mentor that he got a crick in his neck.

"Miss Ada, I don't know what you mean."

"Yes you do. You like Tea. Just say it."

"Is there any point? She doesn't like me."

They stepped across the street together, walking toward the church parking lot. "Of course there is a point. And I'm glad to see it."

"You are?"

"Yes. No man should be alone. No woman neither. And it would be so nice to see two people who are in need of one another come together. It would be even nicer if y'all realized that at the same time. Only…"

"Yes ma'am?"

"Tea requires patience. And I think one reason why men haven't taken to her is that they get impatient. For the wrong thing, if you know what I'm saying. She's not going to give her heart easily to anyone. But once given, it will be a sweet reward. Are you patient, Jack Darwent?"

Was he?

"I'm this old and haven't gotten tangled up yet." He pressed the button on his key fob to open the door for her.

He eased Miss Ada into the passenger seat and went around to the other side to get in, taking off his jacket first because the warm May day was getting to him.

"I see. And I know we've talked about why before. I suspect, and you'll forgive an old lady for speaking plainly to someone she wants for her grandson-in-law…"

His head swiveled again and they both laughed.

"No, seriously, be gentle with her. She'll come along. And you will too."

"Me?" Jack's voice went up a bit as he pulled out of the parking space into the street.

"Yes. You have some things to figure out too, don't you?"

He backed out carefully, straightening the car on the road. "My movie, the cookbook, all kinds of things."

"I mean your daddy."

Her wise words stopped him in his tracks.

"Don't go getting twisted up with Tea until you get all that fixed with your daddy first. People think those things don't matter, but they do. When you leave that stuff alone and don't tend to it, it will fester. Tea is down here, working on herself. You driving around the country, making your movie and all, but you need to make a stop up there in Tennessee and have a talk with him. When you do, then talk to Tea about what might be. But not before then. Understand?"

"Yes ma'am. I do."

She leaned back in the seat, closing her eyes. "Good. Because I do want some great-grands. They'll be pretty babies and I want to see them. But not before I know you have taken care of yourselves first. That's all. I'm tired."

"Yes ma'am."

He drove the rest of the short distance home in silence, thinking about the road ahead and when he could squeeze in a trip to Tennessee.

Was Althea worth it? A knot pulled tighter inside of him.

He knew she was.

Chapter 18

E VEN WITH TEA'S LITTLE SPILL yesterday, stalking on four-inch heels across the beautiful town square was nothing new at all for someone who had lived in New York for a good portion of her adult life. Others would have been discomfited at the feeling of their heels sinking into Georgia red clay, but not her.

No. What unsettled her was the way Jack Darwent had been just now.

Why did men say women were the ones who were crazy and changeable? Clearly the man was loco.

The crowds in Mason's had settled down and she was glad, because she would love one of their Bloody Marys. Again, not great for her stomach, but great for her state of mind.

She swung open the door and the entire Mason clan was inside at work. Monique came over to her, ready to bump fists.

"I need a Virgin Mary. Like now."

"With the works?"

"The works?" Tea's face went quizzical.

"Dad bumped it up. You can have it with a baby fried

157

chicken on it, an Angus cheeseburger slider with pepper jack, and a skewer of grilled shrimp."

"Oh no. I've eaten. Just the regular."

Monique ushered Tea to a patio table, away from her nosy family, and got her the drink. The first sip of the cool beverage went right to her brain and smoothed all the rough edges away.

"What is the problem, Tea? Was it your grandmother?"

"Oh no. She's fine. I mean, that was all unexpected this morning, but she's fine."

"Good. I know you don't like PDA, so…"

Tea took a bite of crisp celery, chewed and swallowed. Such a great teeth cleaner. "No, that's not true."

"It isn't? Well, I always thought that of you."

"No. I don't like everyone knowing my business. There is a distinct difference."

"Well, you should have just texted me to come over, because look at these fools." Monique shouted towards her four sisters, who all of a sudden had chores to do that were near their table. They scattered.

Monique sat down.

"I didn't want to go home."

Now she had her friend's attention.

"Say what?"

"I didn't want to go back to Granda's with them."

"Why not?"

"It was time for Granda's nap and I didn't want to be in the house with him by myself." Which sounded silly now, because she could have gone into her own room and shut the door. She could have demanded that he go back to his houseboat and she would see him tomorrow to prep for the feast. Why didn't she think of those alternatives rather than running over here to Mason's?

"Whoo girl, really?" Monique leaned forward. "You

know that every woman in this town and up and down the coast has been trying to find out that man's game. He's a dream."

"What about our family's recipes? They need protection."

Monique leaned back in her chair, slapping a towel on the edge of the table until she was forced to take a sip of her drink again. "Ha! Good luck with that, girl. Tell yourself that."

"I can't go falling for him. He's trying to take my grandmother's intellectual property." She shoved some more celery into her mouth. To stuff it up.

"Is he, Althea Louise? Can't you?"

Monique's nosiest sister—the baby of the family, Lydia—had worked her way to the next table over. "You. Get out of here. That table is clean," Monique ordered.

"I can clean where I want."

Monique pushed her glasses up on her nose. "Scram, I said. She's my friend, not yours."

Lydia went back to the counter area, disappointed. Allie couldn't help but laugh. "You don't know how many times your family made me glad that I was an only child."

"Yeah, same. I loved getting a glimpse of your solitude. But seriously. Do you think he's after her recipes?"

"He said he was. Shouldn't I believe him?"

"Well, friend. They have to go somewhere. I think a movie or a printed cookbook is a very grand way to hold up her legacy. That's why I didn't think anything about it. I mean, I'm not an intellectual property lawyer. As a librarian and archivist, my whole thing was about getting them down in some way. And you never seemed to be interested."

"Cooking just wasn't my thing."

"Well, I recall some attempts you made at our house. You weren't awful."

"You mean Jeno's Pizza Rolls and premade cookie dough?"

"I mean the time we made spaghetti for my family. It was good."

Tea chewed thoughtfully on the last of the celery, relishing the cleansing quality of the vegetable in her mouth. She had buried that memory. Monique and she had been eleven, and it was one of those times her parents went off on a trip by themselves and she had stayed with Monique.

She always wished that they would take her with them, and she hated them going away with one another, often to nearby Calloway Gardens for a weekend, but they loved each other, and as much as they loved her, they wanted to be alone together.

It was on one of those trips that they went away and never came back.

Had she blocked that memory of her successful spaghetti out?

"Yes. We made the sauce with Ragu. And doctored it up."

"Yes. You did. You added Italian seasoning, and garlic salt and powder and pepper. Then a bit of sugar, you said to offset the acidity of the tomatoes."

"I said that?" Tea sat back in the chair.

"You did. I'll never forget that. Someone of your young age having that understanding."

Her mouth opened in wonder, and all of a sudden it hit her. "Because my grandmother showed me."

"And my parents loved it. We all did. You made meatballs with a mix of ground beef and pork, and baked them with a little extra cheese in the meat mixture."

Her friend's words set her back in the past and she stared off into the square. How could the past be like a ghost that emerged and made you stronger, or, like this memory, weaker?

"That was the last time I ever made anything besides scrambled eggs."

"What a loss." Monique stopped flicking her towel and looked downcast. "It was delicious. I was sure you had inherited your grandmother's cooking ability."

Those words snapped her out of her reverie. "Oh no. No one can do what Granda does."

"No one wants you to."

"I just. I mean. All desire to cook left me after…"

Monique reached over to capture her friend's hand in hers. "I know. I hear you."

The pain of unshed tears pricked at the corner of Tea's eyes. How embarrassing it would be to have a public display of crying over this now, twenty years later.

Get it together.

She sucked the pain back in and tamped it back into the corner where it belonged. "I don't cook. But I'll help prep to be there for her."

"And you'll let Jack have the recipes?"

She shook her head. "He'll have to pay her royalties. He cannot have the property of her mind for free." She finished the cool drink. "I'm going back home now."

"Good. Jack will probably go back to his houseboat. Then you don't have to worry that you'll weaken and kiss his lips." Monique lifted her eyebrows.

She put a finger to her lips and shushed her. "Hey. Stop that."

"Come on, Tea. When was the last time you had a boyfriend?"

"Now you want to talk about my business."

"I've never heard you mention a name. All these years, girl."

That's because there weren't any of note. Not since college, anyway.

She gave her friend a sidelong glance. "I'm too busy. I was always too busy with the firm for that kind of thing."

"I'm just saying, girl. Admit it. And that Jack, he's been giving all of the Milford ladies happy dreams at night."

"Monique Angela!"

Her friend cackled.

Then Tea smiled. "Including my grandmother."

"Especially her. She be looking at him like, yeah, if only I was forty years younger!"

They laughed together and she delighted in feeling light again. She didn't know if it was the cool drink or her friend, but it worked.

The visage of her kindly grandfather hovered in her mind: a man who'd liked to pay hide and go seek with her as a little girl. Until he couldn't. "She loved her Oliver."

"I know. I'm just playing. But someone ought to get the fun of that fine white man. Is that what is stopping you?"

"I didn't even notice."

"You didn't notice what? You not down with the swirl?" Monique elbowed her.

"I know you are." She shook her head at her friend, referring to Monique's past love interest.

"Yeah well, a man is a man is a man."

"Fine."

"Exactly." Monique stood.

"I cannot believe you. No."

Monique stood over her, looking around for any more nosy sisters. "I see how he looks at you. He wants to be more than friends."

"Excuse me?"

Her friend's eyebrows went up and they giggled. "See, you have been too busy with these trade secrets. You don't even know what I'm talking about."

"I do. But it's not for me." Tea pushed the drink away, needing to walk home. She opened her purse and took out a twenty, handing it to Monique. Monique held up her hand, but then she took the money and tucked it into her apron pocket.

"You think about what I said. You've made partner. Isn't it time for you to sit back and enjoy your success?"

"Maybe."

"Maybe." Monique parroted her. "Get out of here."

She stood up and waved at all of the Masons, getting ready to walk home. When she came out of the restaurant, she saw Jack's car parked at the corner. With Jack in it. She turned around, trying to see who would see them. *Dear Lord, word would spread like a Milford track star at this.*

"What are you doing here?" She bent down to his level/to the open window.

He yelled out from the driver's seat. "Get in. Thought you and your hat might need a ride home. You wearing those heels and everything."

"I could have walked."

"Well, you don't have to. I'm here." He popped open the door and she slid in. "Don't tell me you were still hungry after my fabulous huevos."

"No, gringo. I was thirsty."

"Ahh. So you wanted a little hair of the dog."

"I'm used to having a Virgin Mary for Sunday brunch." She emphasized the word *virgin*, but all that did was make him grin harder, and blood rushed to her face, so she turned from him and looked out the window for the brief ride.

Before she knew it, he was pulling into her grandmother's driveway. "Here you are, Miss. That will be ten dollars."

She held up her hand. "The only payment necessary will be you signing the contracts that I draw up to make sure that my grandmother receives a portion of whatever you make with your movie and cookbook."

He turned off the car and tilted his head at her. "You seem to be very worried about that."

"I am." She narrowed her eyes, pointing a finger at him. "Because you are a charmer. And charmers leave a lot of pain in their wake."

He smiled. "You think I'm charming."

"I'm going into the house." Allie jabbed her index finger into his impossibly hard chest.

Again.

My Lord.

When will I learn?

"You're going to your houseboat?"

He put a crooked arm up on the open window sill. "I'll tell you what. Your grandmother is going to nap for some time. How about you come with me when you change? We can go for a jog along the river and work off our brunch."

Right now, a run sounded so heavenly. But with him? "No."

"No?" He seemed surprised. *Ha.*

"I'll see you tomorrow."

"That's fine." He popped the door open again. "Need help getting into the house?"

"Absolutely not."

"I offered."

"And I rejected your offer." Tea put a lot of emphasis on the *r* word, and the way his brow crinkled up showed he got the point. She stepped out of his car, making her way to the house, fishing her key out of her purse.

"Oh, Sweet Tea?" His voice trailed out behind her. "Make sure that you have a little bit of dinner I made for you. Miss Ada will show you where it is."

"I don't need anything from you, Jack Darwent."

All she could hear was his laughter floating out of the car window as he drove away, making her into something she'd never known she was.

A liar.

Chapter 19

ONE REASON SHE DIDN'T LIKE to return for the special May feast every year was because of her grandmother's—as well as President Jasper's— insistence that it center around the theme of some important Milford College history or personage. In past years, he had even centered it around himself, which Tea found conceited beyond all belief, but what else could you expect from someone who had remained president for more than thirty years?

Monique never failed to email her or text her every year with the theme, because, as she said, "Shows how crucial we are in maintaining the history of such a place—of a historically Black college early on."

Those words always gave her pause. Why did anyone have to focus on what Milford was or how it came to be? Or that if it hadn't been for Evangeline Casey Milford, the woman who had owned the original plantation the land was on and who'd founded the town with Virgil Smithson, it wouldn't be at all? Why did that matter?

All of these facts chased each other in circles around her head as she woke the next morning to ready herself for feast prep today. She wanted to be useful to her Granda, of course, now that they had made peace, but she hoped that this year's theme didn't dislodge too much in her world.

She woke at 6:30, as the sun rose, to take her jog, a quick loop around campus and down to the waterfront since her ankle, fortunately, had recovered enough. Looking at the marina, she wondered if Jack was up yet. She didn't know which houseboat was his, but they all looked pretty snug and well kept.

Turning around from stretching at the waterfront, she didn't look where she was going, and *bam*! She ran smack into a hot, slick chest.

Jack's chest.

"Good morning." He took out his earbuds and ran a hand over his head. His curls were gone, sleek with dampness that pasted his golden locks to his head and turned them into a darker color.

"Hey."

"You don't seem happy to see me."

"Should I do a jig?" Tea curtseyed.

"No. Just more stretching would be nice."

"You were watching me?" She smacked his arm, a gun that was loaded for bear and as hard as iron.

"Ouch." He laughed a bit. "I bruise easily."

"You should have been more thoughtful before you said that."

"You never know who is watching you. Might be Calvin. He sure looked like he wanted to be your cinnamon roll."

"Well, from what I hear from Monique, half the women of Milford wouldn't mind being on your houseboat."

She started to jog away from him, but he caught her

by the wrist and his touch caused the burning sensation that was usually in her stomach to travel up her arm to her shoulder. *What the…*she almost spoke the rest, but looking up his bare arm and shoulder she could see that he was as stunned as she was.

"Umm. I wondered if you wanted to come aboard. For coffee."

"No. I need to get back to the house and shower." She yanked her arm away from his touch for her own self-preservation.

"Okay. I mean you could shower on the boat, but I guess that's where I'll shower." He showed her all of his pearly whites.

"Nice try. I'll see you later."

She jogged off, glad to have her sea legs beneath her enough to get home and bring Granda to campus to start with the feast prep.

They worked all day and collapsed when they got home. The next day, Jack was already in the kitchen before them, directing everyone assembled to particular duties.

"You, Althea." His deep voice resonated. "You stick with me."

She wondered what he wanted her to do.

Once they were in the kitchen, filled with smells from rendering turkey necks and turkey butts down into gravy and surrounded by four teenage assistants who had been tasked to chop celery and onion, Jack slammed a big bag on the counter in front of her. "Do you know what this is?"

"Cornmeal?" She could read the label on the front of the bag clear enough.

"Yes. We'll make three big pans of cornbread for the dressing. Can you crack eggs?"

"Sure." She knew how to make scrambled eggs for herself.

"Crack them in a small bowl, then pour them in the big bowl so that there will be no shells."

"Got it."

She had gotten through her first dozen when Granda came up to her, a general checking on the command of her troops. "What you doing, Tea? He got you cracking eggs?"

"Yes ma'am."

"Do it properly then. You know how."

Before Tea came here, she might have gotten irritated at that wording. Now, she understood her grandmother's desire for the best possible outcome. In that moment, she knew it was because they had the same work ethic.

She continued cracking the eggs, and when she looked up, Jack was engaged in shaving plump, milky kernels of corn off of the ears. "This is for the eating cornbread that we'll make later," he explained. "The cornbread for the dressing won't have fresh corn in it."

"We never had that growing up."

"It's a touch that Miss Ada appreciated," Jack informed her, letting those long lashes wave up and down and up and down…

She put down an egg. "I'm sure you aren't doing anything that my grandmother wouldn't approve of."

"Well, here's something that you might not be used to." Jack reached beneath the table and lifted a bag of sugar.

She felt triggered. "What is that?"

"We're going to put sugar in this cornbread."

"Oh no. I'm going to tell." Something inside her made her want to laugh at how silly she sounded. She? Tea? Sounding silly? It had been years since she'd had this sense of play.

"You won't say a thing. This here is a Tennessee secret and we're proud. And like I said, eating cornbread is different than dressing cornbread."

Just in that moment, Granda came by, looking like a fierce little Napoleon with her hand tucked into her chef's jacket, a smaller, more crisp replica of what they all wore.

"You two stop that playing and get to work. If I can't trust you to be an example to these children, who can I trust?"

"Yes ma'am." Tea stuck her tongue out at Jack and he wielded a wooden spoon at her.

Afterward, while she drank a cup of coffee, Jack set up some camera equipment in the corner of the kitchen, setting it on one of the shiny silver counters. He came to her with a clipboard with a stack of papers on them.

"Will you sign this release, Sweet Tea?"

She swigged the last of the coffee. "I didn't really want to be on camera. I thought you were filming my grandmother."

"I am. I had in mind a grandmother/granddaughter story. Your Granda here is going to show you how to prepare muscadines for the grape pie."

Tea looked over the release and it was boilerplate, so she signed it, wondering if Connie was okay, since she had not sent the papers to protect Granda's IP down to her yet. "Wait. I need makeup."

Don't I?

For the first time in years, she didn't feel the need to put on anything to take her color down two shades.

"No. I want a natural look and a natural interaction. Just act natural. I've framed the shot." Jack beckoned to Granda, and set a bowl of muscadines, an empty bowl, a knife and a cutting board in front of them. He went to get his camera, and focused on them. "Ready? Three, two, one…action."

Right on cue, Granda declared, "These here muscadines, they aren't the kind of grapes you can buy at the Kroger. You have to get these out from the woods somewhere."

Tea couldn't help it. She blurted, "It's awful, Granda. Why are they building timeshare houses up there?"

"Up where?"

"Where we used to get muscadines. Up by March's woods."

Her grandmother ran her hands over the bowl of grapes. "Oh yes. Well, we have to keep the town going, Tea. Keep it active, keep it thriving. Lots of people are appreciating Milford for its closeness to the water, so they want places to live when they come to the coast."

Something in Tea's heart sank at those words. Granda went back to the grapes and picked up the knife.

"Cut the muscadine in half, pull the fleshy seed out, then cut it again and put it in the bowl. Sometimes you can try to save the seeds and dry them out so that you can get some muscadines to grow in your backyard, but they are mighty particular. They never came up for me."

"Might as well try," Tea suggested.

"Indeed. You're young and you might as well try." Granda handed the knife to Allie, who began to cut the grapes as Granda had instructed.

"We need you to tell the courtship story of the grape pie." Jack spoke from behind the camera.

"Courtship?" Granda looked confused for a minute, and it struck Allie once more how old her grandmother appeared to be. She should have been here more often. Why had she let hard, bad feelings deprive her of closeness to the only immediate family member she had left in the world?

"Of Mama 'Manda and Papa Virgil."

Granda raised up a hand in acknowledgement. "Oh yeah. Well, Mama 'Manda, we have found out, was born up in Ohio and she went to school up there at the only school they would let a Black lady go to in them days, Oberlin College."

"A well-known college."

"Yes. Some call it the cradle for HBCU schools because they were just about the only ones who let the Black people go to college before the civil war."

"Keep cutting and prepping the muscadines, Tea," Jack said.

She did as Jack bid.

"Anyhow, she was brought up there by a white lady, cause her mama died when she was young."

Tea stopped cutting. "She did?"

"Yes."

"I never knew that about Mama Manda." The knowledge soothed her somehow. Made her know she was not alone.

Granda watched her cutting those muscadines. "Lawd yes. She was even younger than you when you lost your mama. She was a baby—just seven."

"Oh my." How hard that must have been for Mama 'Manda. There was always someone worse off than you. Tea steadied the knife in her hand.

Granda didn't see her tremble. Just a bit. "So her papa had the keeping of her, and this white lady, she raised her, taught her homemaking and such. So we think it was this lady what taught Mama 'Manda the grape pie. When she came down here to teach the Milford slaves how to read and write, she brung the recipe with her."

Granda sighed and continued. "Virgil Smithson was

the head of the town. He didn't want no strange Northern woman down here teaching the slaves her fancy ways, but when he had some of that pie, Lord, he fell in love with her and had to marry her."

Jack interjected. "So, the town founder fell in love with her pie?"

Granda looked at the camera head-on, which made Allie giggle a little bit. "No. He wasn't the founder. He was the mayor. He was in charge. Mrs. Milford, this was her land and all the enslaved folks worked it, but Papa Virgil had the trust of them. He knew how to talk to them and get them to do the most work 'stead of beating them up. That's why when freedom came, she told him to organize a town of their own and she made him be the mayor. He was a blacksmith, a mayor and a preacher."

"Sounds like a man of great prominence."

"He was. But that pie brought him low."

"As well as Mama 'Manda's beauty." Tea added, glancing at some blind-baked pie crusts beside them in metal squares. This way they could freeze the pies unbaked, bake them on the day of the feast and keep them warm over Sterno heaters.

"Yes, Lawd. She was beautiful. She put me in mind of you. You both look the same."

Tea pulled a hand back from the bowl of cut grapes and faced her grandmother. "I've never heard you say that. I thought you thought I looked like my mother."

Granda took the bowl from her. "What would make you think that? No. Mama 'Manda laid hands on me as a child with the most gentle touch. And I remember her face. It was old by then, of course, but that's the face you got. You have her face, even if you are taller."

A wind blew into Tea's bones, warming her to her core, making her think deeply, for the first time in a very long time, about the gentle woman who was her three-times-great-grandmother.

She got the feeling that Mama 'Manda would have been proud of her.

In that moment, that knowledge was enough.

Chapter 20

J ACK'S FRAMING OF THE SEGMENT with Allie and her
grandmother filled him. Like being satisfied after
a good meal. She might want to sue him, but seeing
these two ladies together, each a spectacular success in
her own way, was right and good.

His filled heart brought words of joy to his lips. "You
both are amazing. This is great stuff. Keep going."

Miss Ada preened a bit and Tea and Jack laughed
together at her antics. "There isn't much more to tell,"
Ada said. "Whenever they told me the story, though, they
said that their love story continued a tradition of people
in our family who tended to fall in love very quickly."

"Like love at first sight?" Tea laughed.

"What's so funny?" Jack asked.

They watched her grandmother add sugar and flavor-
ings to the fruit, getting ready to put it in a pot on the
stove to cook down. "I put in lemon. Some don't, but
it brings out the flavor to me, especially if you have a
sweet batch of muscadines."

"Because everyone knows falling in love at first sight is
ridiculous." Now it was Allie's turn to stare into the camera.

God, she takes my breath away.

He spoke up over the pounding of his heart. "I don't know. Stranger things have happened."

"Tell me who, Granda."

"You need evidence, Miss Lawyer?"

Tea spoke to Jack, staring into the camera again. "You're going to have to cut all of this out. This has nothing to do with grape pie."

"Go on." He looked through the viewfinder once more. He wanted it all on tape.

Granda thought. "Well, your mama and daddy. They only knew one another for a few weeks at freshman orientation before they fell in love. Me and Oliver. We were on the protest marching lines together for a week before we knew. My mama and papa. They came together at a union meeting. My grandparents. They came together at the Atlanta exposition. And that takes me back to Mama 'Manda and Papa Virgil. Old Mrs. Milford commanded them to get married right away when she came down, because Milford was a Christian community and she wasn't going to have no living in sin."

Miss Ada arranged the square pie tins. Then Jack adjusted his frame to watch the older woman stir down the grapes into a thick jammy filling. Moving back to the pie tins, her hands moved quickly with surety as she braided the pie crust edges for "extra pretty," as she said.

"How in the world were they talking about living in sin back during Mama 'Manda's day?"

"Seems like you forgotten some particulars, Tea. Or now you understand I have plenty of evidence. When Mama 'Manda came here, she didn't have no place to board. She was supposed to be a man. Back in them days Papa Virgil wanted a man schoolteacher. That's what Papa Virgil ordered. So the man teacher would have stayed in the barn. But Mama 'Manda being a lady, she couldn't stay in the barn and she had nowhere else to go, so they had to get married so she could live in his house."

"That's crazy, Granda."

"It's the kind of crazy that got you here, Tea. Watch that mouth of yours."

"It is a pretty remarkable story, Miss Ada." Jack had to defend Tea's exclamation.

The older woman's hands stopped moving. "So you defending her, Jack?"

"Miss Ada, I'm just saying. I see what Tea is saying. To have to marry a woman you hardly know so she could teach school for the entire community was quite a sacrifice on Virgil's part." He had to stop himself from saying Papa Virgil. These people had come alive for him, almost as if they were a part of him.

"Not to mention on Amanda's part," Tea countered.

Miss Ada dusted her hands. "Well, he did the right thing. 'Sides, he had that little girl, March, already. She had to be taken care of, and wasn't no man who was a blacksmith, and a mayor, and a representative gone do it. He needed 'Manda's help."

"He might have hired someone," Jack put in helpfully. Tea threw him a grateful look. He liked it.

Granda scoffed. "What is wrong with young people today? Black men in the 1800s did not go hiring folk. Family came in and did it, or you got yourself a wife when yours died. That's all he did. And I'm glad he did it. We wouldn't be here if he hadn't. We come from the youngest son. Stewart was my great-grandfather and your two times great-grandfather, and if you had some babies, he would be their three times great-grandfather."

"Where did that come from?" Tea stood up a little

straighter.

"Thirty-two ain't getting no younger, is all I'm saying. Just think on it."

Tea waved her hands. "Granda, you didn't even like babies. You told me so yourself."

Miss Ada stirred the pot, looking very contemplative. "Yes. I have a plan for that. Bring them by every once in a while until they are two. Then let me have them."

Jack laughed and turned to face one of the student helpers, who said they were all finished cutting up the celery and onions, and what was next?

Who ever knew what was next? All he knew was that he liked to see her smile.

The day was long and satisfying. When Jack took the ladies home in his car after a hurried dinner of a side dish sampler at the cafeteria—because how else would they know what was good?—he escorted them into the house, and turned to her.

"We didn't get in our run this morning. How about we take a walk to the waterfront and I show you my houseboat?"

She raised her eyebrows. "I'm covered in cornmeal and flour and you're still restless?"

"Yes, I am. I'm a high-energy kind of guy. What were you going to do, anyway?"

"Take a shower and get some work done. I have a case to take care of."

"Is that really necessary? Are you behind?"

There went her cute nose.

"Well, no, but…"

"Well, put on one of those one-piece things you have and let's go."

Miss Ada waved her on. "Go on, Tea. You know I'm going to bed soon."

"Are you going to bring that infernal camera with you?"

"I don't understand why you don't like it."

Tea shrugged her shoulders. "It's alternate reality."

"So you prefer reality?"

"Will you all get along and jibber jabber outside my home?" Miss Ada turned from them and walked to her wing of the house, muttering all the way about the foolishness of youth.

Their eyes met and they both laughed. "OK. I'll be back."

"No showering. You're Okay. Honest."

More than okay. From where he stood an arm's length away, she smelled like his best honey cornbread and grape pie filling.

Ten minutes later she had on some sunshiny yellow thing that resembled, in a more sophisticated way, what kids used to wear. She wore flat yellow shoes to match and she appeared like a living, walking, breathing sunbeam to him.

They walked down the street together back toward the campus, and in the dimmer light, yet hotter heat of early evening, everything took on a bit of a haze.

To make conversation he said, "Miss Ada wants us to get the pecans."

"Yes, and I still need to get up to Charlotte this week."

"For?"

"Some work on my suit."

"Tell me about it."

"Tell you?"

"Well, I can be a sounding board. I do have a degree."

"I recall it well."

"So you can talk legalese to me and I'll understand."

"Wait. Just give you my thoughts and you'll hand them back to me all sorted out."

"Sure. Why not?"

"There's a problem with confidentiality. But I guess I can stop before I head into trouble territory." So she spoke to him, but instead of him straightening out her woes with a rather straightforward trade secrets case, she soothed him, like a good forkful of macaroni and cheese would.

"Sherry has to give up the tea. Literally. It's not hers."

"But it *is* hers. It was her grandmother's." Allie's pretty face frowned as they headed down the slope to the Milford marina. Most of the boats bobbed gently in the water, but *Gimme Some Sugar* just did her thing, being his stable home.

"Which someone in Cassie's family took somehow. The secret," she added.

"What is the secret?"

"I have signed confidentiality agreements. I cannot divulge that." Tea's arms folded.

"Ahh. I just wanted to make sure you are on your toes. There's my boat."

"*Gimme Some Sugar*? That's the name?"

"Yes." He put his hands in his pockets and rocked back and forth.

"That's pretty cheeky, isn't it?"

"No." Jack donned a serious look. "It's merely asking for what I want."

"Which is? Amuse me."

"Ladies who come on the boat are supposed to give me some sugar."

She stood there, folding her arms across her chest. "Then I am perfectly satisfied to wait right here. All of a sudden I have become a certified landlubber."

He laughed out loud.

"Did my grandmother do it?"

"Of course she did. You've seen her kiss me."

"On the cheek, yes." She rolled her eyes, but was smiling.

"That's what she did. I wouldn't ask her for anything else."

"Well, good."

"It's just fun. That's all."

"So you are a large child, Jack Darwent."

On purpose, he stepped inside her personal space.

Just to see what she would do about it.

Her arms came loose, as if she didn't know what to do with them anymore, and she put them into the pockets of her outfit, rocking back and forth on her heels.

"I'm not a child, Althea. About as far from it as you can get."

When she breathed out, which she was doing very heavily right now, she smelled fruity, like a peach. One of the first of the summer. A fragrant, sweet, ripe peach. Was there anything better than that?

"Hooray for you." Her voice sounded very low, like a whisper. Like she couldn't talk her usual trash talk. Had moving closer to her taken her off her game? "But I'm not following that directive and I'm not getting on that boat."

Well, no. It hadn't.

He stepped back. "I'll bring out some cider and glasses then. Hang on."

She walked over to some benches on the waterfront, a boat or two away from *Gimme Some Sugar*, and sat, arms folded back again.

Well, she'd won that one. He had to give her props.

He went to his boat, dug around, and found a Martinelli's sparkling cider. He opened the bottle and went back outside with the cider and two glasses.

"It's not a Virgin Mary, but it will do."

He sat down on the bench next to her and poured. Putting the bottle down on the ground, he raised his glass up to clink it to hers. She obliged him with a "Cheers."

"To what?" he asked.

"To a smooth feast for my grandmother."

"Yes. Of course."

"And a nice trip for you."

"Ahhh. You wound me, lady. I felt that golden apple go right upside my head that time."

Her eyes widened. "What would you know about anything going upside your head?"

"Miss Luly. She would say it all the time." He took a sip and she did the same. "I should have known I was going to be a foodie. Whenever she would say that, I would think of upside-down cake."

That got a laugh from her.

"So who is your next Southern Treasure?" Her body was inclined toward him.

"I've got several places to choose from. I'll think about it after the feast, and…"

"I thought you were going to leave on Sunday."

"I can stay here and rest after the feast."

She sipped her golden cider and looked down the waterway at some people who were waterskiing. "If you must."

"Cold-hearted. I deserve rest for as hard as I'll work to help Miss Ada pull this off."

"I suppose so."

"Or is it me you need rest from, Althea?"

He had gone for it. He took another casual sip of his cider and looked at the waterway in the opposite direction.

Let's see what she has to say to that.

Chapter 21

WHEN THE SILENCE FELL BETWEEN the two of them, Tea guessed she was supposed to speak or something. Something, the swirly feeling that was not burning her any longer, kept her from speaking.

"Lovely evening," Jack supplied.

"It is."

"Lovely cider."

"It is."

More silence. Then, she spoke. "Granda has enjoyed your visit here, but, well…and I don't want to sound impertinent, but it's time for you to be moving on."

"You do sound impertinent. But I'm sure that's not a problem for you." He drained his glass.

Whoa.

"Umm. Okay. I'm just saying."

"And then what? You're going to go back to New York to your lonely life?"

She raised an eyebrow at him. "Excuse me? You know nothing about me."

Guess he was getting bold. "I see you. I know you are one of those who works eighty hours a week and that you maybe see a play or go to brunch on the weekends and that is your life. Here you are now, what, thirty-five years old, and you are left wondering what there is anymore."

"I'm thirty-two," she informed him, pointing a finger out from her glass.

"Life is so much more than working all of the time." He breathed out with a whoosh, and poured himself more cider.

"Spoken like a true trust fund baby."

"Well, it is."

"Look. When I was at boarding school, I grew up with my share of people like you. People who never had to worry or work a job or count coins or make things last so that I didn't have to call Granda for it. After all, she's basically the lunch lady here. Milford is not a college with a strong endowment. To be honest, it's on its last legs."

"What do you mean?"

She sighed, hating this subject with a passion. "I mean, Milford College may not last much longer."

Jack stood, goblet in his hand. "This place? The one built by your ancestors?"

She nodded.

"You can casually talk about its demise and that doesn't hit you? Upside the head?"

She drained her own goblet. For courage, because she could not fathom what he was talking about.

"Okay. I'll explain."

Shadows crossed his face and she didn't like it. "Good. Help me to understand."

"It's a dream. A lovely dream that has been realized for more than 150 years. And now, there isn't enough to sustain it. There needs to be something else, but no one seems to know what to do in terms of reinvention."

"Why aren't they figuring it out?"

She looked him square in the eye. "Because no one wants to face the inevitable. People don't like to face truths that make them uncomfortable. That's one of them. That the college land is worth more than the college itself. That people want Granda to cook for them so everyone can pretend that the fifty thousand dollars or so out of this event will really help."

He sat down, putting his head in his hands. His distress reached out to her, plucking at the very core of her. "Look," he said. "I've been here the longest of any of the places that I've visited, and well, this place is important. It means something. It matters. The students matter, the faculty matters, what's taught here, the history, it all matters."

Raising her goblet, she wanted to quip, "Black Lives Matter," but he wouldn't appreciate the joke. Not when he was this wound up.

She lowered her goblet. "Well, I'm sorry. It's one reason why I've stayed away."

"That's it? What are the other reasons?" His eyes narrowed as they looked at her. "Because I don't think you're telling the whole truth about why you stay away."

"Well, you don't know a thing about me." She stood up. "That's my cue. Because I don't relish being called a liar."

"That makes two of us."

He stood up right next to her, and took the goblet from her hand, which meant that their fingers had a brief moment of commingling. He kept his fingers on her hand, right there.

She tried to pull her fingers away but he wouldn't let her. "Someone has to do something," he insisted.

"Look, Jack. I'm sure you would love to come in and play white savior to an HBCU, but you have no right. It's not your worry or concern. So after the feast is over, you can take yourself right back to wherever you came from. Really. It sounds like an interesting subject for a documentary and I'll throw in a thousand myself to help your funding, even though we can all play as if you are poor and are in real need of money."

"That was not nice."

His guise was 180 degrees away from what it had been. She felt chilled by it. Desperate, even. What had she said?

What had happened to funny Jack? Jokey Jack, silly Jack, the one who smiled. The one who looked like sunshine, the one who bore a more than passing resemblance to an Apollo statue. That one.

Come back.

But no. Now he was all seriousness and storm. All gray and anger and thunder and rain. Not like night, but like Vulcan, the god who stamped out lightning bolts, intense and intending to shock. Not shock and delight, but shock and awe.

Just because of what she'd said, something that was wrong.

"I think I'll get going. Thanks for the invite, anyway."

Tea deliberately walked away from him, and now here it came. The burny feeling in her stomach crawled up, up, up her throat, threatening to explode in her head.

When she got to the end of the walkway on the waterfront, she turned around, thinking he might follow her. But he didn't.

Well, she'd read that all wrong. As usual.

Was she disappointed?

Did she enjoy his interest?

She walked the rest of the way to her grandmother's house, wondering, for the infinite time in her life, how she always managed to screw up anything that might finally make her happy.

The next day, Jack opted to work with a different crew than the prep crew. Fine. She would ignore him, prepping with great solemnity. Granda came to her as she peeled potatoes, like she was a private on KP duty.

"You going to get the pecans today?"

"Yes ma'am." Tea stopped peeling potatoes. Thankful for the rest.

"You don't have to go now."

"Maybe it's best if I did."

Her grandmother peered into her face. "Something going on with the two of you?"

"Granda, there is no two of us."

"He's working over there and you happy over here peeling potatoes? I don't think so. Tell the truth."

"Granda, that doesn't make him my best friend. He's your friend, not mine."

"I thought all of that had been settled."

"Not with me. Surely you know that I'm a better attorney than that."

"I appreciate you looking out for me, but it's all okay," Granda said. "You'll see."

The offer to help came from her lips so easily now. "I know. I'll just go get the pecans for the pie and then help you shell them."

"You want me to save you some lunch?"

Tea smiled at the elderly woman, who thought that food cured all. She patted her arm and kissed her cheek. "That's fine. Thank you, Granda."

She finished peeling the last of the potatoes and

cleaned up her work area. As she left, she turned back in the other direction and saw her grandmother talking to Jack.

A look of dismay crossed Jack's face and those thick eyebrows of his met in an angry fuzzy caterpillar on his forehead. She quickened her pace, leaving the work kitchen behind and walking hurriedly down the hall to reach her car.

Too late.

"Tea. Wait."

She started to run.

His steps quickened behind her.

She ran faster.

So did he.

"Stop!"

She didn't care what he said. *Run.*

Out the door of the building and across the square toward her grandmother's house. She didn't care that she had left her car behind; she could get back to it. All she wanted to do was to get away from him.

But it didn't work.

His hand closed in on her upper arm and she was stopped.

"What?" Well, at least he was out of breath.

"What do you want?"

"Why are you running?"

"I didn't get my jog in, so I was doing it now."

"Stop. You wanted to get away from me."

"So?"

"Where are you going?"

"You aren't my daddy."

"Are you going for the pecans?"

"Pe-cahns," she said, just to be cantankerous. The old argument of the way the word was said had kept people arguing for decades, it seemed.

"Whatever."

"You know I am. My grandmother went over there and told you."

"She wanted to know what was going on between us."

"Did you tell her that you saw fit to reprimand me? As if I were a child?"

"Come on, Tea."

"No. You come on, Jack."

He stepped up, apparently not out of breath anymore. "Look. You must know a lot of other men you can bully around and they'll back down to you. That's not my style."

His words took her aback.

"I'm not a bully. You are."

"Well, you certainly struck me as one the other day."

"Yesterday."

"Yes. I don't care. I'm willing to stand up to you."

"Well, goody for you." She crossed her arms in a petulant way. Which was childish. She uncrossed them.

"I wanted to go with you to get the nuts." He stood back from her, trying to charm her again.

And it worked.

"Well, come on. I don't have all day."

"We have to go back to the parking lot, though."

"I know that."

"Because you were running away from the cars."

"Whatever, Jack."

He smiled at her and apparently all was forgiven about her rudeness.

She didn't like it, but she was glad about it.

He drove, to keep the peace. The drive to the pecan farm took an hour, and during the drive, they kept the talk to niceties. She really hadn't been with him alone for so long, but it surprised her that she could spend time in his company that long without rancor. She learned that Milford had been the sixth stop on his Southern Treasures tour, and that he had intended to make ten stops.

"I've been in Milford longer than any other. It's just such a wonderful place. When I heard you had stayed away for so long, I just wondered how was that possible. It's great."

"Too many reminders. I had to make my own way in the world. I'm happy in New York."

"Are you?"

"Meaning?"

"If you were so happy, why are you so quick to jump down my throat all the time? Why can't you relax and not worry about time so much?"

"I think in billable hours."

"And now that you are partner, you don't have to think that way anymore."

"It's not easy to turn the switch off." She looked out of the window.

"Yeah. That's why I couldn't opt for that life."

Was he judging her? "It's a privilege to opt for that life. The insurance money from the accident covered my boarding school. I didn't have enough for college. I got a scholarship, but then I needed living money. Going to school in New York is expensive."

"So you got a scholarship, but still had to work to live there."

"Yes."

"So that's why you have catering skills?"

She looked sideways at him as he slowed the car down at the pecan groves, filled with lush trees. "Yes. That was one of the things I did while earning my way through school. It was at one of those events that I met Mr. Pichon."

"And the rest is history. His hand-groomed pick."

Where were her Tums? "You make it sound awful."

He pulled into a gravelly driveway, stones crunching beneath his wheels. "Well. Is this really what you want to do? Or did you just happen upon a career that makes you a lot of money so you could stay away?"

There it was.

All of the questions that had danced around in her mind since she was twelve. She had worked so hard and kept so busy for so many years trying to keep the truth at bay.

He put it to her so clearly. Clearly, it was time for that truth to come out of her.

Now, she told him the reason, the true reason she had been Atalanta all of her life. Running. Always running.

"I didn't want to be the lunch lady."

And the words, these ones that had stayed in her head for so long, sounded so small and hard when she said them.

She wished she could take them back.

Chapter 22

T HE PECAN FARM WAS ANOTHER place where her
life had changed, so she had a fond memory of it.
It was a family-run business, and she well recalled
how her family would obtain pecans at the holidays
from the place, run by several generations of Newleys.

Now, Mr. Percy Newley, the grandson of the original
farmers, was in charge, and had cute toddlers of his own
running around. May was not his high season but, as
he told Allie, "Miss Ada is the best of them all. I made
sure my ladies saved the choicest meats for her. We will
put the pecans in your car while you enjoy the farm."

Intrigued by the family operation, Jack did some
interviews with the staff while he was there. He had a
way with people, for sure. Allie even helped, positioning
the camera while he interviewed the ladies who processed
orders and videotaped two young women who were
making pralines with the last of the season's bounty.

The slab of cold white marble, run through with swirls
of green and blue, was the place where the workers scooped
out the hot blobs of sweetness full of pecans to cool, one
inch apart.

"We have to wait for them to cool," Mr. Percy said, laughing at Tea's raised up eyebrows of intense interest.

"I'm aware of that, sir." She straightened up and tried to rearrange her face appropriately.

"Don't tell me we've found your weakness, Tea."

"I don't have weaknesses, Jack."

Jack reached back to the edge of the slab of marble for one of the pralines, except it still wasn't cool enough, and he bounced it between his two large hands, with a squinched up look of pain on his face.

She glanced at him. "Are you okay, Jack?"

Someone brought him a little white box and he dropped the candy in there, done with his game of hot potato. Mr. Percy gave Jack a disapproving glance, but the two young women who had scraped the large bowl free of the last praline mix elbowed each other with knowing smiles.

"Hold out your hands," Tea commanded him.

"Eh, he won't blister," Mr. Percy waved a hand.

Still, tender red dots erupted onto his hands. "Oh, Jack. Why did you do that?"

"You wanted one."

"I knew that's why he did it," one of the young women crowed. "We have ointment if you would care for some, sir, before you take the tractor ride to the pecan trees." Jack stepped forward, gratefully taking some of the offered ointment and a wrap of gauze on each hand.

Why had he done that? That had to have been the dumbest thing he had ever done. What would Miss Ada say? His help was needed for the feast and here he had gone and burned himself. "I usually have asbestos hands."

"Nothing like a sugar burn to prove you wrong. Come on, Andy is waiting with the tractor." Tea held up the little box with the praline in it. One of the young women waved her off. "Oh no. It's for you. Your boyfriend wanted you to have it."

"Such a romantic gesture." The other young woman said, and she lowered her head. She opened her mouth to say that Jack Darwent was certainly *not* her boyfriend, but what did that look like now after what he had been through?

"Just wait for it to cool now."

"I will." Tea followed Jack out to the tractor, which had a trailer attached to it in the back, with two benches that faced one another.

Once they were seated on opposite sides of the truck bed and Tea had put the white box next to her, they drove off, and Andy explained to them, in boring detail, how the pecan trees were in a state of limbo in May.

"Can you?" Jack gestured to his camera.

"Me?" Tea squeaked. "I can't do it."

He held up his bandaged hands. "I can't do it either."

A wave of heat ran through her, making the May day warmer than it was. She held up the camera. "That's the shot I want. Of the grove. Frame it and hold steady."

She wanted to protest some more, but looking at that little white candy box gave her pause. The least she could do was help.

He sat behind her, and she could feel his invasion of her personal space and his breath on her neck. "Steady. It's like a little painting. It's a vision in your mind's eye. Of what matters to you."

His big body behind her was like a boulder or something, and the surety and certainty of someone so close to her had never been realized before. Everything smoothed over and she cleared her throat. "Umm, Andy won't be able to keep this wagon steady if we are both on this side of the tractor bed."

"True." His breath warmed her neck. "I suppose I should go over there."

"Yes. You should."

"Okay. I will."

He surely didn't seem to be in any hurry, though, and he took his time about it. As he withdrew, he took that playful Jack energy with him and the world grew gray all of a sudden.

Tea took in a breath and was surprised to feel herself shudder inside, like she was nervous or something. How could that be? She was never nervous.

"That should be good enough. Thank you, Tea."

She lowered the camera and watched him as he awkwardly fumbled to put it away in the case.

As the tractor drove back to the front of the pecan farm, where their car was, Tea reached out for the praline and broke off a piece, putting it in her mouth, letting the sweet caramel melt over her tongue, leaving behind the fresh crunchy pecans as a bonus to chew on. Was there anything better than a fresh praline?

She sighed with pleasure, recalling a sweet memory. "Granda would arrange for these people to send me a box of these every Christmas. A dozen would come at Christmas and I would eat one each month."

"Each month?" Jack's eyebrows went up.

"Well, to eat them all at once would have been greedy. So the first of every month, I allowed myself that one. She stopped sending them once I graduated from college, so it's been a bit since I've had them."

"Let me try some." Jack gestured to the box.

It was on the tip of her tongue to say that he should help himself, but he held up his bandaged hands.

Of course.

He couldn't break it off.

She would have to feed it to him.

The realization of having to invade his personal space caused her heartbeat to accelerate, but she breathed slowly to help it slow down. It was just to help him, like she had helped with the camera. That was all.

She broke off what she considered a good piece. Sometimes, the praline edges didn't have any pecans in it, so it was more a middle piece, and she reached out to his mouth.

Jack leaned forward, but he wasn't close enough.

She had to get closer.

Andy stopped the tractor and now it was possible for her to move closer. It didn't matter that the tractor pull was balanced anymore. Now she could go over to his side and feed him the bit of praline.

So she went and sat next to him, the heat of his body radiating off him. He opened his mouth and she found herself praying.

Please, let me concentrate.

What was wrong with her that this man had this kind of magnetic pull on her?

She lifted the bit of praline to his mouth and, God help her, Jack's juicy lips reached out and took the praline from her, his lips touching the tips of her fingers. He took his good old time about drawing back from her, chewing on the praline carefully and thoughtfully.

She pulled her hand back as if she had been the burn victim this time. "Well?" She kept her voice low and curt.

"Pretty good. They have good ones in Texas too."

"Texas?" Andy scoffed as he came around and opened the gate for them to descend. He held up a hand to let Tea down, but Jack jumped down from the tractor bed. "Who wants any of those pralines?"

"Louisiana, too," Jack pointed out.

Mr. Percy shook his head. "I had a box to give you

but now I don't know if I should."

Tea broke in, "Oh, don't pay him any mind. I'll take it. Please, let me pay you."

"No way. These are broken pieces left over. It's a gift from us to your grandma for her good business. I hope the feast goes well. Send her our love."

"Thank you, sir." Tea took the nice hefty box of praline pieces and held them to her.

"But don't let him have any!" Mr. Percy laughed, waving them away.

Tea and Jack walked to the car and looked at each other. His hands.

"I guess I have to drive." Her heart started that erratic pounding again. When would she stop feeling this way, or stop overthinking all of this?

"Well ma'am, I'm supposing you must." Jack held up his hands once more.

"I do fairly well," she said with more confidence than she felt. "I had to get here from Atlanta." Driving gave her something else to focus on instead of his physical presence, which also overwhelmed and confused her. The car had the Sirius XM option and they hopped around several channels, arguing about their musical preferences, which for Tea, was more along the lines of early 2000s pop, while Jack enjoyed '90s R&B and hip hop.

"I'm feeling along the lines of Kanye, where, I'ma let you finish, Taylor Swift," he joked.

"Finish what?"

"Driving us back to Milford."

They laughed a minute and then the atmosphere in the car grew serious. "I enjoyed this trip, Tea."

"Well, it's good to get out of Milford every so often. Don't ask me how I know." Light. She had to keep the mood light. She would not let him get all serious on her. No more.

But he insisted. "Listen. I think we had a good time today and so, let's continue it."

Keep your eyes on the road.

"What do you mean?"

"I want to talk to you about my project. I mean, we are getting along so well here, I want you to come back to the boat so I can let you know what I'm trying to do. Please."

"You don't think we should get back to Granda?"

"Hey. She'll make a plate at work and go home to nap. I'll send a text and someone will get her home. You and I, well, it's only four o'clock. I'll talk to you about *Southern Treasures*, show you what I'm trying to do, and if it runs into dinner, I'll make something or we can order Mason's."

"I don't really think…"

"Come on. Or are you afraid you'll really like my project?"

"Well, I'm not afraid of that. But I can't go on the boat."

Now she was the one smiling, as did he, when she took the exit to the road that led to Milford.

"Ahh. You're afraid of my rule? Well, you did what you were supposed to do, so it's okay to let you come aboard the good ship *Gimme Some Sugar*."

"Excuse me?"

"You gave me some sugar. The praline. So you're good."

She let out a breath. "I see. Yes, you're right, even though you're a true scoundrel. Okay. I'll come aboard and see what this is all about. Yes."

"Great. Park back at the school and we'll get everything all lined up for your visit."

Hey, the only men she had been alone with in years

were her partners at the law firm.
It's high time THAT changed.
She could not disagree.

Chapter 23

WHEN THEY RETURNED TO CAMPUS, they came upon Miss Ada preparing to leave. The old lady carried a white plastic bag with a folded clamshell inside—tonight's dinner, all secure and ready to reheat when she wanted it, after a long day of preparation.

Trent walked along behind her, getting ready to take her home in his car, no doubt. Jack caught himself saying a small prayer of gratitude that the old lady was so beloved and that so many people looked out for her.

"Hey there!" Miss Ada waved. He waved back as he got out of the car, and then he caught her look of horror.

Oh no.

Miss Ada walked over to him. "What happened to you?"

He had forgotten that his hands were bandaged up. He had no pain. Was it because he was having so much fun with Tea? "I burned my hands on a bit of praline. No big deal. They'll be all healed up tomorrow."

"They'd better." She frowned and saw her granddaughter emerging from the driver's side of the car. "Tea, if Jack's hands aren't better, then I got some of my homemade ointment at the house for his burns."

"Yes, Granda."

Miss Ada reached out to them. "Okay. Put those nuts inside. I'ma going back home now. I'm tired and I need to rest up for the morning."

Tea went to her and kissed her on the cheek, embracing her grandmother with her whole self, Jack could tell. Seeing them exchange affection with one another made him want to shed these goofy bandages off his hands. His hands were feeling better, but that familial love, something he himself hadn't had in a very long time, formed a testimony in his mind. If he couldn't have it, he was glad that Tea did. Jack kissed Miss Ada in his turn.

"Save me some of Mr. Percy's praline ends. Don't eat them all, Althea." Miss Ada pressed her granddaughter's hands with affection.

"I won't, Granda."

They watched Travis and Miss Ada depart, then they took the nuts inside and secured them before they headed down to the waterfront to *Gimme Some Sugar*.

The dock swayed a bit and Jack practically jumped on board, and he held out a hand to Allie to help steady her as she walked on the swinging planks. "Your hand," she protested.

"It'll be okay. Come on."

And it was. She walked up the gangway to the boat and leaped on, surrounded at once by a gleaming deck of white oak decorated in navy and white. "This is beautiful."

"Thank you."

"You must be quite a trust fund baby to be able to afford all of this."

"I have enough."

"I've been on the boats of the partners up in Long

Island. This is way better."

The boat was laid out with an upper bedroom and a gathering space. Below decks was a smaller bedroom and even smaller television room. Jack pointed out, "I like to come and splice here."

"Splice your film?"

"Yes."

It was a very small room, though there was a computer, a TV and a small couch where he sat as he worked.

"I'll get started here. You'll get to meet the previous ladies I've spoken to."

"I should have known they were all ladies." Her tone was light and jovial. He could see that she smiled as if she were amused.

"Well, Tea, I'll tell you. In all of my Southern childhood, I became convinced that the only true magic in the world is in the keeping of older women. Even as a small child in Nashville, I've known that. That's why I've finally come to realize that they are the true Southern Treasures, hence the name of my film and cookbook project."

He cued up the footage of the first three interviewees that he had spoken to: Mrs. May Jones, Mrs. Aileen Rutherford and Miss Alma Jean Horston. As the tape played, he was surprised to hear her making suggestions to him to help the pacing between the ladies make more sense.

Before he knew it, three hours had passed by.

When was the last time that had happened?

He ran a hand through his hair. For the first time in a while, he felt a slight sting on his hands. "That was so helpful. You have no idea."

She sipped at a glass of lemonade he had brought her. "They were just things that made sense to me. And maybe, as you continue this project, they may shift around and change. So be open to that."

He nodded his head. "Of course. Hungry?"

"Sure."

"We can have barbeque delivered. I do it all the time. Practically a standing order. What would you have?" He readied his phone. "I order by text."

"A burnt ends salad with extra shredded Pepper Jack cheese and an extra container of the house vinaigrette."

"Sounds excellent. Think I'll have the same."

"What is your standing order?"

"A sliced brisket sandwich with baked beans and cole-slaw, but I can cool it for tonight. Something stronger than lemonade?"

"No. This is fine."

He brought her a fresh glass of lemonade as they emerged to the upper deck of the houseboat, where they could see the sun setting, preparing for twilight, as people went by in boats, playing on the water with the occasional water skier splashing by.

"It's something to see this waterway be used like this. It wasn't something that I ever grew up with."

"Do you think it's a good thing?"

"Yes. Maybe it is. It gives Milford some different options. Maybe some things that aren't the college."

"That still saddens me. That there is so much trouble."

"Well, the feast can change that direction. I hope it will." She sipped the lemonade, letting it swirl in the most elegant way, a way that probably left the taste of sweetened lemon on her lips. That was Tea. Tart and sweet at the same time.

Stop staring at her lips.

He spoke up. "Me too. I want to thank you for helping me today."

"Oh. That. Well, it was fine. My question is," she spread her hands, and he loved the way her heart was in front of him, "What about these Southern Treasures? I love your idea that we are often too busy these days to take in the knowledge of these women. They have a lot to tell us. But how do they become part of things? Did you have the other ladies sign releases? What are they entitled to? Cookbook royalties? A share of the box office or licensing fees when you release the film?"

He ran his hand through his hair. "I thought that capturing their words and ideas for posterity was enough."

She shook her head. "It's not. It's their property, their ideas, their ways of being that have been sifted through your sensibility. They must be compensated for it."

"I'm already struggling to make the picture."

"Do you have investors?"

"Not really."

"You were going to slide in on your trust funds?"

"Yes. Whatever it takes. But I'm out this year, since I've already run through my money."

"Well, you need investors. You need to think of a way to offer shares in this project so you can raise money. Let me see a piece of paper."

He brought her a notebook and she bent her head to her task, writing things, biting her lip in the most adorable way and sipping at her lemonade, until it was empty.

"Here comes our food."

He jogged down the plank and Tea looked up to see the approaching delivery person bringing their food.

Jack heard her sharp intake of breath as the young woman with long braids approached the boat. Thanking her, he took the bag and hopped back on the boat.

"Hey Althea. Hey girl!" the young woman called out.

Jack came to her with their food in clamshells.

"Do you know that young woman?"

"Yes. It's Deah, Monique's younger sister. She's just about the biggest gossip in Milford."

"Well, wave to her. She's seen you here."

Tea did as he bid her too, but her limp wave was not from her heart.

"What's the big deal?" He handed her the salad and bag of utensils and dressing.

"It's not a big deal. It's just, people are very strange."

"Will she tell?"

"Oh, without a doubt." It would have been funny to calculate just how far and how fast this rumor would travel around Milford—if only she had not been at the center of it.

Jack sat down in a wicker chair across from her and picked up his own clamshell, poured the extra dressing on top and went to town. It was an amazing salad.

"Well," he mused as he chewed the last of the great combo of burnt ends, lettuce and cheese. He could have gone for some fries, but he had some here that he could throw in the air fryer if he were that desperate. "Does it really matter?"

He almost wanted to say a prayer to his food. It was the perfect distraction.

She finished her salad, closing the clamshell and looked for a place to dispose of it. "I'm not sure what you mean."

"I mean, does it matter what Monique's sister says? About us?" He took their containers below to his small galley, giving her time to think about what he'd said, to be by herself, and hopefully not wound his feelings with any sharp, lawyerly words. He hadn't ordered any dessert, but he had a slice of cheesecake left over. He quickly prepared a peach topping, flambéed it, plated it and took it upstairs. Just the one piece. To see what she would say.

"Why did you leave for so long?" The sun was setting and he turned on the white lights that surrounded the boat, so that he could see her slim silhouette in the darkness.

"I wanted to make some dessert."

"Oh, we have the praline ends."

"Miss Ada said not to eat all of those. So I whipped up this fruity cheesecake."

"That does look good."

He sat down on the settee next to her. "I brought two forks."

"It's amazing what you can do with your hands." She smiled at him, and watching that sun cross her face and light it up was much better than any Christmas lights.

"They feel better now. Much better."

"I'm glad. Granda would have really had my hide if they were seriously burned with just a few days left to the feast."

She picked up a fork and gathered the perfect bite of cheesecake and rummy peach sauce on her fork. "Ummm. So good."

He took a less particular bite. "I agree."

Together, they demolished the poor cheesecake in the quiet of the setting sun. He took the plate and went downstairs to dump it in the galley sink. He would wash it later. Every minute away from her now grabbed him by the lapels and blew a hot wind of realization in his face. Tea, increasingly, was becoming important to him, and he didn't want to miss anything with her.

He went back to the top deck and held his hand out. "We'll have a long day tomorrow. Come on. Let's really give Milford something to talk about. I'll walk you home."

Her eyebrows went up and she bit her lip. "Excuse me?"

"I'll walk you home. Let's go, right up the square where everyone can see us. So that Monique's sister, what's her name?"

"Deah. Short for Lydia."

"Yeah. Her. Let's make her little bit of gossip obsolete. Let's admit that we had a good time today in each other's company. Even if I did get burned."

"It's okay if I hold your hand?"

"It's more than okay. Sweet Tea. It's just the balm I need. Let's go."

He stepped off the gangway and held his arms out to her. He put them around her waist, carrying her over the water in one smooth movement onto the solid ground, and just like that, they walked, hands linked, up the waterfront, through the square and on to Miss Ada's house, laughing about what Milford said behind them, the entire way.

Chapter 24

INSTEAD OF GOING INTO THE campus kitchen with Granda in the morning, Tea asked if she could come in midday instead. Her Granda was a little taken by surprise, but she patted her hand and squeezed it, saying, "Whatever you need, baby girl. I've got you."

It wasn't that she didn't want to face Jack.

It wasn't that she was scared to face him.

Okay. Maybe she was scared to face him. What was even happening?

Was it a good thing or a bad thing?

It was that she needed time, just a morning, to sort it all out.

So, when she knew that he was at work with her grandmother, she took her jog, came back to the house, showered, and then went to the Milford College library. She dressed in her jeans and black tennis shoes and a tee shirt, carrying her chef's coat so that she could go to the kitchen right after that.

The library of the college had become a hub for the town since the Milford county branch had closed. It brought sadness to her heart, since she had spent many a time in her young years at that branch library, but now, it was a post office. So the youth of Milford came and hung out at the college library instead. This was encouraged by the head librarian, Monique, who ran a tight ship, but who was beloved by all of the young people in town, as well as her library students, for her great flexibility and fun activities.

When she stepped in the door, Monique took her by the elbow and shepherded her back to her office, where books were piled into towers so high, it looked as if her friend were hosting a competition for how many books could be stacked before they toppled over.

"Tell me everything. Every single thing. Do. Not. Leave. Out. A. Detail. Or…" Monique spoke in a hoarse library whisper.

"Or what?"

"Wait." Monique held up her hand and her voice went up. "What are you doing here?"

"I'm talking to you, Monique."

"Umm. That's not what I meant. You should be helping with the feast."

"Well, thank you much. They are frying chicken and they don't believe I can be of any help this morning."

"Well, true. Although every self-respecting Black woman should know how to fry chicken, it doesn't mean we do. So. What's going on with you and Jack?"

"I'm sure I don't know what you mean."

"Girl, you know Deah has given me the report. Tell me what went down."

"We had Mason's for dinner together, as you now know."

Monique clapped her hands. "If I had known he was calling for two salads, but that louse sister of mine took the order and didn't say anything at the time. Heffa.

Wait until I get my hands on her."

"I don't mean to be the cause of sibling rivalry, Monique. That's all that happened."

"Look. You've got to give me something." Monique looked like Pauline on the square, with her finger up.

She paused and folded her hands. "Can't I just be another patron? I did come here for a reason. To do research."

"Ugh. Okay. Whatever." Monique sat back, off her hunt for new gossip.

"We had a nice time at the pecan farm and then had dinner," Tea informed her.

Monique leaned forward, back on again.

"What? I didn't know there was a decision to extend the conversation."

"Well, there was. He asked me to take a look at some of his film and I said yes. It only made sense. I need to get a complete picture of his project before any kind of settlement can occur. I need to know how much time he is spending and how much time these ladies are putting into the project."

Her friend waggled her finger.

"What?"

"He likes you. You know he does. I've seen him looking at you when you aren't watching. He's enamored of you."

Her heart beat a little faster. She squeezed her palms together. "So what?"

"Well. How do you feel about it?"

"I feel...well, he's leaving soon. So he can look all he likes, but as of Monday, he'll be gone and that's it. Bye bye."

"Say what? That's new."

"His project involves going around to all of these old

ladies and getting their recipes. He's not a scammer. He's genuinely trying to capture these recipes and stories. He's a trust fund baby and someone who has to figure out a way to make a mark in the world, and this is what he has chosen." She spread her hands in explanation and Monique stood up, took off her espadrilles and threw them across the room, toppling a tower or two.

Tea shrieked at the toppling books, jumping to the side. "What are you doing?"

"You'll be leaving then too."

"I'm right here."

"No. I mean you like him too."

"Monique. I do not."

"Althea. Yes you do."

"Why do you say that? I'm here to look up something in the law books, if you will lead me to them. Why have I been corralled here in your office imprisoned by all of these books when I have work to do?"

"Because," Monique leaned forward. "You aren't being honest with yourself and you know it. You'll be condemned to stay here all of your days until you are."

She sat back and the friends stared at each other. Monique blinked first. "Actually, I have a summer reading program kicking off in 15 minutes, so I don't have time to see this through. But," her friend shook her dirty, funky espadrille at her.

"But what?"

"After you are finished, you'll come back in here and tell me about the time on the boat."

"I will not. I didn't say I was taking the morning off. I'm still going there to help."

"Well, they will not let you fry chicken if they know what's good for them."

She rolled her eyes as Monique put her shoes back on.

Both shoes on, Monique stood. "Tell me this. What is wrong with saying that you like him? He's classy. He's funny. He's fine as frog's hair."

"Do frogs have hair?"

"No, but I'm just saying. What's not to like? You aren't getting any younger, and…"

"I didn't come down here to find a man. I came to help my grandmother to ensure that she's protected. Now that I have, I can go back to New York and be at peace."

"Tell me something." Monique's hands were on her hips, ready to face a crowd of elementary school kids. "Did you turn on your computer this morning?"

Tea's brow furrowed. "No."

"Ha!"

"Ha what?"

"Since when have you not turned on the computer first thing in the morning? To check on your case?"

"I haven't gotten any texts from Connie that the baby has come. She keeps me well informed of whatever I need to know. I don't need to open my computer. Besides, I'm going to meet up with Sherry because she's bringing down her trademark tea recipe later."

They turned and walked from the office, as Monique guided her back into the stacks, deep and dark with time. "Okay, okay. That explains that. But still, you look… lighter somehow. Give me an explanation for that."

"I just finished jogging."

"Okay. Well, that will have to do. You know the ropes around here. Enjoy, and if you want to come up and help with these first graders…"

"Ummm, no. Thank you."

Monique sighed and turned and left her in the quiet, earthy-smelling stacks. The law books were enveloped in a rich dark brown leather and embossed with gold. The collection had started with the Milford family library's books and had been added onto ever since.

She quickly found the law that she was looking for regarding her grandmother's intellectual property, those recipes and stories. It was good to have her thoughts confirmed about the proprietary nature of recipes. It was a train of thought that had only come into being since the early 2000s, but now, with the increase of women in the legal world and the presentation of certain rulings, her grandmother and all of the other ladies were certainly entitled to a percentage of royalties of the cookbook project.

The film was another matter. Still, she was sure that Jack could be persuaded to share some of the proceeds with the ladies, or their churches, libraries or community centers.

He wouldn't mind.

Why do I know he wouldn't mind?

Because. Now that she knew him, she knew he wasn't a scammer. He was just a trust fund dude, trying to make a documentary. She could convince him that spreading the proceeds of the movie could actually help him get the movie made. He would have less struggle if he shared.

She sat down on a small library stool, the kind of thing on wheels that shorter people used to reach tall shelves. Could Monique be correct?

Well. Yes.

She did like him. More than she'd thought she would. He was here to help her Granda and not hurt her.

So okay. She liked him. She liked spending time with him. Yesterday was fun. Now what?

He's going to leave on Monday. There's no need to get wrapped up in anything.

I won't. It will all be fine.

The more she sat there, the thing loomed larger in her mind. What would she say to him? How would he look at her? What were they doing?

It's okay to have a friend. You have friends. Monique, Connie, your brunch crowd back in NY. The ladies you go to the gym with.

But none of them caused her heart to race like Jack did.

None of them made her forget things like Jack did.

None of them caused her to forget opening her computer like Jack did. She was so eager to get the day started, she had organized herself around finding out about Jack, working with Jack and getting ready for the feast with Jack.

She slumped, her face in her hands. What was wrong with her?

It was good that he was leaving next week. She should do the same. Summer was a slow time for the practice, but unless Granda wanted her to stay longer, there was no need to be here any longer after the feast. Maybe she could talk Granda into coming to New York for a vacation. Now that she had money, serious money, they could fly somewhere and sit on a beach and just be together. For the first time ever.

Something about the thought of being a friend, a real friend with her grandmother made tears come to her eyes. Granda was 82. It was time to do that kind of thing. Maybe they could rent a little villa in Italy. She would text Connie to have her look into it.

She lifted her head and looked at the random book in front of her. It was one of the volumes of law books about Milford, the town. Old ones. She could tell because the books were larger and edged in a funny and uneven way. She wiped the tears away from her face and tried to get the moisture from her hands. She knew from years of dealing with old law texts that she should have gloves on, but Monique hadn't given her any. She thought about getting up and getting some, but her friend was probably knee deep in elementary school kids.

She pulled out the big book carefully and opened it on her knees, letting her eyes adjust to reading cursive instead of small close print. This volume dated back to 1868, and immediately she had respect for whatever it held.

V. Smithson vs. Milford, Constance and Milford, Lucy

V might mean Virgil, her three-times great-grandfather. The one with the scary countenance who looked down at her so sternly all of the time.

She read on.

The case was all about how V. Smithson had a certain amount of land but these women, these Milford women, were claiming that Papa Virgil didn't have any rights to the land because he was a Negro.

"A well-established, respected Negro, but one of that populace who had no right to hold land that should have come to them rightly through the mother of the Milfords' husbands." That would be Evangeline Milford, the woman who had encouraged and helped Virgil to build the town and the college.

Her daughers-in-law weren't claiming the land, but desired to hold it in trust for their children.

But the case was won on the merits because Papa Virgil was a Negro. Even if their mother-in-law had bequeathed it to him.

Fascinating. She had heard many a story of how respected he was, but not that he had ever been denied anything before. She would ask Granda about it.

Chapter 25

WHEN SHE ARRIVED AT THE kitchen, there was a clear frenzy of activity there, but things were winding down. The five or six student assistants were consumed with putting away the fried chicken pieces as they cooled. Frying two hundred pieces of chicken, cooling it and storing it so that it could be reheated to stay crispy was a major task.

She sat down at a table nearby so that she wasn't in the way, and watched her little grandmother delegate. There had been big vats of her specially flavored flour recipe for dredging, so special that she would only use one brand of flour. It always made her chuckle to think about her grandmother carrying a bag of flour up to New York City for her when she'd visited years ago, because she didn't know if they sold any of "her brand" up there in the North.

She was right. They didn't.

Her Granda waved at her, but kept directing a young man to use the tongs in a certain way to put the chicken away for deep freezing.

While she watched, a shadow crossed her and leaned

over on her.

She looked up out from under her eyelashes.

Jack.

Her heart quickened a bit.

"I've been looking for you all morning."

"I'm here now."

"And you want a sample, no doubt."

"No doubt."

Jack folded his arms, but his blue eyes sparkled. "Well, like the little red hen once said, those who don't work don't eat."

"Well, okay. I'll just take myself off and head to Atlanta today." She stood up and they were definitely too much in each other's personal space.

She liked it.

"What's in Atlanta?"

"I'm going to the airport to pick up Sherry. Who has the tea, literally. She's coming here to make her secret recipe of sweet tea tonight."

"Ahhh. Would you like some company?"

"Are you offering?"

"I am. But I need to shower first. I feel as if I've been swimming through an oil slick."

She laughed. "You have, and of course. If Granda permits."

"Well, we'll see."

And sure enough, just as he said that and turned out to face the room, her little grandmother came up in her pigeon-toed way. "I was just thinking about you, love. You get done at the library?"

"I did." She leaned over to give Granda's soft cheek a kiss.

"Good. We'll be doing the setup outside this afternoon. Thank goodness the weather is predicted to be nice. You taking care of the tea after lunch?"

"Yes. I came for lunch. I'm starving! Then I'll get in the car and go to Atlanta to meet with Sherry."

"Fine. I'm looking forward to meeting her."

Jack wrapped his large hand around Allie's waist and pulled her to his side. "Will you need me this afternoon, Miss Ada? I thought I might accompany your granddaughter here."

"Oh no, Jack. You go on ahead. You might want to film after things are set up, anyway."

"I appreciate that. We'll be back later on."

Her grandmother waved her little hand and gestured to the students, who came over with their sampling plates, and another who had a platter piled high with plump, crispy, delicious chicken.

Heavenly.

Not even Jack's presence could keep her from enjoying this food.

"I remember when I was at boarding school," she started in after they had selected the choicest pieces of chicken, along with mashed potatoes, sautéed broccoli and red peppers, and slices of cool cantaloupe. "They had fried chicken sometimes because students like it. The boarding school lunch lady kind of put me in mind of Granda, so I knew it would be good, but not *as* good. But every week, I wouldn't take my share. Or I would wrap it up in a napkin and take it back to my room to eat in my closet when my roommate had class and I could get a free moment."

"What on earth would you do that for?" Granda broke apart her wing, crunching on the dead man's finger portion for more crispies.

Tea crunched on, her stomach happy to be full of good food, and not cramped and full of pain. "I didn't want them to see me. I mean, I would start to eat it with a knife and fork, but then someone called attention to that. So I started saving it so that I could eat it with my hands as I wanted."

Jack wrangled a breast portion, and as the juice dripped down his chin, he caught it with a napkin. Only Granda could make fried chicken so juicy, even the breast, that it dripped down the chin.

"It was the one time, one day in the week when I got to reflect about leaving Milford and what that all meant. It was only later that I realized that I didn't want anyone at school to see me eating fried chicken with my hands. When I was in college I stopped eating it. Whenever I got it in New York, I would always have takeout. But never in a public restaurant."

Jack finished chewing and stared at her. "Why not?"

She lowered her head. "I had a thing in my mind that I might look like some old-time racist cartoon if I ate it with my hands in public. Eating it with a knife and fork made me appear strange, but at least I still looked as if I had table manners."

"Oh, Tea. I had no idea you were dealing with such foolishness. This is the food of our people."

"I know."

Granda put down the now-denuded dead man's finger. "Chicken used to be very expensive to obtain, but once people learned how to raise it, it got cheaper. The college had a department that used to raise chickens for feed and such."

Tea looked at her grandmother, eyebrows raised. "They did?"

"Yes. My mama, Junety. That was how she worked through the school. She got to be well-known for her chicken raising skills. Her skills with chicken are part of what got you here."

She nodded. "I see that now. I saw another interesting document in the library about the land, Granda. I have to ask you a question about that."

"I look forward to hearing that, child."

"But right now?" Jack pointed to her with a drumstick. "What?"

"Eat your chicken. With your hands. Like regular people do."

She picked up her extended chicken leg, as they called it in Milford, and gladly crunched into it, savoring the salty-sweet taste, not caring who saw her.

When lunch was over, Jack went to get a shower on his houseboat, while she sat with her grandmother drinking an afternoon coffee pick-me-up some students brought back from Calvin's coffee shop for them. They hadn't found Tea's order too hard at all, because Calvin remembered it and cued it up for her. Small town life had benefits for sure.

Granda's order was just black coffee. "Black as me," is what she said to Calvin. When she made a face, her grandmother told her, "You are a spoiled one, girlie. I remember when we had to drink Postum and Sanka 'cause we had no money. So when I have it, I want to taste the real coffee and nothing else!" She paused.

"What was that you told me about you saw in the library today?"

"Yes. I was looking up legal precedent for this case, to make sure Jack cuts you and the other ladies a fair deal. Don't look a certain way. That's what I'm here to do."

Granda put her cup down. "I'm just happy someone wants these recipes. I've got everything I need. Any money I get will go to you. So I don't know why you pressing so hard."

With no thought of putting her concoction to the side, Tea told her, "Those other ladies need their share too, Granda. You should be paid for your hard work. That's all I'm trying to do. Anyway, I saw a weird book, a ledger of some kind from back when Milford College first started. It was a court case about the land the college is on. That Papa Virgil lost."

Granda closed her eyes. "Yeah. Umm, let me see. There was some tussling over the land. You know, this was the Milford plantation first."

Tea nodded. She wasn't a graduate of the college, but because her parents had met at the school, she knew some of the history basics. One of the main requirements of the students was that they had to pass a test on the history of the school before they left.

Granda leaned back. "Mr. and Mrs. Milford had two sons. They both went to fight in the Confederacy and both of them were killed. Shot down dead like dogs in the battlefield. Mr. Milford had died some years before the war, so that left Mrs. Milford alone during the war years. Before they had gone to war, both of them boys had married. So when they died, and it was some years after the war, their widows came back to Milford. Mrs. Milford had passed the land to Papa Virgil, wanting him and Mama Manda to start a school here. But those widow women came and started the lawsuit. Took the land away."

"Sounds like Papa Virgil needed a good lawyer." Tea's voice was low. She was a good lawyer, born too late to help her stern ancestor.

"Yes. All he had was what he could afford." Granda warmed to her tale. "Every bit of what he and Mama Manda did went into the school. All of their heart and soul and money. And given when it was, they couldn't get the kind of good lawyer they needed. It was all against them, even the judge. So they lost the case and the land."

Back in her past, she would have shut her ears to a sad tale like this. She didn't like hearing about how her people had suffered. She might have just gone and waited for Jack downstairs. Now, she had a different feeling about it. It was like hearing about her family for the first time, and now, the story would stick. So that she could tell any children she might have this story. Papa Virgil hadn't sat down and given up. He fought. So did Mama Manda. And they still managed to get the school. That was important. Something to be proud of. Something to pass on.

She sat up a little straighter. This visit to Milford had brought so many things to sharp focus in her world. Or maybe it was that she had achieved her goals in life, and now she was free to have new goals.

Like a family?

Maybe with Jack?

Was that possible? Next week, he would be gone from her life forever. So there didn't seem to be any point in thinking about that.

"How did they get the land, then?"

"Well, one of them girls wasn't totally trash. She was kinda sorry about the lawsuit and she stayed in Milford, and taught in the school. Fell in love with another one of the schoolteachers and married him and raised another family."

Tea put a hand to her heart. "Thank goodness."

"Yes. 'Cause in time, the good sister-in-law bought out

the other one, who just wanted the money to begin with, and she left the school to Mama Manda's care. Bless her."

"What was her name?"

Granda frowned. "I don't know. Seems funny that's not part of what we teach."

"Some things get left out."

"That's a shame too. 'Cause there are good people in the world, Tea. Like Jack." Her grandmother winked at her. "God made them duck by duck. You can take him as his own person. His own individual. He's helped me a lot down here and I'm glad to help him with his film."

She looked up and saw Jack approaching her, obviously freshly washed with a navy polo on and chino slacks and docksiders. His hair, slightly damp, curled a little more than usual to his head and her heart beat to see him.

Control yourself, Tea.

"True, Granda, but that doesn't mean that he doesn't owe you a share of his success. Right, Jack Darwent?"

"Absolutely." Jack bent down and kissed her grandmother on the cheek and Granda fairly giggled.

"You ready?"

"Yes. We'll see you later when we bring Sherry back."

"Good. Take care, you all."

Jack held out his hand.

Standing, Tea took it, and they headed out, hand in hand, into the hot May sunshine for the two-hour drive to Atlanta.

Chapter 26

THE LONG DRIVE PROVED THAT Tea, the name that she now preferred and that Jack started to call her, was an excellent road partner. Sure, you can put up with people for one hour, but two is a whole other matter. They agreed on their music selections so there wasn't too much shuffling around on Sirius XM. They agreed when to take a stop on the road up to the Atlanta airport where Sherry was meeting them. He told her his plans for more interviews, stretching as far as Texas and even into Chicago.

"Chicago is not the South," she pointed out.

"Ahh. The southside of Chicago might as well be Mississippi. When Black people from that state left the South, they settled there en masse."

She tapped her chin. "I remember learning something about that in college. The Great Migration."

"Exactly."

"My family didn't do that."

"No. You were the one who migrated."

They smiled at each other, and he was breathless at the wonder of her smile.

"Will we need to take Sherry shopping?"

"No. She arranged for supplies to be shipped to the school, so we're just taking her. She's excited to meet Granda."

"As she should be. Miss Ada is a living legend."

"I'm beginning to see that now. After a lifetime of missing out."

He wanted to kick himself for making her sad; it was the last thing he wanted to do. She looked out of the window at the swiftly passing highway.

"It's not too late. There's still time."

"I thank God for that."

"You do?"

She looked at him. "Yes. I do. I mean, it's been years and years since I've been to Milford AME. I didn't attend church in New York. I'm not comfortable with strangers in such a situation."

"What do you mean?"

"Ever since my parents' funeral." He waited for her to continue. After a moment, she did.

"Church is such a vulnerable place. People are yearning, too open, too wounded, too scared there. It's why I've had a problem with it ever since my parents' funeral. I couldn't stand being that open."

"I see what you mean. I agree, but I've looked at it in a different way. Like it's a safe place for all of that. You're with others who understand your pain and you're all there for the same reason. To have God, and the knowledge that there will be a better day ahead to heal you."

He drove with one hand, the one that hurt less, and reached over and touched her hand with the other, covering it. Her hand was like a healing balm to his, and they sat like that in the car, quiet until they picked up Sherry at the Hartsfield-Jackson airport.

He liked Sherry, a pleasant-faced, middle-aged woman, who was older than they were, but starry-eyed at the thought of her behind-the-scenes look at the preparations for the Milford May feast. She wasn't old enough to be a Southern Treasure, but he never minded talking Southern dishes with someone who clearly knew what she was about, and the drive back to campus passed smoothly.

He parked the car as Tea took Sherry inside to meet her grandmother. The square was abuzz with activity: a DJ setting up equipment, students unfolding tables and covering them in tablecloths. The Milford area itself expanded to accommodate the fifty visitors who came to the feast to sample the good wares of the legend that was Miss Ada.

He had thoughts of photographing all of the setup, but he could get shots in the morning. Every moment he was away from Tea seemed long and boring. Besides, he wanted to see Sherry do her thing.

When he went into the kitchen, the three women seemed a cozy trio, united in watching Sherry execute her secret recipe for sweet tea.

"What's in the boxes?" Jack pointed to a stack of tall boxes near them.

"Filtered water from a Carolina spring."

"We have water here."

Miss Ada shook her head. "It's not that water. She had to make sure that the recipe would turn out. Isn't that right, Sherry?"

"Yes ma'am. There's a certain pH that reacts with the tea…"

"It sounds like a science project," Tea said in awe.

"It kinda is. I went to school for chemistry, when my mother taught me the recipe, to see why it was so special."

"You did? What's your alma mater?"

Sherry's voice rose with pride. "North Carolina A&T on scholarship."

"Another HBCU."

"Yes."

Out of the corner of Jack's eye, Tea turned away. What was going on with her? He moved closer to her and draped an arm around her waist, inviting her back into the circle.

I'm here.

And she turned back around giving him a smile, but the wrinkle of her forehead showed she was still troubled.

"This mixture is going to be the base, and as I make my sugar syrup, I'll put in my secret ingredient."

"A simple syrup is two parts sugar and one part water. Boiled down a bit for the sweetener," he rattled off.

Tea nudged him. "Show-off."

"That's right, Jack. And here are my tea bags." Sherry dangled some tea bags.

"Just regular orange pekoe black tea," Tea observed.

"Yes. This ingredient is not so special."

Sherry went into one of the boxes and dug around in it, lifting out a red plastic bag. She walked over to the stove where the syrup was boiling.

Jack's eyes lit up. "The secret ingredient."

Sherry laughed. "It is. It goes in at this early boiling stage."

She opened the bag and poured it in. A waft of dust rose and went to his nose. Mint, some kind of peppermint. He shouldn't be surprised. Mint had great healing powers, but it was so strong that he was surprised to think it was the kind of secret that could trigger a lawsuit.

"You know what it is, Jack?"

"Mint of some kind?" He peered over into the big pot

where the sugar syrup was cooking. There was a white mound there that dissolved as Sherry stirred.

"Very minty," Miss Ada said.

Tea still had a tortured look on her face. "I need to go to the ladies' room," she whispered to Jack.

"Of course." Was she okay? He was tempted to follow her, but she'd said she was going to the ladies' room, so he prayed she was.

Miss Ada went to the pot and peered down in it. "Girl, that's peppermint. Candy cane?"

"Ahh, you guessed it, Miss Ada. That's what it is."

"It was ground up so fine it looks white, but I see a bit of red here and there."

"It provides a certain kind of background note that's not as overwhelming as mint usually is, but it's still there. My grandmother would buy as many discounted candy canes in the after-Christmas sales as she could to last through the year. Now, I just contract with Bob's candy canes here in Georgia. They send us the broken pieces off of the line, much cheaper and quicker."

"That's so clever. I wish I could put it in my documentary." Jack pointed out.

"Can't you have any deceased Southern Treasures?" Miss Ada demanded.

"Oh, my grandma isn't deceased, ma'am. She's in the home. She's 95 years old."

"Praise God," Miss Ada declared.

"Her mind is still sharp, though. I know she wouldn't mind talking to you, Jack."

"That might work out." Jack usually felt a certain energy rise in him when he tracked down another lead for his film. Now, he just wondered about Tea. Was she okay? "Excuse me, ladies."

He went out into the hallway from the kitchen and

saw her sitting on a bench. "Is something wrong?"

Tea bit her lip. "I just needed some air."

He sat down next to her on the leather-covered bench and put his arm around her. She seemed to like it, fortunately.

"I like Sherry." Tea put her face in her hands and began to sob.

Her sobbing was not natural. Jack was used to her strength, and not knowing what to do, he sat there, patient and quiet. He pulled her softness to him and she melded into him, in a way that made Jack feel that their hearts, which had danced around each other for so long, came together and locked.

"Of course you like her. I like her too."

"No." She lifted her pretty tear-stained face from his chest. "I mean, I didn't expect to." A sigh shuddered from her. "I suppose I should explain. I can't say too much because of confidentiality."

"You can trust me." Jack kept his voice low.

She took in a deep breath. "I'm representing Mama Cassie's Home Cooking, the party that is suing Sherry. I'm the one behind the cease and desist."

He sat back. "Well, how did you come across her, then?"

"When I was in Charlotte to speak to Cassie at her headquarters, I don't know what made me go to see Sherry, but I did. That's how we became acquainted, and when she professed such admiration for Granda, of course I had to ask her to come to the feast. But all of that, the way she makes it, how careful she is..."

"And the trade secret."

"Which is why I left. If I heard her say it, I would have to recuse myself."

"Well, I think you ought to already."

"Excuse me? Why?"

"You're in too deep with the opposition. Do you think Cassie would believe in your capacity to represent her fairly if she knew you had been on the road with Sherry? Think about it. No, you need to take yourself off of this case, like yesterday."

"But this is my first case as partner. What would it mean if I gave up now?"

He pulled her back to him. So much reflected in her eyes. He had to share his heart with her. Now.

"My daddy, as you know, is one of the most famous civil rights attorneys in the Southeast. He knew Martin Luther King, Jr. Had dinner with Martin Sr. and Alberta. Marched on Washington as a teenager. The whole nine yards. He raised me with certain high ideals and packed me off to Vanderbilt to be just like him, a fighter for rights and justice using my Vandy degree. And right up to and including my graduation, I did what he wanted me to do."

"What does this have to do with Sherry?"

"I'll get there, Sweet Tea. Just be patient." He held her hand, because it might make her feel better, but it really made him feel better.

"I went to sit for the bar exam. And I just… I couldn't. You know what that's like. So. I got up and walked out."

"You did what?"

"I walked out of the bar exam."

She shook her head. Clearly the thought was un-imaginable.

"Do you know why?" he prodded.

"No." She gave a little laugh, wiping at her face.

"It wasn't me. It was him. That was his dream. I was such a wastrel in college and in law school, putting forward half the effort. Because that's not what I wanted.

I wanted to go to cooking school. I wanted to celebrate the South in some way. I went and finished it and passed it later, but when I wanted to. Not when he did."

He took a breath. "What do you want, Tea? That's what matters. Do you want to be this barracuda lawyer and shut down Sherry's business? The one her grandmother started so that Sherry didn't have to work for a white woman?"

"Yes," Tea breathed out in a hard whisper. "The grandmother who worked for Cassie's family and had her recipe stolen from her. She didn't know anyone like me who could help her." Tea disengaged her hands from his, wanting to cover her ears.

"I'm sorry. Look. Let's get you back to the house so that you can rest up for tomorrow. It's going to be a long day, don't you think?"

"I do," she whispered. "Thank you. Thank you, Jack."

He put his arm around her as they stood. "Making sure that you are comfortable is all I desire."

Taking her out to the car and making sure that she got back to the house so that she could rest made him feel as if he had fulfilled a mission and had a purpose.

Anchored, not aimless.

Secure, not sorry.

He never wanted this feeling to end.

Chapter 27

THE DAY OF THE FEAST dawned bright, sunny and clear, just as the weather forecast had promised. Because she had been crying, her eyes felt welded shut with gritty glue, but a hot shower and splashes of equally hot water to her face gave her warmth and clarity.

Everything was so topsy turvy since she had arrived in Milford two weeks ago. Had everything gone wrong, or had everything gone right?

She quickly went out to her grandmother, dressed in her black pants and chef's coat in the Milford College colors of green and yellow. Granda was out there, putting on her solid heavy shoes, huffing and puffing, bending down to tie them.

"Here, let me do that." Tea bent down to tie the shoes. "You need some stretchy ones, not these tied ones. I'll send some." The words tripped over her mouth and made her realize that she was not going to be here next week.

"Thank you, Tea. I'm so glad you are here, child."

"Me too, Granda." She stood as they regarded each other.

"I'm going to miss you when you go back up there to New York."

"Aww. I was going to ask you if you wanted to come up with me and spend some time with me for a little bit. Maybe take a trip."

"What a nice invitation. All I can do is think about this feast today. Let me give the idea some thought, okay?" Her grandmother squeezed her hand and she squeezed back.

"I'm glad I'm here to help you."

"The same little Junety."

They winked at one another at yet another old name that Granda had given her when she was small, because Tea's stubborn personality put Granda in the mind of her own mother, Juneteenth Smithson.

They ate a boiled egg and a slice of toast each, took up their coffee mugs and went out the door, where Jack greeted them at the rental car.

By the time they got to Porter Hall, the square was humming with activity. The serving would start at 11 a.m., so there wasn't much time to linger. The feast used to be laid out buffet style, but that had had to change because some guests got greedy with certain dishes. So to control that, people got a portion of everything, the plates were premade and served all at once by students in khaki pants and green and yellow polo shirts.

Sherry volunteered, not just to make sure her prize-winning tea was ready to go, but for anything else that needed to be done. By the time it was serving time, the fifty people who were the special guests at the feast were all present and ready to consume lunch.

When the dressed-up diners came, they were shown to their particular tables. The feast had become an anticipated event, not just by friends of Milford College or those who had given a great deal to the college over the past year, but by selected food writers and bloggers.

There were journalists here from *Bon Appétit*, *The New York Times*, and *Food and Wine*, Tea marveled, as she helped to create plates for the students to serve. Each table held drink offerings of the tea that Sherry had created, water and lemonade.

Tea waved at Jack, who wasn't in a chef's coat today, but a green and yellow Milford College polo. He stood with a student in similar garb. "Why isn't he helping, Granda?"

Granda stood still for a moment, relaxing herself. "He got to get his movie made. He was here during the night, helping to defrost and thaw."

"All night?"

"Yes, child. That's how it usually is. I used to do it, but I'm getting up in years. He said he would supervise for me and I'm glad he did. Made everything so much easier, God bless him."

Like a well-choreographed dance, twenty-five students marched out to their assigned tables with four plates each, heads high, all ready to start serving at noon, precisely. This was all due to Jack's influence? To her grandmother's unique contribution?

What a marvelous thing. Her grandmother was a true genius. Why hadn't she seen that before?

Jack spoke over a microphone. "We are going to have a moment of prayer with the president of Milford College, Dr. Jasper."

The older man, now a bit stooped over but still sharply dressed in a natty summer suit and tie of Milford college colors, held up his hands. "Welcome, everyone, welcome." The crowd quieted instantly. Dr. Jasper was not a preacher, but he had that effect. "I want to say the prayer so that we all may partake while the food is hot."

Instead of feeling as if she were raw and vulnerable,

Tea felt as if warmth and light surrounded her. She reached over for her grandmother's hand and held it in her own. "Dear Lord. We thank you for the gift of Ada Smithson Dailey. These wonderful meals have kept the college going for many a year when things were low and desperate. She just keeps on going, keeps on giving to the mission of this school, to uplift and celebrate those who had been cast down into the depths of society. Lord, we pray a blessing on her and those who have assisted her in the making of this delicious food here today, and always. In the name of the Lord and of those who keep us unified, let us say together, Amen."

And everyone said it. Including Tea. When she lifted her head, Jack was standing next to her and they clasped hands, for just a second, until it was time for the students to parade out with baskets of his hot cornbread, and fresh biscuits with honey.

Pacing back and forth and helping as she could, Tea noticed her grandmother sitting on a stool, giving orders as if she were a general. It hit her then, in spite of the wish of Dr. Jasper, that her Granda would not last forever. She stopped what she was doing and stood next to her, looking around at a scene that was once thought impossible, all kinds of people openly enjoying great food, company, and love.

"This is amazing." Tea clasped her hands. She could not help it; her heart swelled with pride.

"I'm having the time of my life!" Sherry proclaimed, her face dripping with sweat.

"Me too!" Jack came to them. "So many great shots of this marvelous event."

Granda just nodded. "I'm glad you young people enjoy it. I'm not getting any younger. It's getting time to let young folk like you take this on over."

Tea grasped her hand and clutched it, ready to talk her grandmother down from such blasphemous thoughts. "No, Althea. I mean it. This might be my last one where I'm actively participating. I've thought of telling Dr. Jasper once this is all over."

The last thing that Tea wanted to do was be dismissive of her grandmother at such a serious time. "Of course, Granda. Whatever you want."

The older woman spread her arms out. "I wanted you to see what you needed to see. This, what I can do to help the legacy of the school. Before I couldn't show you anymore."

"I see it, Granda."

"It's the best that I can do."

"It's a wondrous thing." Tea hugged the frail body to her and a frisson of panic shivered through her. Why was Granda saying these things to her now?

Time for the dessert plates to go out. Each plate held a small serving of pecan pie, grape pie, a slice of pound cake and a small scoop of buttermilk ice cream.

Heavenly.

The time that people came and enjoyed the feast zipped by so quickly. She had never done so much physical work in her life, but maybe that was a good thing, given that they all needed to work off the richness of the food.

By the time it was 2 p.m., everything was winding down. People had departed, leaving behind a few journalists who had lingered behind to speak to Granda.

Tea and Sherry were supervising students to put the trash in the dumpsters in the back of Porter Hall when a tall man came down the walkway. "Oh my gosh, that's Derek!" Sherry shrieked as if someone had jerked upon her braids, and she ran to him, into his arms, and he twirled her around.

Jack came over to them, camera equipment put away, helping to clear up the square. "Who is that?"

Tea squinted at the man, until it hit her that she knew his rounded contours. "You won't believe this. He's the Uber driver I hired weeks ago to take me to Sherry's."

"Really?"

"What is he doing here?"

The couple came up to them, holding hands. "Derek came for me. Can you all believe it?"

"Sherry, you know I came here for you. And for a plate," Derek grinned.

"Well that too, LOL."

They all laughed. Working the feast was a perk many fought for, because a plate was a reward. They handed him an apron. Sherry and Derek took over the supervision of the trash as Tea watched them.

"Why are you so amazed?"

"I didn't know they were a couple, but I guess they met when I went to Sherry's. How nice for her."

"It's nice for her that she has a ride back to Charlotte."

"It is. I mean, now that it's all over. She could get back on the plane, but from the looks of it, she would probably rather be in the car with him."

"True." Tea looked over at the last table, which was set up with a camera crew still talking to her grandmother.

"It was a great success," Jack said.

"It was. I'm glad I came." She shut her eyes, relishing the feeling of completion and a different kind of success than what she was used to.

Jack poked her with an elbow. "I'm glad you did too. So what's on for tomorrow? Do we just slump down in a corner?"

"Oh, I'm sure Granda will want us at church. I'll make

sure she rests for the rest of the day and that she gets there. I'm guessing you have to hit the road."

There it was. The unspoken.

"Yes. On to scam the next old lady." He rubbed his chin.

"Come on, Jack. You know your approach didn't look that great."

"It didn't. You've made it better. You made a lot of things better."

He picked up her hand, stroking the back of it with his thumb. "What are you going to do about Sherry?"

"I... I don't know."

"Are you going to tell her?"

"Do you think I should?"

"You know the right thing to do, Tea. It's in your heart."

She closed her eyes and sighed. "I'm not so sure some days."

"Well. I think it's for you to decide."

He dropped her hand and Tea was sorry. She had enjoyed the feel of his hand on hers. "What about *Gimme Some Sugar*?"

"I'll keep it here in the marina. After I've driven around for a few more months, I'll sail her down to Florida for the winter."

"Sounds like a plan." She nodded. The journalist interviewing her grandmother shook her hand and the camera crew backed off. "I'll go get her and get her ready to go home. I know she's worn out."

Jack nodded, and she could tell the air between them had changed. What had she done wrong? Why had Jack's personality changed toward her all of a sudden?

He wasn't that enamored of her.

Yes, that was it. Someone as handsome as Jack could

have any woman he wanted. She wasn't looking for anything permanent herself. So why did his distant behavior bother her all of sudden?

He brightened with Granda, making sure to escort her to his car, putting her in front as Tea took the back seat, after they said goodbye to everyone, and he drove them back to the house.

Even when Granda invited him to stay, he told her he needed to get some things ready on the houseboat. "I'll see you in church," he said, reaching over to kiss her grandmother on the cheek.

He gave Tea a flippant little wave, as if she were a second thought, and then he was gone.

Well, she might have expected it. It was just part of a pattern she was used to. Men never wanted to stay or last with her.

But, boy, it was fun while it lasted.

Chapter 28

THE NEXT MORNING, WHEN SHE went out to Jack's car in a stripped-down peach sundress with matching espadrilles and a straw hat, she could tell by Jack's lingering gaze on her that he approved of her choices.

Granda went a little more stripped-down too. "It's summer. Ain't nobody trying to wear all of that."

"Exactly."

Granda had no meetings before church this day, so they were able to march right into the sanctuary, as many came to her and gave her congratulations and honor over the success of the feast. Tea took all of it in, amazed at seeing her grandmother in her most natural state and setting, regally receiving folks in her white summer sheath dress, shoes and small hat.

Jack still went all out with the full Sunday outfit, with striped tie, blazer and light slacks. Today, she sat next to her grandmother and Jack sat next to her, with his arm lightly resting on the chair behind her. The reverend spoke.

"Before we answer the call of the Lord to praise Him, I want to ask Jack Darwent to come forward, please."

Jack rose from his seat as if he'd expected to be called forward to stand next to Reverend Michaels. The two men shook hands and everyone looked at them with expectation. Especially Tea.

"This man has been a blessing to our community for these past several weeks. I mean, in addition to his help and care of our dear beloved Sister Ada. He has been there for all of us in whatever way we asked him to be. Lugging big boxes to clear out storage rooms, driving folk to doctor's appointments, helping out at the school when teachers couldn't teach, reading at the storytime hour…shall I continue, brother?"

Jack held up a hand, indicating that it was okay if the minister didn't continue. A smattering of laughter broke out. "I see you being modest, but I just wanted everyone here to know." The reverend's gaze lingered on Tea, for some reason. "That we have come to love this man and we will miss him. If ever in your wanderings you wish to return here to Milford, know that we always will welcome you with open arms, my brother."

Everyone clapped. It was an amazing thing to see Jack received so well. She'd had no idea of all that he had done to be helpful to the community before she had arrived. But since she had come to know him, she would have to say that she wasn't surprised.

"I'm not good with words like you are, Reverend Michaels. But I just wanted to thank everyone here for welcoming a stranger in your midst. Milford, and my time with Miss Ada and her granddaughter, has meant the world to me, and I'm sure it will form an important part of my film. I hope that when the film is done, I can come back and screen it here or in Porter Hall."

More clapping. People shouted out exclamations, like "I can't wait!" and "Yes, Jack," and "We love you, Jack."

"I love you all too."

Everyone quieted. "Thank you all for your open arms here. Be blessed."

With that, he returned to her side and Reverend Michaels gestured to everyone to stand and sing, "We Are His Own."

Miss Ada, sitting down in her chair, opting not to stand, had whipped out some tissue, dabbing at her eyes. Jack leaned over to her while people were singing. "How was that?"

"Just fine."

"Good."

He sang the song himself, since he knew it as well, but Tea didn't sing. Reverend didn't bother to say anything about her leaving Milford. Why was that? Maybe she hadn't done as much. Or was it because, as someone who was of the family and the community, her coming and going was taken more for granted? Wasn't her own 'return to Milford' worth mentioning?

Or maybe they just don't like you.

Back in the day, such an answer would have suited her. Now, it didn't so much.

What was she supposed to do? Should she return to New York? Admittedly, the thought of going back to the practice and helping Mama Cassie's triumph over Sherry and her invalid grandmother made that terrible burning feeling come back to her. She hadn't realized that the feeling hadn't bothered her lately and she felt better. More healed. More whole.

Maybe she didn't have to go back to New York. Or the practice.

What kind of sense did such a decision make? Of course, she would return to work. She just needed more time. Maybe another week.

What would she do with another week? Stay with Granda? She turned to her left and saw her grandmother, nearly ready to doze off in the close heat of the church.

Inch by inch, she turned to her right. Jack. He had shrugged out of his navy blazer without her noticing. He had worn a short-sleeved shirt underneath, and his muscles—Dear Lord—she did not mean to take the Lord's name in vain, but his muscles bulged out in the most satisfying way. He had laced his fingers together and listened to Reverend Michaels, an intense look on his face. He noticed that she was looking at him and he smiled, and once again, it was like Apollo had come into the sanctuary and beamed at her.

She turned away from him. What could she do?

Her brain honed the minister's message. The beautiful words of Ruth were his text. Maybe Jack was thinking of her, just not in such an overt way. The text was Ruth from chapter one, the passage about leave-taking and how Ruth opted to stay with her mother-in-law and how she found happiness where she stayed.

"When you change as a person, there are times that going back is not a possibility. You've grown. You're different. The clothing doesn't fit any more, for whatever reason. Things have changed. Ruth knew that. I wonder how many of you know it as well?"

The minister's voice softened as his message about leave-taking went into their hearts.

Jack's hand inched toward hers and his touch bumped up against the edge of her hand. She had peace like a river at his touch, but then his thumb, that thumb stroked along the edge of her hand, causing the most unsettling feelings to rise in her stomach.

They were not holy feelings.

Not at all.

To stop him, she slipped her palm under his and they laced their fingers together.

His thumb stopped the naughtiness and she smiled inside.

Jack leaned over, and it was as if their intentions laced together as well.

"Come with me, Tea. Please."

Had he read her mind? Did he know her thoughts? Did he know her heart?

He did. She whooshed out a breath of relief.

She knew, at long last, she knew what to do with the next week of her life.

When Reverend Michaels extended his hands out and asked folk to come forward for the saving, Jack stood up, squeezed her by the hand and tugged. She followed him, closing the doors of the church behind them. The beckoning a signal for the near end, but not quite the end, because the choir hadn't sung the Amen yet.

When they reached the quiet narthex just in front of the church, he said, "Do you know what I'm talking about?"

"I suppose I do." Was everything she heard in there a mistake?

"I have to return to Tennessee first." He ran a hand through his hair. "I want to film the Decoration Day celebration. It would only be for a few days. Then I can go onto the next interview."

"Works for me." Tea didn't know what Decoration Day was, but she was open to finding out on this fun adventure she was going on with Jack.

He stood there, then reached out and grasped both of her hands, gazing at her. "I'm so glad you said yes. I mean, you were such a help on the boat; you…you have quite an eye, you know, and it really helped me see how to put this thing together."

She laughed. "I only did what I thought to do. If it was helpful for you."

"When are you supposed to go back to New York?"

"I haven't given the partners an official date for my return." She shrugged. "It's basically the summer. Most of them will go to their summer homes. I don't have a summer home and I didn't know what I was going to do once I returned to the city."

"Will you talk with Sherry?"

"I think there is an answer for Sherry. I just, I haven't gotten to it yet, and I need time. Time to work it all out."

"Will this time help you?" He squeezed her hands.

"Yes. It will."

The connection in that moment between the two of them seemed so strong and permanent that it only made sense to make it stronger, to seal the deal with something that would pleasure them both. Tea, always the rebel, never had a thought about where she was. She was reaching for what would make her feel good for the first time in a very long time.

So when he reached down, bringing his juicy lips close to hers, she stretched up, as if it were instinct, even if she hadn't kissed a man in years.

The distance between them closed, inch by inch, little by little, so that everything, every possible thing in the world went away in that moment.

Until the church doors exploded open and the choir's "Amen" rang out across them, into the Milford town square.

And then there was silence.

Every mouth that had echoed with joy at praising God fell silent as the reverend, surrounded by choir members in their sand-colored robes and the rest of the Milford

AME church family, poured out, staring at what Tea and Jack were doing.

Tea jumped up and apart from him as if she had gotten the Holy Ghost.

Jack did the same.

A crowd of people, quiet people, silent people, pressing people, questioning people, surrounded them, waiting for what came next.

And, as she had done in the past, without question or acknowledgement, Granda, her tiny grandmother, emerged from the nosy throng and said out into the Sunday afternoon, "Althea Louise. You gone stop your running from the Lord, girl!"

Instead of feeling ashamed or embarrassed, instead of running away, instead of curling up in a corner with her pain at being humiliated in front of the whole town, she did what she'd never thought she would do in that moment.

She laughed.

Without hesitation, she went to her grandmother and embraced her, and soon Granda was laughing too, along with everyone else. So much so that Monique, walking on her way to help her father open up the barbeque store, stopped with a hand on her hip. "Church must be a happening place, Tea, if you are in here laughing with a handsome man and your grandmother by your side."

"Hey, Monique. You know all are always welcome here."

She drew her confused friend into her embrace as well, reassuring her that they would keep in close touch as she told her of her plan to accompany Jack on the road. She looked forward to traveling with this man, assisting him in documenting *Southern Treasures*. With a new friend. Or maybe more than a new friend.

The first stop would be to visit Jack's home and family in the middle of Tennessee, just outside of Nashville. She could hardly wait.

Chapter 29

J ACK HAD NOT BROUGHT A woman home to his mid-Tennessee home in more than ten years. His engagement to Everett—that is, Martha Everett Sloan, but known to one and all as Everett—had been broken once they graduated from college. He was off to Vandy for law school, and he just couldn't keep up the façade any longer that he was that much in love with her.

Driving this road in an RV with Tea reminded him how vastly different he was at thirty-four than at twenty-two. Moving his stuff from the houseboat to the RV he had rented so that Tea could be comfortable, he shrank to think of how silly he'd been, professing to be so in love with Everett. Why could he not see how selfish, small and picky she was at the time?

It was only after a talk with Miss Luly that he was convinced that he had to do the hardest thing in the world and ask for his ring back. Everett carried on for an entire weekend about it, asking him why he bothered listening to Miss Luly, except the words she used were beyond foul. It was when she threw his mother's half-carat diamond engagement ring at him and it rolled into a crack in the sidewalk that he knew he was well rid of her.

"What are you thinking about so hard, Jack Darwent?"

It was good to see Tea with her feet up, literally: bare, narrow and the toes manicured perfectly with peach polish to match her sundress, scrolling through her tablet.

"Just the past. My past. Things have been messy here at home and I just want you to know."

"You've been involved in messy? Do you think I'll cause trouble? I can always get a hotel."

"No. It's not that. I just think it's good I'm bringing you with me at this point in our relationship rather than a later point. I've learned. You'll see and then decide if you want to hang with me or not."

"It's just a week, Jack."

Maybe for her it was. For him, he had a week to convince her that she could be doing something else, something better, something grander with her fierce intelligence. He had looked into that law firm of hers. Oh, they were on the up and up all right, but it didn't sit well with Jack that they were limiting Tea. But that was for her to find out. On her own.

"We can stop and get some lunch or go to the homestead and try to ferret out what is in my Dad's fridge."

"I don't want to be any trouble. We can stop." She punched and swiped on her phone. "Actually, there is a Mama Cassie's in this part of Tennessee if you want to eat there."

"Yes, I think that's a great idea. I want to hear tell of what you are talking about."

The restaurant was the farthest one west of Mama Cassie's Charlotte headquarters, and according to Tea's information, it was only about a year old.

Mama Cassie's was the kind of restaurant that expected RVs and buses full of senior citizens and the like to pull up to their restaurant, so Jack did not have a hard time pulling into a long space and helping Tea disembark into the slightly crowded restaurant, which featured a cute blond cartoon carhop waitress welcoming them all. The character did look like Cassie a bit, Tea thought.

"Tea, please," was the first thing Jack said as they sat down and contemplated big menus listing lots of homestyle dishes for their consumption.

The waitress obliged them and brought two frosty glasses and a basket of warm cornbread squares with little silver ramekins of sweet potato honey butter.

Tea focused in on the cornbread, but Jack was all about the tea. She watched him slurp it past his lips as if it were a fine wine. Swig. Swish. Another slurp.

"It's good, but…"

"But?" A whole world hung on that little word.

"Bracing. Floral notes, different sweetener, but yes, just a hint of that taste. Very similar."

"Ugh." Tea put her head in her hands.

"It's okay. It's going to all work out. Let's order."

Jack ordered the family feast that let them have three meats and six sides.

"We can sample and then take the rest with us. Trust me, you won't regret that." He stretched his hand out to her but she didn't take it. She looked all around the restaurant, looking far less sure than the confident Tea he had come to know.

"What's wrong?"

"I don't know. It's the vibe of the restaurant."

He tapped his hand on the table. "Hey. I'm here. There's no need to be…" He didn't want to describe the way she looked now, pretty eyebrows all in a tangle, shoulders hunched up against the AC, biting at her lips. Was she frightened? Of being with him?

Suddenly, across the wide booth was too far away. He stood up and went around to her side of the table. "Scoot over."

"What?"

"I'll sit next to you. This way we can create a plan of attack for our family meal deal on one side of the table rather than two."

Her face lit up. "You are crazier than… I don't know what. Granda would say a bitsy bug, even though I don't even know what one of those is."

She moved over and he slid in with her, arm around her shoulders against the AC blast.

When the waitress, as well as another server, brought them plates of food, she didn't bat an eyelash. "Crispy fried chicken, catfish, ribs, broccoli and rice casserole, sweet potato souffle, corn casserole, summer squash, green beans, turnip greens and a basket of beaten biscuits."

"Apple butter?"

"Oh yes, coming right up." She dashed away. They surveyed all of the food laid out in front of them, looked at each other and laughed.

"Well, you can never accuse them of being less than generous."

"Sherry's portions were, also. Let's just try things one at a time."

The waitress brought them small plates and they plated things as they went. Jack ate, sampled, offered tastes to her. He had never had so much fun. The meal was not that awesome, but if you were looking for home cooked lite, as he liked to call it, then Mama Cassie's was it.

The server brought them a bunch of to-go containers and they packed it all away, two grocery bags full of food, along with a jug of sweet tea for good measure.

"Well, Cassie sure knows hospitality."

"True. Why wouldn't you want to come back to that?"

Tea turned to him. "Thank you for sitting here and making me comfortable."

He slipped his hand in hers. "Never doubt it. I will always do that for you." He picked up her hand and kissed it, palm side down. "Let us go, Sweet Tea."

He slid out, taking up the bags of food, and offered his arm out to her. "I'm fine, Jack. Really."

"I want you by my side."

She gave him a puzzled look, but she hooked her hand in the crook of his arm and he took her out to the parking lot.

They put away the food and then situated themselves in the RV. "I appreciate what you did back there," she said, picking at the edge of her dress.

He put his hands down from the wheel, not starting the RV. "That's who I am, Tea. If you are someone special in my life, then I'm going to stand up for you. There's no need to say that you appreciate it. It's what should be done."

She stopped fidgeting with her dress. "It's been a long time since I've dated, and it's been an especially long time since I've dated someone so solicitous. Wait. I don't think I've ever dated anyone this solicitous."

"Well, that's those guys' loss and my great fortune." He reached over and squeezed her hand. Lord, he would have kissed her, but she looked so shell-shocked from the restaurant. "Tell me. Do you think all Mama Cassie's places give their customers the heebie-jeebies?"

"The heebie-jeebies?"

"Yes. Like they have the sense of welcome, but they really don't."

"It's not fair to judge a whole chain by one restaurant."

"True." He put the key in the ignition and started up the RV, giving it a good rumble. "To the Darwent home, then."

Truth be told, he knew that he rambled as he told her stories of his Tennessee childhood, but the stories seemed to keep her occupied and it kept his mind off of having to face his father after some years. There was a bit of afternoon traffic heading to Franklin, and Tea ended up pushing the seat back and getting a nap in.

What would his father say to him? There was so much pain and hurt between them after his mother had died, and ultimately he'd decided that he wanted to take a different direction in his life. He would just keep it loose, as he always did, and not rise to his father's bait.

Tea snuffled in her sleep and he smiled. What a piece of luck he had run into when he came across her. He had fallen, fallen hard, even seeing pictures of her around her grandmother's house. That's when he knew he loved her. Thank you, God, that she'd come to a similar conclusion after some time, but boy, had she given him the runaround.

The drive to his father's property involved some twisty roads and he was thankful that he knew his way, because people who didn't would lose signals from their phones and would end up getting lost.

He made one last turn up the long driveway to Lucinda Oaks. In the large spread of fields off to the left, there was a young lady with a long dark braid thrown over her shoulder riding on a horse, maybe a renter. The property had belonged to his mother and his family had inherited it upon his mother's death. The farm was owned and operated under a consortium that comprised his father, his sister and Jack. His share of it was a bit less because he had asked once to sell, to raise seed money for his films. Drew had sent him a check, but didn't speak to him for a year after his request.

Pulling up, he saw a towheaded blonde run off the porch. Her long, lean frame, narrow nose and hollow cheeks looked the same. Bethany.

His big sister jumped up and down like a fool at the sight of him pulling this huge RV into the long driveway. One of the children, probably his youngest niece, waved like crazy. Tea sat up. "Are we here?"

"Yes, Miss Tea. We are."

She looked to his childhood home and he saw the large colonial house through her eyes. "It's lovely."

"The woman with all of the blonde hair is my sister Bethany, with one of her girlies." In spite of his previous trouble, he was glad to be home.

He came down from the driver's side and ran to Bethany, picking her up and swinging her around. "Oh Jack, I'm so glad to see you," she bubbled.

"Me too, big sister. Same." Bethany always smelled like sunshine and wind. He'd known she would change when she got to be a mother, but there was that old sense of familiarity about his sister.

"How is he?" He put her down and put an arm around her, guiding her to the other side of the RV so he could let Tea out.

"Same as always. Misses the hell out of you. I'm so glad you are back, and I see you've brought a lady friend with you?"

Good old Bethany.

He opened the door and handed Tea out. "Tea, this is my big sister Bethany. The little one next to her is one of her brats."

"I'm not a brat, Uncle Jack," the girl child informed him.

"Of course you aren't, Pressley."

Bethany laughed. "That's not Pressley. This is Wendy. Pressley was riding the horse when you came up the drive."

"That's Pressley? She's...she's..." He shook his head to clear it, unable to reconcile the young lady on the horse as his niece. When had she grown up like that?

Bethany hooked her arm through Tea's and he relaxed. "Why are you here with my clueless brother? He who thinks we should all freeze in time until he comes back." At his sister's jovial tone, he could see that, more importantly, Tea relaxed. "Let's get to know each other, Tea. What a cute name."

"Thank you. It's short for Althea."

They turned to the house and there on the porch was Drew Darwent. His father, a bit more slumped over, a bit grayer than he was five years ago, lifted his head and nodded in recognition calling out: "You done making films and ready for a real job, Jack?"

Jack bit his lip, but picked up Wendy, making her giggle. He was grateful for the shield his niece provided.

"Never change, old man."

And as far as he could tell, Drew Darwent had not. Unfortunately.

Chapter 30

MEETING JACK'S FAMILY WAS JUST as if someone had put the key to Jack in Tea's hand. Now she understood. The tension between father and son, thick as the former Berlin wall, surrounded them even as they went into the kitchen and ate Beth's stew, which was not as bad as Jack teased her it was.

"I didn't make it, and it was a great lunch," Tea proclaimed, as she scraped the last of the tender beef from her bowl. She had made the bread and beef bites work out equally, so she was pleased.

"I almost want to ask for more, but I won't." Jack sat back in his chair as Beth smacked one of his hard arms.

"But I will." Drew held out his bowl and Beth obliged him with another helping.

"We had all of this leftover food from Mama Cassie's, but this is so much better."

"Y'all went to Mama Cassie's?" Drew said. "That's about an hour plus from here."

"Yes, the case that Tea is working on is tangled up with them so, we went. A bit undercover."

"Ahh." Drew stopped scooping meat and vegetables

into his mouth. "Tea, is it?"

"A family nickname. Short for Althea."

"Jack is familiar as family to you, Miss Tea?"

"Well…"

"Dad." Jack's deep voice came solid and firm as that wall.

"Well, no harm in asking. Clearly this lovely woman is in need of family. Some one of us should help her to one."

"She has the best grandmother in the world," Jack declared.

"That ain't the kind of family I'm speaking about, Jack. Or do you know what I'm talking about?"

Bethany came up and snatched her father's bowl away. "There'll be no stew if you keep that up, Dad."

"Gimme that bowl, girl." Bethany lowered the bowl back to the table reluctantly. "Just trying to find out what your brother is up to."

Jack said, "When I have something to announce to you, Dad, I will tell you."

Drew dug back in. "Don't slow around. This lady is a prize. So your case has to do with Mama Cassie's?"

Tea nodded, sipping on some lemonade. "I cannot say much, but it's a trade secrets case."

"Beautiful," Drew swallowed. "And brilliant. Probably rich as Croesus too. This one here, she can bankroll your films, Jack. If that's why you have her as a friend."

"No, Dad. That's not why."

The room grew quiet. Too quiet.

Tea could see that Jack wasn't finishing his stew, and Bethany was not eating either. Her heart jerked a bit. Her happy Jack looked so serious right now. Too serious.

"Well, there's gotta be some reason." Drew barked.

Tea cleared her throat and spoke up. "Jack is a great filmmaker. He showed me the rough cut of his movie.

It's wonderful."

"He did?"

Jack smiled at her. "She made great editing suggestions on it."

"What is this film about, son?"

Tea could see that Jack had reddened a bit, but seemed determined to overlook his father's rudeness. "It's called *Southern Treasures*. It's a celebration of older women here in the South and the food they make. Tea's grandmother, Miss Ada, is one of the treasures."

She sat up a bit straighter as she heard Jack speak about his project with pride. *Please, Lord. Let him like it.* She hoped his father would receive the description of his film with love and pride.

"Will this one make any money? So that you don't have to ask to sell more shares of Lucinda Oaks?"

"I hope so." Jack dug back into his stew.

"I'm confident of it. It's really good." Tea picked up her glass to drink the rest of her water.

Bethany set down her own glass. "I would like to see it, huh, Daddy? Maybe Jack would let us see his rough cut."

Drew waved a hand at his daughter. "So that's why you came home? Decoration Day?"

"Not a lot of places still celebrate. I want to film it as well as the food at the celebration."

Bethany sang out. "They asked me to bring a dish."

"Did you say no?" Jack scraped his bowl,

"I said I would "

"So what are you going to bring?" Jack sat back. "Green beans?"

"No one ever brings anything green. So yeah, something with a vegetable."

"Jack makes the most delicious cornbread," Tea put in. "Maybe you want to have some of that."

"What's so special about his cornbread?"

"It has vegetables in it. He made it for the May feast. It was yummy."

"The May feast?"

Tea explained the entire enterprise to Drew Darwent as he finished off his second helping of stew. When done, he wiped his mouth and chin with a napkin. "Now I see. That's how you met. And you came down to see if he was swindling your grandma. Good instincts. No wonder you're a partner already. So, do you still think my son is a swindler?"

"No, sir." Her voice came across strong and clear.

"Well, I still wouldn't turn my back on old Jack. He has a way of disappointing." Drew stood. "I'm going to watch some of the French Open. You all are welcome to join me."

He meandered off down the hallway and Tea saw him disappear behind one of the doors. She turned to Jack and it hurt her to see such pain on his face.

"Well, nothing has changed, apparently."

"He's so happy to see you," Bethany assured him.

"So happy, he cannot stop tearing me down."

"Jack, you know how disappointed he was that you left the firm."

"He might get over it one of these days." Jack pushed a chair in frustration and it hurt Tea's heart to see the sun disappear from his face.

"He will. Meantime, just do what you are doing. I believe in you, Jack. So do the kids. And now you have a friend who believes in you too." Bethany smiled at Tea. "Please. He'll be okay. In the meantime, show me your cornbread. Maybe that's what I'll take."

His entire demeanor changed. Previously he had slumped, reddened and shamed. Now he sat up, looking into Bethany's face, ready to take control. "Well, let's see if the ingredients are here first. You know you all aren't up for too much cooking."

"If not, we can run to the store," Beth said.

"Or I will," Pressley chimed in, coming in from outside. "I do have my driver's license."

"You what?" Jack looked at his niece with fierce intensity. "Wow, I have been gone a while."

Tea watched him pull out eggs, cornmeal, sour cream and other things to get ready to make the cornbread. He was happy again, and that made her happy, even if she had questions about the Darwent family dynamic.

Tea was glad that for the rest of the day, father and son kind of circled one another at a distance as if they were two suspicious dogs. Jack stayed in the kitchen and showed Bethany how to make the cornbread, then he, Tea and Bethany went into the family room to watch Jack's rough cut. His nieces joined them there.

"Why not start a GoFundMe, Uncle Jack?" Wendy asked.

"I have one, but it's not raising enough, to be honest. In the meantime, I feel as if I owe something to these wonderful ladies. From me and my heart, not from other people."

"But it's really good." Wendy said. "Like PBS good."

"Thank you, miss. I appreciate that." Jack shook his head and pointed to Pressley. "I used to ruffle the hair of this one, but she's such a polished Southern belle now."

Pressley put her arms around her uncle. "Go ahead. Once more."

He did it and they all laughed.

They ordered a pizza for dinner, which Drew said gave him gas, so they all took a walk around the compound afterward to walk off the carbs. Jack and the girls ran ahead and Beth and Tea lagged behind.

Bethany stuck her hands into her pockets. "I've got to be honest with you. I've never seen him this happy. Especially not when he was with Everett."

Tea remembered hearing that name earlier, but just said, "He's doing what he loves. A profession that he cares about." She drew the words out, wondering if they applied to her as well. "Who wouldn't be happy?"

"Well, yes. There's that. And you."

"Me." Tea spoke the one word, not as a question, but as a declarative statement. Then she laughed.

"What's so funny?"

"I was going to tell you that we've only known each other a matter of weeks, but then my Granda says there is a tradition of love at first sight in my family."

Bethany clapped her hands. "That's awesome."

"Maybe." She sobered. "I'm going back to New York."

"You are? Well, there's lots of ways to keep in touch these days."

"That's true."

They circled back to the house, seeing Drew on the porch from far away as he watched his son and grand-daughters play a pickup game of football. Jack picked up his littler niece and carried her over the goal line, sending her into vigorous protest.

"What is the circumstance with your father?"

"They've always enjoyed butting heads." Bethany looked off in the distance. "I don't know of a time when they didn't. I just stay out of it."

Tea nodded. "I had my own problem with my grand-mother before I came down. I didn't realize he had his with his father."

"Jack hides adversity well. Just like Mama did. I don't think she was ever that happy with Daddy."

"Why do you say that?"

"Well, his law practice caused him a lot of strife. As we were growing up, someone tried to bomb our house a few times. That's what led us to move out here. There were attacks on Dad's life a few times. We got called names at school. Horrible ones. And Mama couldn't enjoy life as a Nashville housewife. So, she kind of withered away. Bless her."

"I'm sorry."

"Yeah. But her life taught me I didn't want that." They climbed on the steps of the porch to where Drew stood, glass in hand.

"How are you ladies? Getting to know each other?"

"Yes, Daddy," Bethany said.

"Well, that's good. Miss Althea, you're welcome here anytime."

"Thank you, Drew."

"What were you just saying about your life, Beth?"

"I said, I wanted to be something as far away from Mama as possible."

"You kind of fell into it though, princess."

She shook her head. "I guess so. But when Wendy is older, I'm looking to weigh my options."

"Options?"

Tea felt this was a conversation that should be private, and went to move away from the father and daughter, but Bethany linked arms with her so that she couldn't get away. "Yes. Like night school at Vanderbilt."

"Really?" Drew took a sip of his liquor.

"Yes, sir. I sent for the materials."

"Who is going to take care of Wendy?"

"Maybe her sister? Maybe her father. But someone. My college degree had to mean more than just a means to hook Kevin."

"Well, I see. What are you thinking of doing?"

Bethany moved closer to Tea and her skin prickled. "I'm thinking of law school."

"You are?"

"Yes, sir, I am. What do you think of that?"

Drew finished his drink and put down the glass. "Well, I had given up all hope when Jack abandoned his law education. I think that's amazing, Beth."

"Thank you. I've always admired your fight for the rights of others, and even though I'm not a Darwent anymore, I still want to do that."

Drew extended his arms and Bethany went into them. Tea nearly slid down the steps, relieved to be off the hook, so to speak. "You'll always be a Darwent. I'm proud of you. Your brother, on the other hand…"

They all looked at Jack laughing with his nieces.

"He'll always be a child in some way."

Beth tilted her head, and spoke up. "Daddy, you really ought to see his movie. It's good."

Drew nodded. "I'm sure it is. He's a Darwent. But he needs to put away childish things and become a man."

Tea could take it no longer. "Jack is a man, Drew. Really, he's doing the same thing as you are, but he's going about it in a different way. Your work is about humanizing Black people through the law. His medium is through film. He humanizes these beautiful women, both Black and white, bringing them together. It's the same thing and it's beautiful. And I haven't known you long, but I think you're smart enough to see that."

Beth pulled back from her father's chest with a bit of a twinkle in her eye.

Tea turned her head, giving Drew the side-eye. He reached across his daughter with his hand out for a handshake.

"What are you doing, Daddy?"

"Why, I'm welcoming her to the family. Once Jack gets wind of how this woman just told me off, he's going to want to marry her."

Tea took the offered hand and all three of them burst out laughing.

Together.

Chapter 31

THERE WAS MUCH ABOUT FRANKLIN, Tennessee, that had a similar small-town feel as Milford: the town square, the green grass, statues, and a coffee shop that was not Starbucks.

Tea might have had tight knots in her stomach about the day, but the hospitality of Bethany had been so warm, she couldn't feel any other way but relaxed. It was also clear that Drew liked her, even if he still clashed with his son in a way that made her uncomfortable.

Jack slept in the RV, to underline the distance between them, and Tea slept in Jack's former room, which was just down the hallway from Beth. "I want you to feel entirely comfortable," Jack said to her as they parted at the bottom of the steps Saturday night. "We'll get up early and set up the shots for Decoration Day together, okay?"

Everyone—Beth, Wendy, Pressley and Drew—watched them. So Tea squeezed his hand, smiled and headed up the stairs. She almost wanted to smile at the near-swear word that Drew uttered, but she knew it would culminate with something cutting to Jack, so she didn't.

As promised, Jack knocked on her door at six a.m. She put on her leggings, a long tee shirt and a light jacket, put her hair up in a ponytail and followed him quietly down the stairs and out to the RV. In the passenger seat he had bundled a fried egg sandwich in ciabatta with bacon and a small jug of OJ. She ate the sandwich open-faced and drank half the juice.

When he pulled into the church parking lot in the town square, she could see that there were people already in the cemetery, across the street from the church. They had gathered in the dawn, holding rakes, brooms, gloves and large green garbage bags.

When Jack came out of the RV, he handed Tea down and she helped him to set up the camera equipment. The mood was a serious, somber one. Jack nodded at several people, shaking hands and giving out hugs to some people.

"What are they doing?"

"When the sun rises, they will open the gates to the cemetery and then go in to do a good cleaning and decorating of the graves."

Jack gestured to a woman and pulled her aside to do an interview. Her name was Margie and she was the head of the committee. "We do this because we don't forget. We can't ever forget them," she explained.

"What would forgetting mean?" Jack asked

"It would mean that we didn't know ourselves any longer. My mama didn't work that hard to bring me up once Daddy got to liking the liquor too much for me to forget her."

Jack turned off the camera. "That's awesome, Margie. What did you bring for the lunch?"

"Well now, Jack, you are just going to have to find

out at that point."

Jack redirected his question. "I'm asking you as a filmmaker, Margie, not as a consumer."

"You know that I always bring my pretzel salad. At least."

He smiled. "That's just what I hoped. I'm looking forward to it too."

Once he had interviewed several different subjects, the crowd thinned out and he went into the RV to get himself and Tea some coffee from the Keurig.

He brought her the coffee in a "You are My Sunshine" cup.

"So what happens now?" she asked.

"In about an hour, a certain group of ladies will return to the church basement and begin to fix lunch. I'll talk to them about the menu."

"None of these town women are your Southern Treasures?"

Jack looked down at the cup of coffee he held and Tea turned to him. "You don't have one from your own hometown?"

"No."

"Why not?"

"We've always been considered a little outcast, a little quirky here. The Darwents, I mean."

"So now you know how I felt in relation to Milford."

The realization seemed to hit him like the growing dawn. "I do. I really get it."

"And I came to peace with it all. What's behind it?" Tea took a sip of the fortifying coffee. It wasn't her special, but it was handmade by Jack, so she liked it.

"Dad's career, I think. Civil rights pioneers aren't that well respected around here."

"So you blame your father?"

"No. A lot of what he has done is very important. I just have seen how it has cost him a lot. He didn't seem to understand what it has cost us, though. Or care. That living in the shadow of being outcast cost my mother a lot, I think."

"Is she there?"

"She is."

Tea looked to the graveyard. "You don't want to decorate?"

Jack's blond curls bounced as he shook his head. "We had long talks about that before she died. She's not really there. She lives in my heart. And in Beth. I see a trace of Mom in Wendy's face. That's where she is. Bethany will come when she brings the cornbread and do what is necessary."

She completely understood. Graveyards were places of comfort to some, but she didn't know who. Even when she was in Milford, she didn't see any reason to go see to her parents, buried in the college's graveyard. Seeing that same date on their similarly aged headstones was too much a reminder of her loss.

When the women came trailing back, she and Jack followed them down into the church basement, adjusted their camera, and Jack filmed some more interviews with the ladies who were charged with Decoration Day lunch.

"Don't get it confused with Memorial Day. That's the mistake a lot of strangers make." One of the ladies gave Tea a good, inspecting look.

"No, ma'am," Jack kept his tone respectful.

"This day existed before Memorial Day and was celebrated all through Appalachia."

"Have you ever been to any other celebrations?" Jack asked.

"No indeed. I must be here in Franklin to pay homage

to my family. Honor thy mother and father so that the days be long upon the land, that's what the Bible says."

"Yes, ma'am."

"And our menu stays the same, so that we can be comforted by the memories of those who have gone before us. "

Except that it didn't. Would the women rebel when Bethany brought in Jack's cornbread? Tea certainly hoped not.

Bethany came down the stairs with her plastic container filled with squares of the cornbread. "I'm here." She handed the cornbread off to Tea. "I'm going to go fix Mama's grave." She lowered her voice. "These women are just catty enough to leave it to me to do, and then what would they say?"

"Where are the girls?"

"With Daddy. He's bringing them later."

Tea watched her turn and go back up the stairs. One of the women approached her and indicated the cornbread. "Is that for us?"

Tea held up the long plastic dish and the unusual way the squares of cornbread looked through the plastic was evident. The woman put a hand to her chest. "Oh my. What is that?"

Opening her mouth, Tea readied herself to speak in a defensive tone, to counter the woman's questioning, but Jack came behind her and slipped a hand to her waist. She could feel his body heat right behind her—alive, strong, supportive. "Hey there, Mrs. Winstead. I made some cornbread and I thought you all would want to add a little spice to the spread this year."

The hostile look in the woman's eyes softened completely as she reached her hands out to take the container, grabbing it in the center and sandwiching it in her hands instead of taking it from the edges where Tea grasped it. "Well, hey, Jack. I'm so glad to have something you made. Was it a cooking school recipe?"

"It was a Jack Darwent recipe."

"Oh, well, I'm going to set it up on a platter then."

"You do that, Mrs. Winstead."

The woman sashayed away from them, saying, "Look at what Jack brought for the Decoration Day meal!"

Jack whispered in her ear. "You need to stick with me."

"I was just going to help Bethany."

He gestured. "Go ahead then. I'm not ready to shoot yet."

She turned to face him. "Don't you want to come too?"

Something weighed heavy on his heart. "No. I don't want to. It's Bethany's thing."

"What if something happened to her? Then what?"

He held up a hand and waved her off. "I just…it's something I can't do. Like how you left the church when you were twelve. You didn't go see your parents' graves either, while you were in Milford, did you?"

She shook her head. He had her there. She moved to the door and up the stairs, seeing Bethany take a few shopping bags out of the car. "I can help."

Tea grabbed one of the bags from Bethany and they walked across the street. As they did, Bethany greeted folks who were walking in the other direction, ready to wash up and head in for lunch. Most of them were friendly, but they did regard Tea with interested glances.

"I bet they're wondering who you are, Tea," Bethany said when they were in the clear, walking across the beautiful green of the small churchyard cemetery.

"I can see that."

"Well, I don't blame them. I'm wondering who you are too."

Tea put a hand to her chest. She hadn't seen that coming.

"Are you a friend for Jack? Are you going to break his heart? 'Cause my little brother has had a lot of heartbreak in his life. He's looking for a soft place to land in this hard world."

The graves were all decorated with flower wreaths, gaily colored springtime ribbons, some plastic and some cloth. Bethany stopped in front of a stone on the edge of the cemetery. The stone was high and well-maintained and was meant for two. "Darwent," it read on the top. The bottom had space for two names and the one on the right said "Lucinda Kent, Beloved Mother, Wife, Friend, 1963-2000." The other said "Andrew Jackson, Husband, Father, Lawyer, 1953-." There was no death date etched on his side.

The Christmas wreath in front of Lucinda's grave was shrunken and brown with a frayed red and green plaid bow on it. Bethany picked it up and pulled out fresh green wreaths with pink bows on both of them from her bag. Why were there two?

"Here." She handed Tea a small spade and together they worked to put a wreath on Lucinda's grave and plant new impatiens near the headstone.

There was something about digging in the ground together that healed Tea in some way, and she wondered if she hadn't made a grave mistake—literally—in not going to see her parents' burial site.

Soon, Beth stood up. "Okay. Once more."

She moved back a bit to the grave on the other side of Andrew Darwent. Tea looked at the gravestone of that one. "Eulalie Jackson. Mother to all, servant to none."

"Is the wreath for her?"

Bethany nodded. "Oh, you thought that Jack didn't want to come here because of Mama? Oh no. It's because of Miss Luly. She's buried here on the other side of Daddy."

Tea could now see that the second grave had the exact same old Christmas wreath that needed to be taken up by the headstone. "This is Miss Luly?"

"Yes. She raised both of us when our mother died. We loved her as if she were our Mama. Jack insisted in this wording on her headstone. Turned the heads of a lot in this town, but I was glad he stood up for her."

Tea felt as if she were getting fresh insight into Jack at the sight of his devotion. "This is why he doesn't want to come?"

"Yes. He loved this lady."

"I guess that's why he feels so attached to my grandmother."

"Maybe. But it's because he has a tender heart. I hope you have a care for it."

Tea said nothing, but knelt down in the soil to help Bethany plant impatiens over the grave of their beloved nanny. She stood and wiped her hands down. "Well, we can get ready for lunch."

"Thank you for letting me help you."

Bethany regarded her. "Thank you for loving my brother. He's a kind man and he deserves love."

As she followed Bethany out of the cemetery, Tea reflected on what wasn't spoken—did she love Jack?

She couldn't answer.

Chapter 32

Now that Tea was here in Franklin, Jack saw it all through her eyes. Everyone was well-meaning and loving to him. But they had to love her too. And so far, they did. Bethany, the girls and even his father. So what was he holding onto that made this homecoming so hard?

In the church basement, they all sat down to the meal of salmon croquettes, macaroni and cheese, broccoli casserole, whipped potatoes, sautéed carrots, the cornbread, and strawberry shortcake, with sugared biscuits. Someone had brought a stack cake, something that would occasionally pop up in this Tennessee valley, but not all of the time. He made sure to get an interview with that baker before sitting down to his meal.

Watching Tea eat and enjoy her food, laughing with his family, made him look again at what he had. He was blessed. By a lot, and he could do no better than to share that bountiful blessing with Tea, who had a lot with her grandmother, but still could use support.

What was she to him? A friend? A potential spouse? A business partner?

His everything. He was falling in love with her and he

didn't want her to go back to New York. What was there for her but a lot of money? Money wasn't happiness. It wasn't family. He wanted her with him and he would do what he needed to get her by his side.

He could only pray that she understood.

And returned his love.

"Jack? I hate to bother you. But could you autograph this?"

He turned around to see Mrs. Winstead thrusting some sheets of paper at him. "Why, what is this, ma'am?"

"I saw there was an article about you on the Southern Living website. I didn't know you were so famous, Jack. How wonderful. What a legacy you are creating with this film."

She turned to his father. "You ought to be proud of him."

"I am," Drew said, drinking more of his lemonade. "He's done fine. It's not what I would have done, but your children aren't your own, as they say."

Jack sat up a little straighter, tempted to make sure there was no wax in his ears distorting what his father had said.

"True enough, Drew. I'm so intrigued to make the grape pie recipe. I remember hearing my grandmother talk about making such a thing and I have always wanted to try that."

He signed her papers and handed them back to Mrs. Winstead with a satisfied flourish. Then he turned around and saw Tea, looking at her phone with a great deal of interest. What was she doing?

"Grape pie?" Drew said. "That sounds mighty interesting."

"Yes, it does," Tea agreed. "It was one of my grandmother's recipes. She showed it to Jack." She held her phone out to him. "Only, I don't see that you've mentioned her or given her any credit in this article, Jack."

He took the phone and thumbed through it. Scrolling through the ads and the article and passing by the picture of himself looking like the adventurous documentarian. It was the photo he used for fundraising. Then there was a picture of him taken during his cooking school days in his chef's coat.

He scanned the article quickly. She was right. There was not one word about Miss Ada.

"Nothing's there. Not Milford, not the family. Nothing." The tone of her voice grew harder and harder. Bethany laid a hand on her arm, which was outstretched to get her phone back. "Maybe there was a mistake. Right, Jack?"

"Son? Bethany is asking you a question."

How could the look on his father's face go from joy in him to disappointment in one second? Bethany too. He couldn't even face his nieces. Wendy just said, "Uncle Jack?"

A question, not a statement.

"That's not the piece I gave them."

"Then what did you give them, Jack?" Tea said, making him wish he was called anything else.

"I negotiated for an online feature in advance of the print edition."

"Did you get money for it?"

"The editor is an old friend, and when she heard about the project…"

"I said, did you get paid for that?"

"Well, yes."

Drew hit the rickety church table with an open hand. Disappointment shone in Bethany's eyes.

Worst of all, Tea stood. "That's not what we negotiated.

Not at all."

Jack spread his hands. "It's one part of the project, not all of it."

"So you took advantage of the time lag between your signing and your lawyer's agreeing, is that correct?"

She didn't even wait for him to answer. She snatched up her bag and everyone, all of the people in that church basement, knew that Tea, the lone Black person in the entire place, was not happy.

"Where are you going?"

"Anywhere. Away from you."

He stood too, arms spread out, far from caring who saw or heard him. "Tea. Come back."

"Sit down, boy. She doesn't want to."

Bethany went after her and after some meaningful looks from his nieces, they followed their mother outside.

And they did not return.

When Bethany came back, he was perched on the steps of the RV. "Where is she?"

"She asked me to take her back to the house and then to the nearest Enterprise. So she left. I don't know where she went."

"This is a mistake. That's not what I agreed to on the website."

"Can you fix it? For the online and the print versions?"

Bethany had just handed him a light saber. Or maybe a golden apple. To get his woman back.

"Yes, that's the answer. Thanks, kid."

"Jack. You deserve to be happy. None of it was your fault. You have to let the past go."

Her words sounded like complete sense to him, but it still made it hard to believe. "You think?"

His sister laid her hand on his arm. "Jack, I know it. You deserve to be happy. This woman, this Tea, she's it.

You've found the other half of you. Some of us are still looking, but you were lucky enough to find her. In the weirdest way, she's just like you."

"What about you, sis?"

"What about me, Jack? It's why I'm telling you. I kind of jumped the gun on things. I just wanted to marry to get away from Luly's control. And then since Mama was gone, I felt that there wasn't anything for me. Kevin wasn't right for me. I mean, I have two beautiful girls from him, but I don't have love. You have love. She's a great woman, Jack. Not a girl. A woman. You have to go to her. Tell her that you love her. So you can be happy."

Everything Bethany said made sense. And he stood, willing to do whatever he could to convince Tea to come back to him.

They hugged one another.

"She didn't leave that long ago. You can still catch up to her."

"What did she rent?"

"I saw her leaving in a midnight blue coupe," Bethany broke in.

Jack nodded. "Got it."

"Text me when you've caught up with her, and then see what happens. Love is magic, Jack. Pure magic."

He got in and started the engine, then waved to her and the girls as they stepped away from the RV. The group of grave tenders surrounded the rear of the RV, waving too.

Drew came out of the church. Jack put the RV in park and went out to his father. "Leaving us again, son?"

"I've gotta find her."

"Well, I understand. She's a pretty remarkable woman." He grasped his son's arm. "She's going to help you go far. Maybe she'll even help you get back into law."

"Don't count on that, Dad." Jack reached out and Drew pulled him into his embrace.

For the first time in twenty years. Since Jack's mother had died.

Some of the old slights, pain, and resentment coagulated together, forming a scab over the hurt, helping his heart heal.

"Hey, I tried. Be safe." Drew slapped his back several times. "And you're welcome to bring Tea back anytime."

"I will."

Jack swung up again into the front of the RV and drove, full bore, onto I-40, determined to beat Tea to Charlotte.

Charlotte had some stupid highway perimeter around it, which meant that he had to drive around the entire city one more time than he wanted to. So when he pulled up into the little gravelly parking lot of the small meat-and-three diner, Sherry's, it was late.

He did not see a midnight blue coupe in the parking lot and his heart sank just like Melanion's must have when he chased after Atalanta.

He swallowed, but his saliva had left him. If he missed her…well, he could just continue on to Milford. No loss.

But it was a loss to think about time without her. To not be with her was unbearable.

He went into Sherry's and the restaurant was relatively empty. The dinner rush was over. A young woman with a crown of braids on her head looked at him. "We closing."

"I'm looking for Tea. I mean Sherry. Is she here?"

"I'll go get her for you." The young woman sauntered to the back and came back out with Sherry.

"Jack. What are you doing here?"

"Was Tea here?"

"Yes, she was here earlier. She took her rental back

to the airport."

He scrubbed his hands down his face.

"Is she going back to Milford?"

"Milford? No, she seemed as if she was going back to New York."

He sat down in one of her booths. He hadn't expected that. New York. So she didn't feel as he did. She wanted to go back to her New York life.

Well, going around talking to old ladies about the past may not have sounded like the most fun to her. But he thought she was having a good time. At least he was.

Sherry touched his shoulder. "Are you okay? Bring him a glass of water," she instructed the young woman.

"I'll have tea if you have it. It's the best."

Sherry lowered her head with pride, but she drew it herself and handed it to him, frosty and delicious.

"Thank you."

"You're in love with her, aren't you? Did you tell her?"

The cold in the glass of tea seeped through his fingers into his soul. "She's gone back to New York. How can I tell her anything?"

"You could call her. Or why don't you go there? Let her know."

He touched his cold tongue to the roof of his mouth to warm it, to avoid a cold headache. "She's going back to her New York life. What can I promise someone like her?"

Sherry sat down in the booth across from him. "Love."

"She's mad at me. She thinks I stole the grape pie recipe." He told her the story.

"Have them yank the article and fix it."

"I did. It didn't seem to be enough."

Sherry put a hand to her forehead. "There has to be some way."

He stood. "I'll figure it out. If you don't mind me using your facilities, I'll hit the road."

"I'll give you a fresh refill of my best."

"Thanks."

When he came back out, a paper cup was filled to the top and there was a plastic milk jug next to it full of the tea.

"Thank you, Sherry. So much."

"You're welcome."

Then it hit him. Like a lightning bolt, it came to him. The way he and Tea could be together and everything could be resolved in Milford.

He practically ran out of Sherry's place, trying to get back to Milford with all deliberate speed, hoping that he could get a flight out of Atlanta first thing the next day.

Chapter 33

W HEN TEA GOT BACK TO her office building, something about it looked small. The grandeur she
had imagined that it had wasn't there anymore. Walking
down Madison Avenue, she noticed so much more.
People were in parks, playing, selling fruit and trinkets;
folks were walking to work, to the subway, to wherever
they had to go. It brought to mind everything that she
had felt when she first moved to New York after she had
finished with college. But in a new and different way.

Where was everyone going?

Why was everyone going so fast?

How had she learned to get caught up in all of it
without even questioning it?

Did she even want to be part of this anymore?

Just the mere fact that she noticed it meant that, in
some way, she was no longer part of it. The parade had
passed her by.

And that was okay with her.

She clicked into the lobby and caught the elevator as
usual, but yet, the marble looked shabby, the elevator
button numbers were worn away. And when the doors

opened onto her firm's floor, she could see that it was in bad need of redecoration.

The brown of the carpet looked like mud. Bad mud, not a vibrant red like Georgia mud. Everything in here looked drab and turned down. Why had she never noticed this in all of the years she had worked here? So many years of her life, twelve years spent here gladly, and in all of that time, she'd never noticed that she had been entombing herself.

"Hey boss!" Connie waved at her and Tea's face lit up to see her. Well that was one good thing. She wanted to be a good boss, not someone that folks dreaded to see. "You look wonderful! I love that dress on you."

Tea lowered her head to look at what she was wearing. A vibrant magenta silk sheath instead of her usual choice of black, navy, gray or brown. This dress, along with the accompanying flowered pumps with a much lower heel, made her feel happy, springlike.

She should dress like this much more often.

"Thank you, Connie. So good to see you too. And you're still with child."

"Of course. I had to wait for you to come back so we can do cleansing breaths together during my labor." They grinned at each other, but Connie's grin left her round face first and she lowered her voice.

"The partners told me to let them know when you arrived."

Tea had expected that.

"Well, let them know I'm here. I'll be in the conference room in a minute." She headed to her office and Connie followed.

"Coffee?"

"No. Not right now, thanks."

"Really?"

283

"Really. I'm good."

Connie followed her into the office and closed the door. "What happened?"

"What do you mean?"

"You seem, refreshed or something."

Tea nodded, going around to the back of her desk, noting all of the sad mess that resided there. She sat. "I do have a different view on things than I did before. Even a new name."

"A new name?"

Turning in her chair to face Connie she spread her hands across her stark desk. "I went back to my old Southern nickname. Call me Tea."

"Okay, Tea. Are you coming back? To stay?"

She met Connie's eyes. She deserved to know the truth. Connie had been an excellent source of support for so many years and she had a stake in whether her boss was here or not.

"Coming back, I felt that I could. Now that I'm here, I'm not sure I can. It's hard to explain. But I feel as if I've outgrown this place."

Connie leveled her with her own look, nodding slowly. Tea matched her nodding, not sure of what she should say.

Tea folded her hands. "You should have a nice long time with the baby. Six months, not six weeks. I'll pay you a generous severance so that you can take your time looking for a…"

"Well, hallelujah!" Connie threw up her hands, not too high, but then she rested them on her shelf of a baby.

"Excuse me?"

"You don't know how long I've been waiting," Connie paused. "Althea. Tea. To see you emerge. And now it's happened. I don't know how it happened, but praise

God. You finally did."

Tea smiled slowly. "Yes. I see what you are saying. Yes, I have. And I'm so glad that you have received your notice of unemployment so graciously."

"I'm so happy for you, I cannot imagine feeling any other way." Connie grasped her hands, then let go. "What are you going to do?"

"My options feel open." Tea hugged herself.

"I'm glad. Well, after you face the dragons in the conference room, I'll be in here getting your things together and I'll arrange for them to be shipped wherever you say. After you finish this case?"

Tea shook her head. "No. I'm giving up the case."

"You are?"

"Yes. That's one of the things I'm going to tell them." She stood.

"Well, good luck. They won't be happy to hear that."

"I have a lot of news they won't be happy to hear." Tea came around to the other side of the desk where Connie stood. "Thank you so much. For everything."

Reaching down, she hugged Connie, and her baby.

"Be blessed, Althea. I mean Tea."

She did feel blessed. Retrieving a bottle of water out of her mini refrigerator, she went to the conference room where they were waiting.

The Three Horsemen.

Instead of looking apocalyptic, they were just three sad, gray-looking men on a beautiful early June day in a conference room with no windows. Missing life. Watching it from the sidelines.

She had been entombed with them, but now?

She was free.

"Good morning, gentlemen."

"You look so....refreshed." said Ellis, the one who'd

always had a crush on her.

"Thank you."

Pichon hit him in the shoulder. "It's good to see you, Ms. Dailey. Do you have anything to share with us on the Mama Cassie's case?"

"Turns out that Mama Cassie stole that recipe. I cannot, morally or ethically, represent her."

Pinchon's thick white caterpillar eyebrows raised up. "That doesn't stop us. I'm sure that you found the hole in the case."

"The hole, sir, is that Sherry's grandmother, who is 95 years old and still in a nursing home in Charlotte developed the recipe. It's hers. I obtained an affidavit from her myself."

"What would you do that for?" Pinchon's fist balled up.

"Because I believe her and I don't want to rip off Sherry's grandmother." She stepped forward with her folder in hand, opened it, and slid an envelope across the table to him. "This is the amount that Mama Cassie's will pay to Sherry's as a settlement and a percentage of all iced tea sales."

"I don't see her agreeing to that."

"Well, she will or I'll represent Sherry in court against her." She opened her folder and brought out another envelope that looked like the first one and slid it across, saying "I'm tendering my resignation from the firm."

Ellis, the one who had the crush on her, stood. "You can't quit on us. You're one of us."

Turning to him, she gave him one of her biggest smiles. "Oh, no. I'm not."

"What do you mean by that, Ms. Dailey? We made you a partner in good faith." Pichon's wrinkled face seemed to become more wrinkled in a millisecond.

"The only reason you made me a partner was because Mama Cassie's needed a Black lawyer to take this case on. I'm one of the very few lawyers in the country who is a Black woman with my depth of specialty and experience. So they came all the way up here for me and you made me a partner."

Her crush boy sat down, mouth open.

"Well, I would not agree with you on that. It was time for you to be a partner. We aren't an affirmative action kind of firm."

"Oh, I know that, sir. I earned every bit of my partnership. And the letter there lists my terms for me to get my share."

Pichon's grasping fingers reached for the envelope and ripped it open.

"You cannot have this." His hands shook.

"I most certainly can and will."

He handed it off to the next partner and their mouths all dropped open in turn.

"I'm distressed to learn that this is the way you treat us after we took you on so young."

She nodded her head. "I'm sure. I'm distressed that you took me on, cheating me of what was equitable over the years because I was so young. That's why I want that amount, and no less. Or I'll see you in court."

Boar, the quiet Horseman, stood up. "You can't do that."

"Oh, I will do that. And I know you have it. The partnership that you offered me so that I could be the face of this particular lawsuit is worth it. You knew it was a great deal of money to me. Now, you should pay me what a great deal of money is to you."

Ellis started sweating, while the air went out of Boar. She wanted to laugh. But she didn't. Coveting her was one thing. Money was another.

"We will need to confer, of course."

"Sure. I'll turn my back, if you like." She hadn't been born yesterday. She wasn't leaving that room until they gave her what she wanted, check in hand.

She turned around and the door opened and there, right before her eyes, dressed in the most expensive, finely cut Italian suit, complete with a just-so folded pocket square and stick pin, was Jack Darwent. With a looming pregnant figure behind him.

Connie.

Her knees went weak.

"Good morning, gentlemen. Am I late?" Jack's voice boomed out.

Pichon stood, his knobby knees creaking. "Who might you be?"

Jack smoothed down his tie, tucking his hand into his lapel. "Well, that depends on what Ms. Dailey says I am."

"Excuse me?" Boar said.

Fixing his baby blues on her face, Jack spoke directly to her as he stepped into the room right next to her. "If Ms. Dailey needs a lawyer in this moment, and she's willing to retain me, I'm happy to provide that service."

The ever-faithful Connie handed Tea a dollar, which she handed to Jack.

"So you are her lawyer? Well, isn't that rich?" Pichon sneered. "After all we have done for this…"

"Beautiful lady. I'm sure that's what you meant to say." Jack picked up her hand in his, brought it to his lips, and kissed it.

"But she's far more than that, and I'm sure that you know it. She's intelligent, fierce, loyal and wonderful."

Boar put in, "You don't sound like a lawyer."

"Oh, but he is. Even I was surprised to find that

out," Tea said, calling for a cleansing breath to still the thrumming feeling rushing through her. He had come here. For her.

"But if you want me to be more to you, so much more, after I've had Southern Living retract that unfortunate article that should have never gone to press, I'm available for that as well, Ms. Dailey. It's all up to you." Jack had not let go of her hand yet and she was grateful for that.

"I don't think this is appropriate, at all." Ellis pouted.

"You wouldn't." These were the only two words that passed her lips that betrayed that she knew he had the hots for her.

But he would never, ever have the opportunity to know a thing about her. Because her heart was given over to this man, this Jack Darwent who stood right in front of her.

"I'm so very sorry, Tea. Please, please forgive me."

"What is there to forgive?" She kept her voice cool, but inside of her lava bubbled.

"The disrespect that I paid to your family heritage. I would never ever want to profit from that. I need you to help me with this film. I need you by my side. I need you in my life. Please say yes."

Connie, situated by the door, sighed audibly.

"What is going on here? This is most unusual."

"Shut up, Pichon," Connie said.

Tea wanted to laugh at the shocked look of the lead partner, but she couldn't, because this was a serious thing Jack was asking of her. Should she go with him? Just as she had so recently been freed of the chains of the firm?

"I'll consider it." Was all she could say. A pretty generous thing in that moment, she thought.

Jack moved closer to her, so that he was standing right over her. "Well, that's fine. I appreciate being considered. Considering."

He wrapped a hand around her waist and thank God that he did, because a strange sensation fogged her brain. How could that be when she had always had good sense?

She didn't. Not right now.

His face came nearer to her and she realized in a split second that if she didn't move out of the way, he was going to kiss her. She could move her face one inch to the left and he would get her cheek. Or she could let his lips, those soft, juicy lips, come right for hers.

She had spent years making sure she slept with Carmex on her lips, waiting for this opportunity. For this moment. For this man.

Tilting her chin up, just a little bit, she met his lips with hers, melting, sliding, tingling in warm welcome and she, knowing that she must have been struck by lightning because of the electricity coursing down her spine, felt him press her to him right in the small of her back and she parted her lips to him, for him.

Because she was found.

Finally.

Chapter 34

T HE VERY NEXT SUNDAY, TEA gave her grandmother the surprise of her life when she walked back into the AME sanctuary—fully fueled with a cup of Calvin's coffee, of course—to tell her that she was leaving New York City to come back to live in Milford. Her grandmother couldn't resist giving testimony in church that morning.

But then, so did Tea. Jack assisted her up to the front, and every head in the sanctuary bowed and nodded at the gesture of affection between them.

"Thank you to my grandmother who could not contain her joy at my coming back to live in Milford. I'm so excited for this next chapter in my life. But I also want to announce a few things in regards to Milford College, if I may."

The church congregation rumbled a bit. The pastor gave a nod and the president perked his ears up, leaning forward. "I had been running away from Milford and what I am for a very long time. I'm done running. I've found home again. I've returned to Milford, which I thought I'd never do. I always hated that saying." She laughed. "That doesn't mean I'm going to stop traveling." She gave a nod and a wink to Jack. "But Milford will be my home base. As such, I want to do things to help. I've been offered, and will finally accept, a position on the Board of Trustees for the college."

Everyone applauded and the sound enveloped her like an embrace. The last time she had felt so secure, her parents were walking the earth, that last morning before she went to school.

"I also want to establish a scholarship in the biology department in my father and mother's names. That's where they met, and if it weren't for their college romance, I wouldn't be here today. It's no longer painful to talk about them and I want them both to be remembered. I want to honor them. Always. Thank you for your understanding, patience, and love."

She went to return to her seat, but then Jack jumped up and came to stand next to her, forcing her to stay there at the mike.

"This town is a blessing. The best blessing I've ever had, and the day I decided to come through Milford, I knew I had found a place I will be happy to return to when I'm finished making my documentary. But I also want to say that the college and the work that it does is important to me. I want to establish a regional culinary department, a Food Studies department. I will also use part of the proceeds of *Southern Treasures* to endow an annual full ride scholarship in the name of Mrs. Ada Smithson Dailey to study Black foodways."

The look on her grandmother's face was one of shock and surprise, but Tea applauded him, and her, so glad that her grandmother was happy.

Granda stood and went to the mike, prepared, Tea guessed, to give one last bit of testimony. "I'm so happy to have my granddaughter and this young man in my life. They have been my joy this year. But, and I'm going to say this in the full view of the church…"

Everyone paused. As did Tea. What could her grandmother possibly say?

"If you all are going to get on the road to collect these recipes in that RV together, you best get ready to let me come along and go too. I guess it's time I see something of the world, and so I'm going to invite myself along with you all."

Tea squealed and reached over to hug her grandmother, as did Jack. She had been worried about what her grandmother wanted to do to travel, and now she knew. She would have the best of both worlds with her family by her side, as well as a very special friend, who was so much more than that.

She had found all the happiness her heart could hold, and when the minister said, "Let the church say Amen," Tea spoke it, openly—happy to make a joyful noise.

The End

Grandma's Biscuits and Gravy

In a memorable scene in *Sweet Tea*, Althea's grand-mother Ada challenges Jack to make the best biscuits he can—and he passes the test. Later on, Jack has the opportunity to make lunch for Althea, and he thinks to himself that he loves to see a pretty woman enjoy his food. There are a lot of ways to make biscuits, and this old-fashioned recipe will impress just about anyone.

Prep Time: 15 minutes
Cook Time: 20 minutes
Serves: 6

Ingredients

BISCUITS
- 2 cups flour
- 1 tablespoon baking powder

- 1 teaspoon kosher salt
- 1/2 cup shortening (butter, lard or vegetable shortening)
- 3/4 cup milk or buttermilk

SAUSAGE GRAVY
- 1-pound breakfast pork sausage
- 1/3 cup flour
- 3 cups milk
- salt and black pepper, as needed

Preparation
1. Preheat oven to 450°F.
2. In a large bowl, combine flour, baking powder and salt; cut in shortening until mixture has a crumbly texture. Add milk and mix into a dough, adding flour as needed until dough pulls away from side of bowl.
3. On a lightly floured surface, roll or pat dough ¾-inch thick. Using a biscuit cutter, cut out biscuits, place on a baking sheet. Bake for 15 minutes, or until lightly browned on top.
4. To make gravy: pan fry breakfast sausage until fully cooked, breaking up large pieces. Using a slotted spoon, transfer cooked sausage to bowl.
5. Add flour to pan dripping and whisk until golden.
6. Slowly add milk and whisk over low heat until thickened.
7. Add reserved sausage and stir to blend. Season to taste with salt and black pepper.
8. Serve split biscuits topped with gravy.

Thanks so much for reading *Sweet Tea*. We hope you enjoyed it!

You might like these other books from Hallmark Publishing:

South Beach Love
The Secret Ingredient
Murder By Page One
Wedding in the Pines
A Waterfront Wedding
Rescuing Harmony Ranch

For information about our new releases and exclusive offers, sign up for our free newsletter at hallmarkchannel.com/hallmarkpublishing-newsletter

You can also connect with us here:

Facebook.com/HallmarkPublishing

Twitter.com/HallmarkPublish